MACALLISTER

By Ritchie Perry

MACALLISTER
FOUL UP
FOOL'S MATE
GRAND SLAM
BISHOP'S PAWN
DUTCH COURAGE
DEAD END
ONE GOOD DEATH DESERVES ANOTHER
YOUR MONEY AND YOUR WIFE
HOLIDAY WITH VENGEANCE
TICKET TO RIDE
A HARD MAN TO KILL (published in England as NOWHERE MAN)
FALL GUY
GEORGE H. GHASTLY
BRAZIL: ITS LAND AND PEOPLE (non-fiction)

MACALLISTER

RITCHIE PERRY

PUBLISHED FOR THE CRIME CLUB BY
DOUBLEDAY & COMPANY, INC.
GARDEN CITY, NEW YORK
1984

For Lynn, with all my love

Library of Congress Cataloging in Publication Data
Perry, Ritchie, 1942–
MacAllister.
I. Title.
PR6066.E72M3   1984   823'.914
ISBN 0-385-19231-2

Library of Congress Catalog Card Number 83–16490

MACALLISTER

CHAPTER 1

The Doberman squatted patiently on the gravel, watching me out of the corner of his eye. He was waiting for me to get out of the car. I lit myself a cigarette and looked across at the house. It was a sprawling, ivy-covered mansion which had had almost two centuries to blend in with its environment. The years of weathering had given the building an air of permanence and durability. Most of the trees surrounding it were as old as the house. From behind the house I could hear the sound of a motor mower at work. This was an intrusion: the twentieth century didn't belong here.

The house itself seemed deserted. My arrival hadn't brought anybody rushing to the door; only the Doberman had shown any interest in me. It was my turn to look at the dog. His mouth hung open, giving me a good view of his teeth, which were large, white and very sharp. I slid across into the passenger seat, putting more distance between us, and the sudden movement made the dog tense slightly. There was a click as the car door opened, which made the Doberman rise leisurely to his feet. He looked as though he was enjoying the game.

I moved no more than a few inches at a time, and it took me over a minute to ease myself out of the Capri into the drive. For a long moment I stood still on the gravel with the open door as protection. Now I could look across the roof of the car at the dog. He remained in the same place, ears pricked hopefully. Carefully, step by step, I edged towards the back of the car. I left the door open behind me. My feet were making little scrunching noises on the gravel. When I reached the boot, I was at the point of no return, and the dog knew this as well as I did. He knew his patience was about to be rewarded.

"Come on then, you bastard," I said.

As I spoke, I stepped clear of the Capri. The dog didn't need an invitation: he came at me fast, covering the distance between us in six fluid strides. Although I had both arms up for protection, he had sufficient momentum to knock me back a couple of paces. I had to fight to keep my balance, then I was struggling to hold him away from my face. Even with both hands on his collar, it was a losing battle, and after a few seconds I gave in. His tongue was wet and smooth on my cheek, his breath warm and fetid.

"All right, all right." It took all of my strength to push him down. "The game's over."

Rex didn't believe me. I had to scratch his ears and thump his rump a couple of times before he'd settle down. He kept close beside me as I walked up the path. The front door was solid oak apart from the small glass spyhole. I listened to the bell tinkling inside the house for a while, but as entertainment, it soon began to pall. Googan must have given his domestic staff their annual day off.

The dog padded along like a shadow as I followed the crazy paving round the side of the house. The traffic on the main road was no more than a faint murmur in the background. There was only the sound of the mower to disturb the peace and tranquillity—that and the noise of laughing children. I would have liked a place in the country myself, and my bank manager would have liked me to be able to afford one.

Nobody noticed me at first. It was Googan himself using the motor mower. Either it was a new toy or he'd had too much to drink with his lunch. Whatever the reason, the swathes he was cutting across the lawn were distinctly serpentine, but this wasn't a criticism I was likely to voice to his face. Googan wasn't a man to cross. Even when he was bouncing around in the bucket seat of the mower, there was no mistaking his size and power. And it wasn't simply physical power. Googan was what the Krays and Richardsons had aspired to be: he had almost as great a say in what happened in London as the Greater London Council. The Luton area was only a hobby of his. This was where he generated enough legal income to keep the Inland Revenue happy.

Bonita was over by the pool where the children were playing. She was sprawled out on a sun lounger, idly flicking through a magazine. If you liked your women dumb, blonde and nubile, she scored full marks in all three categories. Bonita was Mrs. Googan, mark three. As Googan himself grew older, his wives became younger. I doubted whether Bonita was much more than twenty. The skimpy white bikini she was modelling showed exactly why she was living in luxury in Aston Clinton. I didn't blame her for making hay while the sun shone: she'd only have a few years before the sand in her hourglass figure started trickling downwards. It wouldn't be many years before she was regretting the open box of chocolates beside her.

It was her stepchildren who spotted me first. There were three of them, ranging from six to eleven, and they all came out of the pool in a rush. I managed to muster an indulgent smile while they soaked my second-best pair of trousers. In any case, I preferred the wet hands to Bonita's lingering kiss of welcome. They were less likely to make me spend the rest of my life watching the world from a wheelchair.

"That's enough, children," Bonita said. "Leave Uncle Frank alone. He's here on business."

The children ignored her. Even at their tender ages, they knew all about human relationships. They understood Bonita's place in the household perfectly: she was simply another one of Daddy's toys. She had no more real authority than the house itself or the Rolls-Royce tucked away in the garage.

"Go on," I told them. "I want to see how well you can swim."

By now Googan had seen me. He raised a hand in greeting but the mower didn't stop. As far as he was concerned, I was just one of his employees.

Bonita linked her arm through mine and propelled me towards the patio doors. I could feel the soft pressure of her breast against my arm. She smelled nice as well, of sun and chocolate. Provided she didn't talk, Bonita was a very attractive woman. Until you remembered who her husband was. Then she had all the appeal of Typhoid Mary.

"It really is good to see you, Frank." Bonita had a breathless, little girl's voice which always put my teeth on edge. "I keep telling Tony he should invite you out here more often."

"I'd like that." The lie came automatically. "There's one thing you have to remember, though. I'm kept pretty busy trying to hustle a living."

"Why not do more work for Tony then? He has plenty more business he could put your way."

"He'd end up taking me over. I don't want to be owned."

Especially not by Googan. I didn't mind handling the collections for his finance company. Everything was legal and aboveboard, and besides, Googan paid well for the service. Allow his foot too far in

the door, though, and that would be an end to my independence.
Googan was naturally acquisitive.

The whisky Bonita poured me made a sizable dent in the bottle.
Once I had it in my hand, we went out beside the pool again. It
wasn't wise for us to spend more than a few seconds out of Googan's
sight. There was nothing going on between us, but I wanted to be
sure Googan knew this. I sipped at my drink while I watched him
play with his mower. This was no more entertaining than the door-
bell had been. Rex had settled down beside me and I scratched his
head companionably. He was the only member of the household I
really liked.

It was almost twenty minutes before Googan decided he'd mas-
sacred enough grass and dandelions for the day. Bonita had a gin
and tonic and a kiss ready for him by the time he joined us. Although she didn't have many duties, those she did have had to be
performed well. Googan drained his drink in two long swallows.

"How are you doing, Frankie?" He really was a big man and he
had a voice to match. "I must say you're looking bloody seedy."

"I'm fine, Mr. Googan. Just a bit short on sleep."

"I bet you are, you dirty sod." The friendly nudge he gave me
would probably leave a bruise for a week. "That's what comes of
trying to burn the candle at both ends."

I smiled politely, pretending he'd invented the cliché. Hypocrisy
was one of my fortes. Fortunately the pleasantries were at an end—I
wasn't important enough to merit more than one attempt at a joke.
The kids continued to splash and shriek in the pool while I followed
the Googans inside. He had one of his massive paws resting on
Bonita's buttock. If this was doing anything for either of them, it
certainly didn't register on their faces.

Bonita had been allowed a free hand to decorate and furnish the
house. The end result was a testimony to what could be done with a
lot of money and no taste. On a small scale, it looked the way Ver-
sailles might have done with Attila the Hun as the interior decorator.

"Well, Frankie." Googan had sunk back into one of the zebra-skin
armchairs. "How did your collection go?"

"So-so." Basically I was very modest. "A couple of names on the
list weren't at home. I'll have to get back to them. I'm not too happy

about one of the cheques either. It can probably bounce down to the bank on its own."

"But all of the others coughed up."

"They did."

Googan already had the envelope I'd handed him open. He riffled through the contents without bothering to make a proper count. I wasn't deceived. His accountant would be checking later, and I'd be held accountable for every penny that might be missing.

"Do you want to settle up now, Frankie, or can you wait?"

"I'll wait."

I'd had my fill of Googan for the month. Just being in the same room with him made me feel vaguely unclean.

"Suit yourself. I'll have one of the boys drop the money in to you with next month's list."

"That's fine by me."

I pushed myself to my feet.

"I've got a better idea, Tony." Bonita was smiling at me over her husband's shoulder. "I have to go to the hairdresser's tomorrow. I can pop in on the way."

"There's no need to put yourself out." I said this very quickly.

"It won't be any trouble." Now there was a slight edge to Googan's voice. "Bonita likes you, Frankie. If it was anybody else, I'd be jealous."

Despite the smile, the warning came through loud and clear. I promised myself I'd steer clear of the office the following morning. There was nobody I less wanted to be jealous of me than Googan.

As I came out of the garage, I could hear the phone ringing inside the house. So could Mrs. Cameron, the lady who lived next door. Her whole life was dedicated to poking her nose into other people's business.

"Your phone is ringing, Mr. MacAllister." She was shouting through her kitchen window.

"So it is. Thanks."

There was no point in hurrying. If it was important, the caller would be phoning back anyway. By the time I reached the front door, the ringing had stopped. On my way through to the kitchen I collected my daily haul of mail and I was sorting through it when the ringing started again.

"Hello, Frank MacAllister speaking."

"It's about time. How the hell are you?"

For a moment the familiar voice didn't register. Then the penny dropped.

"Robert?"

"In person. It's your lucky day, Frank. I've come to spend a couple of days with you."

"I'll hang out the flags. Where are you now?"

"I'm up at the airport."

"Alone?"

"Alone. I didn't bring Angela with me on this trip."

I was disappointed. Angela was one of my favourite people. She was also the sister of my late wife.

"I suppose you want me to drop everything and come to collect you."

"Heaven forbid. I'll grab myself a taxi. There's a whole fleet of them outside."

"Fine. In that case I'll see you in about twenty minutes."

"You can bet on it."

I discovered I was smiling to myself as I put down the phone. The incident was typical of Robert Latimer. He'd always acted on impulse, even in the Army. Whenever he came visiting it was the same story: the phone would ring to say he was at Luton, Gatwick or Heathrow—once he'd even rung me from the phone box round the corner. It didn't occur to him that I might resent such short notice. As it happened, I didn't. Robert was welcome any time he chose to turn up. I held a very special place in my heart for people who had saved my life, although, to date, Robert's was the only name on the list.

There were some clean sheets in the airing cupboard, and I threw them on the bed in the spare bedroom. Then I made myself some coffee. I only managed a quick sip before Robert was at the door.

For such a big man he was wearing remarkably well. Part of it could be explained by his suntan: it was the deep, permanent tan of somebody who spent most of his life in Portugal. The rest was down to his obsession with physical fitness. And to a wife who resolutely

refused to pander to his sweet tooth. There was no more flesh around
his midriff than there had been when we'd first met. Sucking in my
own stomach was an involuntary reaction. I still worked out a couple
of times each week but I was only going through the motions, the
motivation was no longer there. I might have more hair around the
temples and less wrinkling around the eyes but I'd never been able to
match Robert's physical condition.

For a few moments we simply grinned at each other like a couple
of kids. It was almost six months since our previous meeting, the last
time Robert had been in England. I didn't go to Lisbon any more.

"Aren't you going to invite me in?"

"Since when have you needed an invitation?"

Robert laughed and threw his holdall at me. I caught it and
dropped it inside the door of his bedroom on the way down the hall.
This delay gave Robert the opportunity to hijack the rest of my
coffee. I had to settle for a mouthful of cold milk straight from the
bottle.

"So what brings you to Luton this time?"

"Big iron bird that fly above the clouds." He was as good at ac-
cents as I was at levitation.

"Very funny. How about a sensible answer?"

"It's business. I have a meeting in London tomorrow morning."

This was the usual reason. Robert ran a successful business in
Lisbon, exporting everything from ceramics to sardines. We'd built
the company up together after we'd left the Army. It was the money
I'd made in Portugal which had paid for the bungalow, and it had
also subsidized the first couple of years while I'd been putting the
Agency in order. My father had been a very sweet man, but unfortunately he'd had all the financial acumen of a brick outhouse.

"How long will you be staying this time?"

"Two days, possibly three. It all depends. By the way, Angela
sends you her love."

"You can send mine back to her. How is she?"

"Worried." Robert was grinning at me over the coffee cup.

"Worried?"

"That's what I said. She's wondering what state I'll be in after a
couple of nights on the town with you."

"It's going to be that sort of visit, is it?"

"Too bloody right it is. I've got a lot of celebrating to do. At least, I will have if tomorrow goes as well as I hope."

I didn't bother to ask Robert what he had on the boil—I knew he'd tell me all about it in his own sweet time. Besides, I wasn't taking him too seriously. Ever since I'd known him, Robert had had something big waiting for him just around the next corner.

"I'll tell you what," I said. "You can buy the drinks. I'll see to the meal."

"Fork out for the wine as well and it's a deal."

"Done."

Some of Robert's enthusiasm had communicated itself to me. This had always been the way. He'd done the leading and I was the one who tagged along behind.

CHAPTER 2

The hangover was even worse than I'd anticipated: my headache seemed to go all the way down to my toes. Robert didn't do anything to make me feel any better. By the time I'd lurched downstairs, he'd already finished his morning calisthenics. He'd also showered, shaved and dressed. The eggs and bacon were out of the fridge and the fat was heating in the frying pan. If I'd had the strength, I'd have thrown something at him. I wanted company in my suffering.

"One egg or two?"

"None."

My tongue felt too large for my mouth. If there had been much more fur on it, it would have needed grooming.

"Come on, Frank. You've got to eat."

"I'll munch a bottle of aspirin." Washed down with a double Alka-Seltzer. Robert was grinning derisively.

"You're getting old," he jeered.

"I'm not arguing. The age I feel, there should be a telegram from the Queen on the doormat."

In the end I did manage a couple of slices of toast. After a bit of grumbling, my stomach decided to accept the offering. The coffee Robert made me didn't do any harm either.

"How did we get home?" I had only the haziest memories of the later stages of the previous night.

"With great difficulty. You insisted on driving."

"That must have been fun."

"It was, believe you me. I'll say one thing for you, though. You drove a hell of a sight better than you walked. You must have collided with half the lampposts in Luton."

My head had started throbbing again. I tried a change of subject to see whether this made any difference.

"What train are you catching?"

"The nine-thirty something."

I looked at my watch. Robert still had almost three-quarters of an hour.

"I'll drop you off at the station. I have to go that way."

"Are you sure you're up to it? They bury healthier-looking people than you every day."

"It'll be a different story once I've cleaned myself up."

"Sure. The way your hands are shaking, I'd forget about shaving. Who knows? A beard might suit you."

As I headed for the bathroom, one thought consoled me: my day could only get better. I'd no idea how wrong I was. My day was about to get far, far worse.

Harpenden was famous for Eric Morecambe, not its immigrant population. It was one of those Hertfordshire towns on the fringes of the commuter belt which attracted money the way nectar attracted bees. West Indian citizens like Jeremiah Cranston were hidden away in the back streets, where they wouldn't do anything to disturb the comfortable middle-class atmosphere.

The dilapidated terraced house Cranston lived in looked as out of place in Harpenden as he did. I hadn't expected anything different. The only duty of a landlord which Googan took seriously was collecting the rent. House improvements and repairs he preferred to ignore.

Whatever the state of the house, Cranston himself appeared to be thriving. I stood six feet in my socks, and he topped me by several inches when I was wearing shoes. When he answered my knock, he had a big, friendly smile splitting his beard. I guessed he'd lose his smile round about the time he learned who I was.

"What can I do for you, my man?"

Cranston had a deep, resonant voice. He also had a pronounced Jamaican accent. As soon as he'd finished speaking, he lubricated his throat with a mouthful of red wine, which he'd brought with him in a tin mug. Although it was barely eleven in the morning, he already had a mild buzz on. It made my head ache in sympathy. There was probably some connection between the wine and the smile he still had in place.

"My name is MacAllister. Frank MacAllister. Here's my card."

"Oh, shit." Cranston managed to put quite a bit of feeling into his voice. "You'd better come inside."

I followed him through into the living room. Somebody had made a good job of the decorating, but there were indications that Cranston's life was on a downswing. It was obviously some time since anybody had done any cleaning, and the impressive collection of empty wine bottles in the fireplace suggested a possible reason for this. On the mantelpiece there was an equally impressive collection of unopened mail. Several of the unopened letters would undoubtedly have originated from the Googan Finance Company.

"You're wasting your time, man." Cranston had dropped into an armchair. It was the nearest to a wine bottle which was still half full. "I can't afford to pay. How much do I owe anyway?"

I took the sheaf of neatly typed papers out of my briefcase. Up to a point, Googan was a stickler for the legal proprieties. He only resorted to strong-arm tactics when it came to a choice between this and taking his claim to court. He had been making an ass of the law for too long to have any great faith in the legal process.

"Shit." There was even more feeling this time. Cranston was building up to a command performance. "It can't be this much."

"It soon mounts up. You're way behind on the loan repayments and the rent."

"But I only borrowed five hundred pounds, man. That was over a year ago." Now a sense of outrage was becoming apparent. "It says here I owe six hundred pounds on the loan alone. That can't be right."

"The figures are all there."

"It's extortion." Cranston had difficulty getting his tongue around the word. He looked to his wine for help.

"Maybe," I conceded, "but it's perfectly legal. The terms were spelled out for you on the application form you signed."

If pressed, I could have managed quite a lengthy monologue on how the finance company operated. It thrived on human gullibility and greed. People in desperate need of cash seemed to have an infinite capacity for blinding themselves to reality. All the advertisements were geared to exploit this, and the punters seemed to believe Googan was some kind of Lutonian Santa Claus. None of them spared a thought as to why he was being so generous.

"I can't pay." Cranston had reverted to his original theme. "That's all there is to it."

"You have to pay. That's the law. It says here you have a good job with the local Council. You shouldn't have had any problems meeting the repayments."

This was the part I really hated. The figures were in front of me. I knew exactly how easy the repayments would have been for Cranston. All he had to do was work twenty hours overtime a week and cut out luxuries like eating.

"I've been made redundant, man." Now Cranston was sounding plaintive. "I haven't worked in two months, not since my woman walked out on me."

Cranston sipped some more wine and I counted the empty bottles. I was wasting our time but there was one last thing I could try. Cranston needed saving from himself.

"A token payment and a promise would be enough to keep the finance company off your back. Say one month's rent and a couple of weeks on the loan repayment."

My suggestion made Cranston laugh out loud. He dug into his pocket to produce a handful of copper and silver.

"This is all I have."

"How about selling something?"

"Why the hell should I? I can't pay and that's it."

The fresh infusion of wine was changing Cranston's mood again, and amiability was giving way to belligerence. He was beginning to see me as part of the system which was intent on squeezing him dry. Now would have been a good time to leave. Unfortunately, my conscience was at work. I had to warn Cranston what he was letting himself in for.

"Don't you have any idea what the finance company is likely to do if you refuse to pay?"

"A court can't make me pay what I don't have."

"It won't be settled in court. That's the problem. Mr. Googan has his own ways of dealing with people who mess him around."

"Is that a threat?"

Despite the amount he must have had to drink, Cranston came out of his seat surprisingly fast. Standing over me, he looked immense.

"I was trying to give you some good advice."

I was wasting my breath again. He'd reached the stage where he wanted to relieve his frustrations by hitting out at somebody, and I happened to be near to hand.

When he swung at me, I rolled off the sofa, and I kept on rolling until I reached the wall. Fast as I was, I barely had time to scramble back to my feet before Cranston was on me again. This time I ducked under the blow and scuttled to the far side of the table. Although this was no permanent answer, it did at least buy me a breathing space.

A couple of deep breaths and I was on the run again. Fortunately, I had one advantage: for all his size, the West Indian was no fighter. Every swing was telegraphed well in advance. He was also wasting an awful lot of breath on the constant stream of profanity. On the debit side, the room was far too small for prolonged evasive action. I couldn't keep dodging him for ever—sooner or later one of his wild swings was bound to connect. I didn't want to damage Cranston but I failed to see how this could be avoided.

A little bit of pain was all that was needed to bury my pacifism. When one of Cranston's fists grazed the side of my head, it almost took an ear with it. It was time to stand up and fight like a man, and I elected to do so with a chair in my hands. Although it splintered on my second strike, this was sufficient to drop Cranston to his knees. I didn't allow him an opportunity to take his revenge; instead I used my weight to force him face downwards on the carpet. To be on the safe side, I pushed one of his hands up between his shoulder blades. He could almost tickle the back of his neck.

From there on it was all over. I allowed Cranston to buck a little until he appreciated how painful this could be. Then I let him swear at me for a bit longer. When he became too repetitious, I hoisted his wrist a few inches higher.

"Sweet Jesus Christ." Cranston's voice was plaintive. "You're breaking my arm."

"You're the one who wanted to fight."

Cranston only needed a few seconds to mull this over. "I don't want to fight any more," he announced.

"That makes it unanimous."

I was careful to back off to a safe distance, just in case. It was an unnecessary precaution. Cranston's mood had changed again—now depression had succeeded belligerence. Over the next few minutes I didn't do anything to cheer him up. By the time I'd finished my explanation he had no illusions at all about what was likely to happen if he didn't meet his debts.

"Oh, shit," he said, burying his head in hands the size of shovels. "What do I do, man? Just tell me that."

This was a familiar question. I'd heard it more than once since I'd been representing Googan.

"That all depends. You're absolutely sure you can't raise the money?"

"Not in a million years." Cranston managed a laugh of sorts. "In my family, I'm the rich one."

So I explained the alternative. Cranston didn't like it at all. He maintained that running wasn't his style, but after I'd said a bit more about Googan's enforcers, he changed his mind. He was a realist at heart.

It was almost six o'clock in the evening before I reached home. Most of my afternoon was spent in Dunstable, where I'd gone to discuss security procedures with the manager of a small engineering firm. Although I didn't mind pocketing the consultancy fee, we both knew we were only going through the motions. If the rumours I'd heard were anything to go by, the next visitor was likely to be the official receiver.

Once I'd finished there, I drove back into Luton to my office in Park Street, where there was the usual pile of paperwork waiting for me. So was John Stubbs, the other operational member of the Agency. He'd spent the last three days in Yorkshire trying to track down a missing person, and they had been three fruitless days. After some discussion, John and I agreed we should give it another week before we admitted defeat. Marcia thought we should jack it in immediately, and, as usual, she carried the day. Although she was only the secretary, she was the one indispensable member of the Agency. Nobody else knew where the tea bags and toilet rolls were kept.

The excesses of the previous night were catching up with me again when I parked outside the bungalow. I felt tired and my headache was trying to get going again. I hoped Robert didn't have anything too strenuous planned for the night ahead. I also hoped he'd remembered to get the paella under way. As far as I knew, there weren't many dishes he could cook, but those he did were absolutely superb. I was already salivating as I went up the path. I even managed a friendly wave to where Mrs. Cameron was lurking behind her net curtains.

Thirty seconds later my mouth was dry again. It wasn't paella I could smell as I stepped through the front door—it wasn't anything nearly so pleasant. I pushed the door very gently. The massive surge of adrenaline had swamped any last vestiges of my hangover. I wasn't sure I could cope any more. There had been too many years of soft living, and workouts with the likes of Cranston were no training for what faced me now.

The biggest stain on the carpet was in a direct line between the living room and kitchen doors. There were smaller stains on either side. Beside the kitchen door there was a smear on the wall; on the radiator, lower down, a handprint was clearly visible. Somebody had been losing a hell of a lot of blood. For a long moment I stared at the telephone on the table, a mere two paces away. I had to fight to keep my hand at my side. Robert might have cut his thumb opening a tin, or he might be playing a practical joke. I believed this the same way I believed I'd grow roots if I stayed much longer by the front door.

I kept close to the left-hand wall when I moved forwards. The first door I reached was to the bedroom Robert was using. It was wide open, and I could see most of the room reflected in the mirror on the wall opposite me. There was nobody there. Nor was there any blood, just a hell of a mess. Robert's clothes were strewn across the floor and his holdall had been ripped to pieces. An equally thorough job had been done on the mattress. Whatever had been happening, it was no accident.

The study on the far side of the hall looked the same as it had done in the morning. Two more cautious paces took me to the living-room door. I pushed it all the way open with my foot. This was habit as much as anything. By now I was fairly certain there was nobody else in the house with me. Nobody alive, anyway.

The table just inside the door was tipped over on its side and the lamp which should have stood on it was in pieces on the floor. There were several spots of blood mixed up with the glass. Apart from these, the only other stain I could see was over by the fireplace. As I watched, it grew larger. For a second I thought my eyes must be playing tricks on me. Then another globule of blood hit the carpet. It was dripping through the ceiling from my bedroom. A patch of ceiling above the fireplace was stained a reddish brown. This stain was spreading too.

"Oh, Christ."

Suddenly I was running, all caution thrown to the winds. The trail of blood ran all the way across the kitchen. It led to a small pool at the foot of the stairs. From there on the spots were much larger. I took the stairs two at a time, praying as I'd never prayed before. A continuous trail of blood led from the head of the stairs into my bedroom. I slowed down again. I didn't want to face what I thought was waiting for me.

For a wonderful moment I thought my prayers had been answered. I was sure the body hunched in the far corner couldn't be Robert's. It just wasn't big enough. Then I remembered that death made everybody look smaller and I took a second look at the contorted features. This time there was no mistake. As I started downstairs again, heading towards the telephone, I was having to fight to keep my stomach down. There was nothing at all I could do about the tears rolling down my cheeks.

"Cigarette?"

"Thanks."

My hands were rock steady as I lit it. Shock, I diagnosed. The shakes would undoubtedly come later. I knew the memory of what I'd seen upstairs would stay with me for a lifetime. I'd have a new nightmare to add to my repertoire.

"Ready to talk, Frank?" Teague asked.

"Do I have any choice?"

"Not really."

We were sitting in the study. Apart from the young plainclothesman over by the door, we were alone. The rest of the house was a maelstrom of policemen, doctors and photographers.

"Look, John," I said. "That poor bastard upstairs with his guts in his lap is—was—my best friend. He was more like a brother than a brother-in-law. I'm afraid I'm not going to react well if you press the wrong button. Why don't I take you through my day? When that's out of the way you can start the questions."

"Go ahead if that's what you want."

It took twenty minutes for me to lay out my day for him. I knew exactly what Teague wanted and I gave it to him: names, places, times and addresses. The CID man by the door noted it all down. When I'd finished, he slipped out of the room for a few seconds. Somebody would be detailed to check it all out. For the time being I was all the police had.

"That sorts you out, Frank. How about the victim? What did you say his name was?"

"Latimer. Robert Latimer."

"Address?"

Teague raised his eyebrows when I gave him the address in Estoril. It only took me a few minutes to give him the rest of Robert's personal details. Then Teague started the questioning. He was very thorough. With the various interruptions, it was nearly an hour before we entered the realm of speculation.

"O.K., Frank. That seems to cover most of it for the moment. Tell me something, though. What do you think happened?"

Teague wasn't simply encouraging me to talk, he was genuinely curious. He wanted to know whether we'd been thinking along the same lines. This wasn't a game I particularly wanted to play.

"That's your line, isn't it? You're the detective."

"Aren't you supposed to be one as well? It says you are on your office door."

Teague couldn't resist the temptation to needle me a little. Although we got on quite well together, he didn't really approve of private detectives.

"Investigating homicides isn't one of the services I offer."

"I suppose you are more at home collecting the rent for Tony Googan."

His smile was designed to forestall any possible offense. He didn't push his question any further; there wasn't any real need to do so. Both of us had a pretty fair idea of what must have happened. The killer had probably been waiting in the house when Robert returned from London. This was what the scratches on the door and the mess in Robert's bedroom seemed to suggest. It was clear that the killer had been looking for something, either information or a specific object. When Robert had refused to cooperate, the murderer had used his knife, and he'd continued to use it for quite some time. The blood in the hall had almost dried when I'd come in, but on the stairs and in the bedroom it had still been wet. The killer had stalked a wounded Robert around the house. He'd stuck him with the knife every time Robert had failed to come up with a satisfactory answer. This was an image which hovered unpleasantly at the back of my mind. Like Teague, I'd have liked to know what the questions had been.

"Did Mr. Latimer have any enemies?"

"Not that I knew of."

"You say he ran a successful company. Did he have any business rivals?"

"Probably. You don't get to be successful without trampling on a few toes."

"You can't be more specific than that?"

"Not really. There weren't any serious competitors while I was in Lisbon. I'm not quite sure what the situation is now. I only saw Robert for a few days each year."

Teague brought out his cigarettes again. "You say the two of you used to be partners."

"That's right."

"Why did you split up? From what you tell me, the business was doing well."

"There was an accident." Even now this was something I found difficult to talk about. "My wife, father and children were all killed. After that I didn't want to stay in Portugal—there were too many memories."

There was more to Teague than being a good policeman—he had a certain sensitivity as well. He realized that he'd hit a raw nerve, so he changed the direction of the conversation again. I answered his questions automatically. The initial shock had passed but the grief and anger were still there. I wished I knew who it was that Robert had been to visit in London. So, I suspected, did Teague. For the moment he was simply groping around in the dark.

Eventually he ran out of questions, and this brought us to the point I'd been dreading.

"What about Mrs. Latimer?" Teague enquired. "Somebody will have to break the bad news to her."

"I know."

"Do you want me to handle it?"

I most certainly did. More than anything else in the world, this was a responsibility I'd have liked to duck, but, unfortunately, I couldn't. Cowardice wasn't an adequate excuse.

"I'll see to it, thanks." Although I'd no idea how. What could I possibly say to her? All I knew was that it was something I owed to Angela. She'd offered me a shoulder to cry on when I'd needed it, and now was the time for me to repay the favour.

CHAPTER 3

Robert and I had been only six months away from freedom when the
Army posted us to Oman. This had been bad enough, but a three-
month stint in Akhdar was the final straw. If our minds hadn't
already been made up, Akhdar would have been enough to decide us
against staying in the Army. The town was sixty miles from Salala,
flanked on two sides by the sea. It boasted a jumble of flat-roofed
houses and a couple of antique forts; otherwise there was nothing
except the heat, the sand and the insects. And, outside the perimeter
fence, the local variety of Marxist guerrillas, the Dhofar Liberation
Front.

Intelligence had put their total strength at five hundred warriors.
This meant there were probably several thousand of them lurking in
the surrounding hills. To combat them there were ten of us Royal
Marine Commandos. We were backed up by twice as many askaris,
the local firqa and twenty-five gendarmes. We had a Browning and
an 81-mm. mortar to defend ourselves with, and the gendarmes were
the proud possessors of a 25-pounder which should have been in the
Imperial War Museum. Together with our rifles and some light machine guns this was our total firepower. The guerrillas had heavy
machine guns, antitank rifles and mortars of all descriptions. They
also had an 84-mm. Carl Gustav rocket launcher which Intelligence
didn't know about, which we were destined to learn about the hard
way.

Fortunately, the guerrillas didn't seem to prize Akhdar much
more than we did. Although they did lob a few 75-mm. shells and
mortar bombs over the perimeter fence, they left us pretty much
alone. They didn't even bother our patrols too much. We knew it
couldn't last. As Captain Farley was fond of repeating, they were

simply biding their time. The guerrillas were waiting for the monsoon to get properly under way, then the rain and cloud would rob us of our air support, leaving us entirely on our own. These pep talks of Farley's did wonders for our morale.

Salvation day was July 15, the date we were due to be relieved. After that some other poor bastards would have the pleasure of defending Akhdar. All of us, with the possible exception of Farley, were praying that the guerrillas would keep biding their time until then. When we went to bed on the night of the fourteenth, we thought we'd made it, but we were wrong. At dawn the following morning the guerrillas mounted their biggest offensive of the entire war, and its target was Akhdar.

The gendarmes on picket duty outside the perimeter were the first to learn of the offensive. They were overrun at six in the morning and all four of them were killed, but before they were killed, they put up enough of a fight to alert the rest of us. Robert beat me to the roof of our barracks by about half a second. We were both there in time to see Farley become the first Marine casualty of the engagement. As senior sergeant, Robert automatically assumed command.

Our initial assessment of the situation was hardly encouraging, and nothing we saw afterwards did anything to modify our attitude. There were hundreds of guerrillas and they weren't concerned about casualties. As soon as one attacking group was cut down, another came forward to take its place. We were hitting them with everything we had and it just wasn't enough.

Before the battle, I'd never thought of Robert as a hero, but now I had to revise my opinion. Our barracks was in the middle of what we jokingly called a defense line, and the two forts manned by the askaris and gendarmes stood on either side. It was Robert who selected targets for the Browning and mortar, and it was his tracer which gave the lines of fire for the light machine guns. In between times he was picking off the leading attackers with his rifle. I was doing my bit too but I lacked Robert's enthusiasm. This was my first real battle and I'd have liked to be somewhere else.

One place I wouldn't have liked to be was the fort over to our left, where the gendarmes had their 25-pounder. Inevitably, it was attracting the brunt of the guerrilla fire. The clay walls of the fort had been built long before armour-piercing rounds had been thought of, and they were slowly disintegrating around the defenders' ears. By half past eight, the return fire from the fort was becoming increasingly sporadic. When Robert tried to get through on the radio, he couldn't. It was my turn to be a hero.

"Somebody has to get over there, Frank."

"And I'm elected."

"It seems like it, old son. I'd go but I've got to keep by the radio. You should be able to make it all right."

I peered through the smoke at the fort, almost a quarter of a mile away. There was no real cover for me to use.

"I can try."

"Good man." Robert was even beginning to talk like an officer. "Take Hancock with you. I'll coordinate the covering fire from here."

Hancock was no more enthusiastic than I'd been. By now there was no firing from the fort at all.

"For Christ's sake, Frank," he complained. "For all we know the bloody place has been overrun."

"That's what we're supposed to find out. Come on."

Even with the Browning and a light machine gun providing covering fire overhead, the journey was a nightmare. The leading guerrillas were almost up to the wire—in places they were no more than a hundred yards away. There was no question of making a direct run for the fort. I'd dash forward while Hancock protected my back, then I did the same for him. It was a miracle that neither of us was hit.

We were halfway across when the 25-pounder opened up again. This gave us the encouragement we'd needed. Besides, we were as near to the fort now as we were to the barracks. It was only another couple of minutes before I was sliding down into the gun pit. Hancock was so close behind that his boots caught me in the small of my back. Once we'd taken stock of the situation, we wished we hadn't bothered to come. One of the Omani gunners was quietly bleeding to death, and three other Omanis were already dead. The only one who was still functioning was a corporal. He was another hero—despite a scalp wound, he was loading and firing the 25-pounder on his own. The metal shield in front of him was riddled with bullets.

I lent a hand to the corporal while Hancock blazed away with his rifle. Although we were safe from the Carl Gustav in the pit, our situation was hopeless. The guerrillas were no more than forty yards away. Any closer and they'd be using grenades.

Hancock was the first to be hit. A round from an AK-47 hit him smack between the eyes, killing him instantly. Less than a minute later, the Omani corporal took a bullet in the chest. I was beyond fear by now. I loaded and fired the ancient artillery piece like an automaton, knowing it was only a matter of minutes. Some of the guerrillas were actually through the wire. It wouldn't take them long to outflank me.

Reprieve came in the shape of the Omani Air Force. The first I knew of their arrival was when the two Strikemasters came screaming in on their first strafing run. Robert must have been talking them in by radio because they came dangerously close to the gun pit. Within minutes, the guerrillas were driven back by the deadly hail of cannon fire. I would have been cheering if I hadn't known how short a time the Strikemasters could stay over the target area. Then they'd be out of ammunition. After their sixth run they were on their way back to base and no other jets appeared to take their place.

I decided to get out too while there was a temporary lull in the fighting. I wasn't to know I'd used up my ration of luck for the day. All morning people had been shooting at me: hundreds of rounds had been aimed in my direction and I didn't even have a scratch. When I came out of the gun pit, there was just one shot. I heard it almost as I felt the numbing blow in my thigh. Then I was down on the ground, gazing stupidly at the blood welling from my thigh. Although there was no pain yet, running was out of the question.

Other guns had opened up by now. Bullets were kicking up the dust all around me. I scrambled back into the gun pit, sobbing with frustration and fear. This would have been the time to surrender but there were no white sheets to hand. Besides, most of the guerrillas couldn't read or write—they hadn't even heard of the Geneva Convention.

With only one good leg, there was no question of manning the 25-pounder any longer. I grabbed my rifle and crawled to the lip of the pit. The guerrillas were surging forwards through the wire again. Some I hit but a lot I didn't. One of the survivors lobbed a grenade which fell just short. While splinters of rock and metal whizzed through the air above me, I covered my head. I was still sobbing. I didn't want to die defending a few worthless square metres of Oman. If the guerrillas had asked, I'd have given it to them. But they didn't ask, they just kept shooting.

There had been no time to slap a dressing on my thigh, and the wound was hurting abominably. Worse still, I was losing a lot of blood. I felt sick and disoriented. There were moments when I nearly blacked out completely.

When I first heard the engine of the jeep, I thought I was hallucinating. Even after I'd seen it speeding across the rough ground towards me, I couldn't believe my eyes. Nor could the guerrillas. For a few seconds we all held our fire. We were too busy watching the madman at the wheel of the jeep. He was travelling so fast that the vehicle was airborne over the worst bumps.

Suddenly the spell broke but it was too late: by the time the guerrillas opened fire again, the jeep was already going out of sight behind the remains of the fort. This inspired the nearest group of insurgents to attempt to rush the gun pit. I shot three of them before they went to ground again. I was reloading my rifle as Robert slid into the pit behind me.

"You crazy bastard," I said. "What the hell do you think you're doing?"

"I took a wrong turning. And you say 'sir' when you address your commanding officer. Can you walk?"

"No."

"In that case, you'd better hop bloody fast. Come on."

The maniac was actually smiling at me. With Robert half carrying me, we made it to the jeep in five seconds flat. Robert had left the engine running. He didn't waste any time on ceremony as he bundled me into the passenger seat.

"Hold on tight."

I held on. Just about every guerrilla in the area had been waiting for the jeep to emerge from behind the ruins. They even had a couple of mortars zeroed in on us. We seemed to be driving into a hail of bullets. I closed my eyes and prayed. Every jolt sent a bolt of agony down my leg, and the seat beneath me was slick with blood. These were the least of my concerns: at that moment I'd have willingly sacrificed a leg to make it safely to the barracks.

We very nearly made it too. The jeep was no more than fifty yards from the barracks when the mortar bomb landed right underneath the front wheels. After that I was flying. There was barely time to feel surprised before I came down to earth again. I stayed huddled where I was behind the wreckage of the jeep, whimpering out loud. I'd had enough—at least until Robert's blood-streaked face appeared above me.

"Get moving," he yelled. "We're nearly there."

"I can't. Leave me here."

"Like hell I will."

He started to crawl, dragging me behind him. The pain was indescribable. I kept screaming at Robert to leave me alone. He ignored me. I called him every filthy name I could think of. He still ignored me. Somewhere along the way I quietly passed out. It must have come as quite a relief to Robert.

I didn't recover consciousness until I was aboard the helicopter which eventually flew the wounded out. The same helicopter had flown in the troop reinforcements which drove the guerrillas back into the limestone hills. At the hospital in Salala, an officer popped in to tell me what a famous victory we'd won. I smiled politely and pretended to be pleased. As far as I was concerned, he was talking about a different battle.

Back in England it was pretty much the same. A famous general pinned on a medal while I lay in my hospital bed. Robert received his standing up on the parade ground. A less famous general spent the best part of a morning trying to persuade us to sign on again. He kept telling us that the Army needed men like us, but we told him it would have to struggle along without us. There had to be easier ways of earning a living.

For the next year or so Robert and I kept in touch by post. After my leg had healed, I joined my father in the detective agency in Luton. Robert, always more adventurous, set out to see the world. His letters carried exotic postmarks like Lagos, Luanda and Lima. Then he reached Lisbon and the travelling stopped. I followed his romance in his letters, so it came as no great surprise when I received an invitation to the wedding.

After I'd actually met Angela, I couldn't understand why Robert had delayed so long. The two of them were obviously made for each other. Angela didn't simply have looks and personality, she had money as well. She came from one of those émigré English families which had been in Portugal almost since port had been invented. At the wedding I met Angela's sister, Jane. We barely had time to discover that we liked each other a lot before I had to return to England. Some three months later, Robert unexpectedly turned up in Luton. As usual, he had been brimming over with ideas which made a lot of sense. Part of Angela's dowry had been a position for Robert in the family business. Although it paid well, Robert had wanted to be his own boss. According to him, there were a lot of small factories in the Lisbon area producing cheap, high-quality ceramics. At the moment this pottery was manufactured almost exclusively for the domestic market, and Robert's idea was to export it to Britain. For this he'd need a partner and I was his choice.

It didn't take me long to make up my mind. Whatever my father might say, the Agency wasn't profitable enough to support the two of us. This had been in the pre-Googan days and money had been tight. Besides, I'd fancied the opportunity to work with Robert again.

With Robert's father-in-law's backing and connections, there had never been any question of failure. Within a year the company was making a profit and he was my father-in-law as well. The period which followed was the most satisfying of my life. If it hadn't been for the accident, I'd undoubtedly still have been living contentedly in Portugal. And, perhaps, Robert would still have been alive.

I had plenty of time for my stroll along memory lane. The French flight traffic controllers were on strike again, and this meant the TAP flight from Lisbon to Heathrow was delayed. It was after midday before its arrival was eventually announced.

I was in the concourse when Angela came through the barrier. From a distance she always reminded me of Jane. Angela had the same build as her sister and the same dark hair. She even walked the same way. It was only as she came closer that Angela assumed an identity of her own. Her mouth was fuller, the blue eyes were larger and slightly further apart and there were a few more freckles around her nose. This time Angela's face was paler too. She'd only had fifteen hours to absorb the tragic news. It had obviously hit her hard. She covered the last few yards at a scampering run, dropping her

suitcase as she came into my arms. I held her close, my chin just
brushing the top of her head. We attracted several amused glances
from the people around us, who probably thought they were witness-
ing a lovers' reunion. With Angela's face pressed against my chest,
they couldn't see that she was crying. Nor could I, but I could feel
the wet of her tears through my shirt. It was almost a minute before
she raised her face to me.

"I'm sorry, Frank. All the way here I've been promising myself I
wouldn't cry."

"What's a broken promise or two? It's better out of your system."

Her face went back against my chest again. She was really sobbing
now, and I could feel the little spasms racking her body. The contact
disturbed me more than I'd have cared to admit. It was a long time
since I'd held a woman so close. My brain knew I was only offering
sympathy, but other parts of me weren't quite so sure. Angela must
have sensed the change of mood because she suddenly pulled away.

"I'm making an exhibition of myself. Let's get out of here."

"If that's what you want. I'll take the suitcase."

Heathrow was as crowded as usual. I breasted a passage through
the sea of bodies with Angela following in my wake, and by the time
we reached my car, she had herself under control. While I drove, she
spent a few minutes with her mirror repairing the damage to her
make-up. This had nothing to do with vanity. Angela was thinking
of me: she didn't want to be the cause of embarrassment.

I watched her out of the corner of my eye. The previous night I'd
suggested that it might be better for Angela to stay in Lisbon, to let
the police come to her while I handled the other arrangements. Angela had refused, and I still thought she'd been mistaken.

"That's better." Her handbag closed with a snap. "Tell me what
happened, Frank."

It was almost a command.

"You're sure?"

"Robert was my husband. I want to know exactly how he died."

I compromised. Although I didn't feed Angela any lies, I glossed
over some of the gorier details. Even in the sanitized, deodorized
version, it wasn't a particularly pretty story.

"Who could possibly do such a thing, Frank?" Angela wasn't crying but all the pain was there in her voice. "Why did it happen?"

"That's what the police are trying to find out. At the moment they don't have any more idea than you do."

"I mean, was it some maniac? Did he just walk in off the street and kill Robert for kicks?"

"It could have been like that. Nobody knows for sure yet."

Perception was something else Angela had in common with her sister. Despite her distress, she was quick to sense my reservations.

"You evidently don't think it happened like that."

"No, I don't."

I still wasn't going to lie to her. Angela considered my answer for a few moments. I'd always realized that this was a conversation we'd have to have sooner or later, although I'd have preferred later.

"What exactly are you trying to say, Frank?"

"To be honest, I'm trying to say as little as possible. There will be plenty of time for us to discuss this later."

"What's wrong with now?"

"O.K." I paused, picking my words very deliberately. "I don't think Robert was a chance victim. Somebody wanted him dead."

"Is that what the police think too?"

"I don't know. They don't take me into their confidence."

Angela started to shake her head. "You're wrong, Frank. Robert didn't have any enemies. Everybody liked him."

"That's what I thought too. And I don't claim to be infallible either. I've simply told you what I think."

"You're mistaken then." Angela almost sounded fierce. "It just doesn't make sense. What reason could anyone possibly have for harming Robert?"

This was a very good question—one I'd been asking myself ever since I'd discovered Robert's body. Perhaps the driver of the blue Datsun two cars behind us had the answer. Whether he did or not, he'd certainly be worth talking to. Then he could explain why he'd been following me since I'd left home that morning.

CHAPTER 4

Even in mid-afternoon, there were a couple of roulette wheels working at Sergeant York's. So was the blackjack table. Nearly all of the gamblers were Chinese. This was probably why their restaurants had to stay open so late at night: they had to earn back the money they lost gambling during the day.

Apart from a couple of little old ladies trying to supplement their pensions, Googan was the only Caucasian playing. Kerridge, one of his goon squad, was standing behind him. The bodyguard seemed far less interested in the roulette than he was in the breasts of the young West Indian croupier. His breathing deepened noticeably every time she bent forward to rake in the chips. And there were a lot of chips to rake in. The Chinese were scattering theirs across the baize, and the little old ladies were almost equally profligate with their 25-pence investments. Googan, by contrast, was playing to win. I knew he'd quit while he was ahead.

I slipped onto a spare seat at the blackjack table. After half an hour I was £3 ahead. I could have done better selling clothespegs door to door. Fortunately, Googan had won enough for the day. When I saw him go to cash in, I scooped up my own chips, and we reached the cashier's window almost together. Kerridge had seen me coming and contrived to be between us.

"It's MacAllister," he said.

"I can see that. How are you doing, Frankie?"

"Not too well. Can I have a word with you, Mr. Googan?"

Googan accepted a thick sheaf of notes from the cashier. Only then did he check his watch. It was a crystal Corum which must have cost considerably more than my car. He was living proof that crime paid bloody well.

"I can give you a quarter of an hour."

"Thanks. I appreciate it."

After I'd collected my own much thinner sheaf of notes, I followed him to one of the tables. Kerridge sat opposite me, beside his boss. He stared at me as though he was debating which limb to break first. This was the way he looked at everybody. Apart from big-breasted West Indian croupiers, that is.

"Well, what is it, Frankie?"

"Somebody was murdered at my house yesterday."

Googan nodded. "I read about it in the newspapers."

"Latimer was a friend of mine. A very good friend indeed. I want to find out who killed him."

This time Googan didn't even bother to nod. So far I hadn't said anything to interest him.

"You know just about everything that goes on in Luton, Mr. Googan." Despite his lack of interest, I forged determinedly on. "I thought you could probably find out whether or not anybody local was involved."

"I probably could. Tell me something, though. Who is it doing the asking, Frankie? You or the police?"

His voice was dangerously soft.

"Me." I positively oozed sincerity. "This is just between the two of us. Not a word goes any further. I'm asking you as a personal favour."

"Favours are an expensive luxury."

"Maybe not this time. It looked like a professional killing. It could even have been a contract job."

Now Googan was interested.

"That part wasn't mentioned in the newspapers."

"Surely you don't believe everything you read. After all, I've seen the articles about you. I'm sure you're not like that at all."

Googan laughed. Kerridge accompanied him with a guffaw. Suddenly the atmosphere was a lot less tense.

"I'll be seeing you, Frankie." Googan had risen to his feet. "Look after yourself."

"I'll do that. Thanks for your time."

He'd ask one or two questions around town about the murder. I was positive of that. Whether or not he passed on what he learned was a different matter. Of course, there was one other possibility. It was the reason the palms of my hands were damp. If there had been a contract, Googan would be the logical person to take it up.

The blue Datsun was still with me when I drove to the police station to collect Angela, and it was high time I did something about it. When I went inside, Angela was still closeted with Teague in his office. I seized the opportunity to hustle myself a coffee and a couple of sandwiches from the canteen. I had missed breakfast and Angela hadn't wanted to eat on the way back from Heathrow. If I'd been Irish and gone much longer without food, the IRA would have started singing songs about me. Either that or elected me to Parliament.

Angela was looking pale and strained when she eventually emerged. It had been a long session. Although I'd asked Teague to go easy with her, he'd had his job to do. I put my arm round her and Angela leaned her head on my shoulder. She'd do a lot of leaning on me while she was in Luton. I was the only real friend she had in England.

"Do you mind waiting for a minute or two, Angela? I'd like a quick word with Inspector Teague."

"Perhaps you'd like a cup of tea or something, Mrs. Latimer." Teague was playing the gentleman. I suspected that Angela had impressed him.

"Tea would be lovely, thanks."

We left Angela in the capable hands of a WPC. Once we were inside his rather spartan office, Teague perched on the edge of his desk.

"Well?" he enquired. "What is it?"

"Do you have anybody following me?"

"Should I have? I thought you had a watertight alibi."

"There's somebody very interested in what I'm doing. He's been behind me all day."

"Where is he now?"

Now I had Teague's undivided attention.

"He should be parked somewhere near the station. He's driving a blue Datsun."

"Registration number?"

"I don't know."

"How about a description?"

"He wears glasses."

"And?"

"That's it."

"Christ Almighty. And you have the nerve to call yourself a detective."

"What do you expect?" I was as exasperated as Teague. "I've been doing my best not to scare him off."

"I'm sorry." Teague's anger had dissipated as fast as it had arrived. "I've had a long, trying day."

"You're not the only one."

Teague stood up and paced across to the window. He whistled tunelessly to himself while he considered how best to handle this new development. When he spoke again, he still had his back to me.

"It could be the killer, you know."

"Possible but unlikely. It's a really sloppy tail. Somehow that doesn't fit with the picture I've built up of the murderer."

"All the same, it's something to bear in mind." He was silent for a few seconds before he continued. "How do you feel about it, Frank? Do you want him off your back? Or can I let him run a little? See where he goes?"

By now Teague had turned to face me. I knew which answer he wanted me to give.

"It's entirely up to you, John. Provided Mrs. Latimer is covered, I'm easy."

"You'll both be covered. Where are you going from here?"

"The Strathmore. Mrs. Latimer has a room there. It might be a good idea for me to stay at the hotel as well."

"It would make things easier for me. Give me five minutes to make the arrangements. I'll let you know as soon as I'm ready for you to leave."

"Fine. There's just one more thing. Will you be needing Mrs. Latimer any more?"

Teague bit his bottom lip while he thought about my question. He looked almost as tired as Angela.

"I will at some stage. It would be handy to have her around if anything crops up. On the other hand, I won't make an issue of it. I assume you want to pack her off to Lisbon."

"I'd like to. That's where all her friends are. I can't be with her all the time."

"O.K. If she wants to go, she can. I can always contact her by phone or through the Portuguese police. Come to that, I might be able to swing a free holiday on expenses."

"You'll be lucky. How about the inquest?"

"I think I can fix it so she doesn't have to attend."

"Can you do the same for me? You have a signed statement."

"That might be more difficult. I'll see what I can do."

I hoped he was successful. Angela wouldn't be the only person going to Lisbon.

Angela and I had dinner at the Strathmore. Although the food was good, neither of us could muster much of an appetite. We were simply going through the motions. Our lack of enthusiasm communicated itself to the waiter. We had to reassure him that we had no complaints about the meal or the service.

Angela had had a long, traumatic day. I fully expected her to retire to bed directly after we'd eaten but she didn't. She preferred to accompany me into the bar. I suspected that she didn't want to be on her own. We managed to get a table in one corner, and I settled Angela down with her drink before I went across to the public phone. To my surprise, Teague was still at the police station. He must have been expecting my call because I was put straight through to him.

"Have you had any luck?" I enquired.

"Some. The man who was following you is called David Pierce. He's from Dunstable."

The name rang a faint bell at the back of my memory.

"You traced the registration?"

"We did." I could hear the weariness in Teague's voice. "Mind you, we could have saved ourselves the trouble. He packed up for the day about half an hour after you arrived at the hotel. My boys followed him to his home. Guess what he does for a living."

"I don't need to. You're about to tell me."

"I thought you might know him. He's a private investigator."

Now I knew why the name had been familiar. We'd never met but I had inherited a couple of his clients. From what I'd heard, Pierce was strictly small-time.

"Perhaps he's trying a spot of industrial espionage. He probably wants to know what makes me such a success. What do you plan to do now?"

"It's already done. Pierce is sitting in one of my interview rooms. He's not likely to be one of the principals. It was a waste of manpower following him any longer."

"Has he been able to help you?"

"Not really. He doesn't even know who hired him."

"You're sure he's not just protecting his client?"

"Of course I am—this isn't a Hollywood B movie. Pierce is falling over himself to cooperate."

"So it's a dead end."

"More or less. If you call in tomorrow morning, I'll give you the details."

Some of the disappointment must have shown on my face. When I rejoined her, Angela realized at once that something was wrong. I gave her a brief résumé of what had been happening. Although she didn't say as much, she was clearly upset because I hadn't taken her into my confidence earlier. She was equally upset to learn that Pierce wasn't likely to be much help. So far we couldn't even be sure that he'd been hired by Robert's murderer.

"The police don't seem to be making much headway." Angela sounded depressed.

"Give them a chance, love. It's early days yet."

"I read an article in a newspaper a few months back which said that most murder cases are solved in the first twenty-four hours or they're not solved at all."

"It may well have done, but that doesn't necessarily mean it's true." I could remember saying pretty much the same thing to Googan earlier in the day. "Teague is a good policeman."

"So you keep telling me." Angela obviously wasn't convinced. "Be honest with me, Frank. Do you think the murderer will be caught?"

"I honestly don't know."

"You're ducking again."

"Not really. It's an impossible question to answer."

"In that case I'll phrase it differently. What do you think the odds are?"

Angela was a veteran of the Estoril casino. She expected a serious answer. In the end I decided to err on the generous side.

"Sixty-forty," I said.

"For or against?"

"Against."

To my surprise, Angela didn't ask the obvious question. Instead she finished off the rest of her drink. The alcohol had brought a little colour back to her cheeks, although this still left her much paler than I liked. I'd preferred her tears to this new, strained control.

"I'm not very good at expressing sympathy but it's there all the same. I know what you must be suffering. I can remember how I felt after the accident."

"There's one big difference, Frank. You were actually there. You know why it happened, you know how it happened. I don't. All I know at the moment is that Robert was butchered. Nobody has even had the courage to tell me exactly how Robert was killed. Can you understand what I'm trying to say?"

"Of course I can."

Angela probably wasn't aware of the tears trickling down her cheeks. I could feel a responsive tickling behind my own eyes.

"Then you should understand why I can't let it go, Frank. If I can't have Robert, I have to have a reason for him not being there any more. Most of all, though, I want the man who murdered him caught. I won't have Robert mouldering in his grave while his murderer walks free."

I nodded. There was nothing else I could do. Angela wasn't really asking for vengeance, although it must have been there at the back of her mind. She wanted an explanation which could satisfactorily account for her loss. It wasn't my place to tell her there never was a satisfactory explanation.

"You say the police only have a forty-sixty chance of success," she went on. "Those odds aren't good enough for me—not nearly good enough."

"So how do you improve them?"

"I don't. You do, Frank. You're a detective. You were Robert's best friend. I want to hire your services."

I couldn't pretend that this was a surprise. I'd seen the request coming all night.

"Teague wouldn't appreciate it," I pointed out. "The police don't welcome people like me interfering in their affairs."

"I'm not asking you to interfere." Angela was leaning forward, her intensity undiminished. "If the police deliver the goods, that's fine. If they don't, I'd like you ready to take over."

"Don't let's get carried away. If the police don't make any progress, what makes you think I'll fare any better? I collect debts and trace missing daughters. Murder investigations are way out of my league."

Angela shook her head impatiently. "You'll have the motivation to make up for your lack of experience. You won't have any other cases to distract you. There won't be any deadline."

"O.K. I'll concede all that, but there's still a very good chance that I won't get anywhere. What then?"

"I haven't thought that far."

What Angela was saying was that she'd never give up. She had all her sister's determination and fixity of purpose.

"Tell me something, Frank. Why do you think the odds are against the police succeeding?"

The question caught me slightly off balance. Earlier on Angela had passed by the opportunity to ask it, and I'd thought it had been forgotten.

"It's just a feeling, really. I know Robert was killed here in England but I don't think that's where the answers are. I think they're back in Portugal."

"Why?" Angela had no intention of letting me off the hook.

"It wasn't a chance killing, I'm sure of that. He wouldn't have had much opportunity to cultivate personal enemies over here—he'd been in the country less than twenty-four hours."

There were other reasons as well, but for the moment, I preferred to keep them to myself. I was waiting for Angela to use what I'd just said as another lever. She didn't bother—she relied on a direct appeal.

"Will you help me, Frank? I need you."

"On one condition." I was having to harden my heart. "You fly back to Lisbon tomorrow morning."

"I can't. What about the funeral?"

"What about it? It's going to be in Lisbon."

"There's the body."

"Leave the arrangements to me. I'll fly over on the same flight as the coffin."

"There's the police as well. Won't they mind me going?"

"That's already fixed. I've spoken to Teague about it."

Angela managed a smile. It might not have been much of a smile but it was a definite improvement.

"Give me a lift to the airport, Frank, and it's a deal."

"You're on. Would you like another drink to seal the bargain?"

On my way up to the bar, I reflected that Angela's powers of persuasion had been wasted. My attitude was the same as hers: if the police drew a blank, nothing on earth would stop me from taking up the trail. I wanted Robert's killer almost as much as Angela did.

CHAPTER 5

Apparently Pierce hadn't been any help at all. I guessed that he must have been desperate for business, otherwise he'd never have agreed to keep me under surveillance. If I was honest, there were grey areas in my own work. My association with Googan wasn't something I'd ever boast about. However, I did have certain standards—I always made sure I knew exactly what I was getting into. If only to protect myself, I needed to know the law was on my side. Pierce obviously wasn't quite so concerned.

Despite his protests to the contrary, he must have known about Robert's murder. He must have realized the risks he was taking. If he'd had any doubts at all, the way he was contacted should have removed them. Accepting work from somebody called "Smith" over the telephone was almost a crime in itself. Pierce didn't even have a phone number to go with the false name: "Smith" had arranged to telephone Pierce for his reports. Beyond any shadow of a doubt, Pierce had known he was involved in something extremely dubious. This was probably why Teague still had him at the police station. He needed to be taught some kind of lesson.

Teague and I discussed this over coffee in the canteen. Angela was back at the hotel packing her things. I hadn't told her that the seat she'd be using had originally been booked in Robert's name. He'd have been using it if he'd still been alive.

"What exactly was Pierce's brief?" I enquired. "Have you managed to establish that?"

"It was pretty straightforward." I'd no idea how many hours' sleep Teague had managed but he still looked deathly tired. "Pierce was simply instructed to keep you under surveillance. He was to report where you went and whom you met."

"He wasn't on the lookout for anything in particular?"

"Nothing. What do you make of that?"

"Let me ask you a question first. Mrs. Latimer wants to retain me to find her husband's killer. She knows you're doing everything possible but she wants me as a back-up, just in case. Do you have any objections?"

The face Teague pulled was an answer in itself. "You're perfectly aware of the official attitude, Frank. I share it."

"Isn't this a little bit different? The murder may have been on your patch, but I think you'll have to go further afield to find a motive."

"Go on." Teague wasn't giving anything away.

"You've heard it already. When he arrived in Luton, Robert told me he was hatching something big. To be honest, I didn't pay too much attention at the time—Robert was always that way. I'm pretty sure I made a mistake. Robert was involved in something big. It was important enough to get him killed."

"That's pure hypothesis."

"Maybe. Can you come up with anything better?"

"What exactly are you getting at?" Teague knew perfectly well.

"Whatever it was that Robert was planning, the plans were made in Portugal—Luton is simply the place he happened to be killed. I have to go to Lisbon for the funeral. While I'm there I want to do some digging."

"That's a problem for the local police. I don't give a damn what you do in Portugal."

"Is it all right to make a few enquiries over here before I go? I'll only be going over ground you've already covered."

There was quite a lot of haggling left to do. Teague might not be able to stop me asking questions but he could make life very difficult for me. I needed his authorization without making any definite commitment to him. Teague wanted me controlled; he also wanted to make sure that I fed him any scraps of information I did pick up.

"What about Pierce?" Teague asked once the ground rules had been established. "You didn't answer me before. What do you make of his mysterious Mr. Smith?"

"The same as you do probably. He's either the killer or somebody connected with him."

"You don't think there may be a connection with your work at the Agency?"

"It's most unlikely. I haven't handled anything sensitive recently. Besides, the timing is all wrong. I don't believe in coincidences."

Teague nodded. "I'm not over-fond of them myself. That leaves us with one big question. Why should the killer have any interest in you?"

My shrug was genuine. "Your guess is as good as mine. Perhaps he thinks Robert took me into his confidence."

"But he didn't?"

This was a point Teague kept returning to. No matter how many times I told him, he didn't quite believe me. Premeditated murder had to have a motive. Until Teague found one, he was groping in the dark.

"Robert didn't say a thing. I only wish he had."

"That makes two of us." Teague examined his fingernails. Like the rest of him, they were well looked after. "Let's recap. The way you see it, Mr. Latimer may have been in possession of dangerous information. Agreed?"

"Agreed."

"Furthermore, the murderer might not be sure whether or not he passed this information on to you."

"I suppose not."

"That being the case, the murderer might decide he'd be safer with

you out of the way. I don't want to frighten you, Frank, but that's
the way it seems to me."

"I'm already frightened," I told him. "That's one of the reasons I
want Angela back in Portugal. She might be at risk too."

Teague nodded. He didn't point out that she might equally be at
risk in Lisbon.

"Don't be too worried if you find you still have a tail. It'll be one
of my men."

"That's fine by me. If it makes life any easier for you, I'll give you
an itinerary for the day."

"I'd appreciate that. There's one other thing as well. I'd like you
to sleep at your place tonight."

"Why?"

"Just in case the killer does decide to come back after you. I'll
send two of my lads along to keep you company."

"That's a pretty long shot, isn't it?"

"Who knows? We might be lucky."

Besides, long shots were about all Teague had in his armoury.

The Britannic offices were in the main airport block at Luton. I
headed there as soon as I'd seen Angela safely off. A small group of
ground hostesses was standing outside the entrance. Their blue uni-
forms were smart and freshly pressed, and their ridiculous little hats
nestled on their heads at jaunty angles. It must have been the beginning of their tour of duty. Later on in the day they'd wilt a little. One
of them, an attractive brunette, gave me a smile as I passed. I'd spent
almost a month working at the airport the previous year and she
must have remembered me from then.

The receptionist in the Britannic front office was definitely new.
However, she'd been there long enough to learn that only a very few
people were admitted to see Alan Thorne without an appointment.
She obviously didn't consider me to belong to that number. Her boss
hadn't taken her into his confidence about his alimony payments, or
how I'd sorted them out for him.

"I know he's busy," I said. "He always is. Just tell him Frank
MacAllister would like a quick word with him."

"I'll try."

She made it perfectly plain that she didn't expect me to have any luck. While she was gone I flicked through some promotional brochures. Package holidays were what Luton airport was all about, and Britannic had regular flights to most of the usual resorts. It also ran a few to others off the beaten track. I flicked through the glossy photographs and tried to remember when I'd last had a proper holiday. Without Jane or the twins to go with me, I hadn't bothered.

"Mr. Thorne will see you straightaway, Mr. MacAllister."

The receptionist sounded surprised. She was also resentful. It was as though I'd undermined what little authority she had.

"Thanks," I said. "I can find my own way."

Thorne was lolling back in his swivel chair when I went in. He was a short, rotund man with very clear blue eyes. He'd lost a bit more hair since we'd last met. I'd have been going bald too if I'd lived as long as he had with his bitch of an ex-wife.

"It's good to see you again, Frank. Grab a pew."

I sat down where I could look out of the window. On the tarmac, a gaggle of holidaymakers was filing towards an Airbus.

"I read about what happened the other night." Alan was all sympathy. "The police have been up here as well. It must have been a nasty business. Was he a close friend?"

"Very close. He's one of the reasons I'm here. I have to ship the body back to Lisbon. I was hoping you might be able to arrange it for me. If it's possible, I'd like a seat on the same plane as the coffin."

Thorne pulled a face. I knew I was asking a lot. "We only do a couple of flights there each day. When did you want to go?"

"Sometime tomorrow."

Teague had promised me the autopsy would be finished before then.

"I'll do my best but I can't promise anything." Thorne was scribbling busily on the note pad in front of him. "The Lisbon flights are always fully booked, and there aren't usually many cancellations."

"See what you can manage. If it's not on from Luton, I'll have to use a scheduled flight from Heathrow. I'll take first class if that's all that's available."

"You don't want to do that." Thorne had pulled another face. "It's money down the drain. Give me five minutes. I can tell you one way or the other by then."

It took him less than three. Neither Britannic nor any of the other airlines operating from Luton could fit me in at such short notice. However, there were no problems at Heathrow. Thorne managed to book me on an afternoon TAP flight. He also made arrangements to have the coffin driven up to London. This was his way of making amends. He'd never considered his obligation to me to have been fully covered by my bill.

Consequently, he was quite pleased when I made a second request he could handle. As the police had already asked to see the flight list, it only took him a couple of minutes to hunt it out. He had all the answers at his fingertips as well. All the passengers had been part of a package except for Robert and a Mr. A. J. Oliveira. Both of them had made use of last-minute cancellations. This alone was enough to make Oliveira interesting, but there was considerably more to it than this. Oliveira appeared to have vanished from the face of the earth after leaving the airport.

"Did the police talk to the flight staff?"

"Those that were available."

"And?"

"Nothing. None of the hostesses could remember your friend or Oliveira. You know how it is on a package flight, Frank. The girls are so busy they only notice the bloody nuisances. It's only the drunks and gropers who make any impression."

"Did both of them make return bookings?"

"Mr. Latimer did but not Oliveira."

"How easy would it be to find out whether Oliveira has already flown back to Portugal? Or when he's planning to fly back?"

Thorne's laugh was devoid of any amusement. "It's virtually impossible. Oliveira isn't exactly an uncommon name. And there are a hell of a lot of carriers flying to Portugal. The police have got me trying for them but I don't expect much joy."

So that was that. I hadn't really anticipated much more.

"Is it all right if we take a look around?"

"Help yourself. If you like, you can pack my suitcase while you're about it."

He grinned and shook his head. "It's against union rules. We're baby-minders, not domestics."

The two CID men had arrived shortly after my return from the office. They were typical of the new generation of police detectives: young, scruffy and armed. Jeans and leather jackets had replaced raincoats as their badge of office. Their names were Bright and Anderson, but so far I hadn't worked out which was which.

While they prowled about the house, I settled down in the living room. The stain on the ceiling above the fireplace was a painful reminder, and I felt better with my eyes closed.

It had been a hectic afternoon. I had no real idea how long I'd be staying in Portugal and there had been a lot of arrangements to make. Fortunately, Marcia was worth her weight in gold rather than the pittance I paid her. She'd joined the Agency while my father had still been alive. She knew far more about its day-to-day functioning than I ever would. I had no reservations at all about leaving her in charge while I was away. Knowing her, Marcia would probably be taking some of the workload from Stubbs's shoulders.

The sound of the phone ringing in the hall jerked me out of my reverie. One of the CID men answered for me. He talked for a couple of minutes before he called me.

"It's the gaffer," he explained. "He'd like a quick word with you."

I accepted the receiver from him.

"Smith has just phoned Pierce," Teague informed me. "I thought you might like to know."

He'd advised me earlier that Pierce would be escorted back to his office in Dunstable. Teague had hoped that when Smith phoned for his report, he would be able to trace the call.

"How did it go?"

"Not too well. Smith wasn't using a local phone. He was in a call box in London. The best we could do was tape what he said."

"Can I listen to the tape?"

"Sure. I'll play it through for you now."

The recording ran for more than five minutes. Pierce did most of the talking. He'd obviously been briefed about what to say. From the little Smith did contribute, one thing was apparent.

"If that's Oliveira," I said, "he speaks remarkably good English."

"I thought the same. Whoever Smith is, he isn't a foreigner."

"He seemed very interested in my visit to the airport."

"That came through loud and clear. The shame of it is, he didn't make any arrangements to contact Pierce any more."

"I suppose there's not a great deal of point. He knows I'm going to Lisbon tomorrow."

"True. He'll send Pierce his cash through the post and that will be that."

There wasn't much more Teague and I had to say to each other. Another possible line of enquiry seemed to have ended in a dead end, and, as far as I knew, Teague had nothing to replace it. Forensic had failed to come up with anything useful. The Portuguese police hadn't managed to trace Oliveira at the Lisbon end. Even Mrs. Cameron next door had let us down: she'd been out shopping the afternoon Robert had been killed.

I only managed a couple of steps down the hall before the phone started ringing again. As I snatched up the receiver, I assumed Teague must have forgotten something. I was mistaken.

"I'd just about given you up, Frankie."

"I've only just arrived home, Mr. Googan."

"It's lucky you did. I wouldn't have bothered ringing again. You know that matter we were discussing yesterday? I've been making one or two enquiries. There was no contract out on your friend Latimer."

"You're sure?"

"I wouldn't say so otherwise." This was a reproof. "Unless it was a cowboy killing, nobody local was involved. Is that any help to you?"

"It helps a lot. I really appreciate what you've done."

"Appreciation I can live without. Just trim some of the fat off your next bill. I'll be seeing you, Frankie."

The two conversations had depressed me. There was still no real starting point to my investigation. The two detectives waiting for me in the living room didn't do a thing to cheer me up. They were wasting their time too. Nobody would be trying to kill me. With the amount I knew about Robert's death, I wasn't a threat to anybody.

Once upon a time it had been a nice part of Shepherd's Bush. This had been when Shepherd's Bush had still had nice parts. Now the area was on the slide. A lot of people would have said the West Indians and Asians crowding the pavements were the cause, but I preferred to think they were the effect. Whatever the reason, the only sign of prosperity in sight was parked at the far kerb. It was a maroon Rover 3500. If the car had been mine, I wouldn't have wanted to leave it untended for the day. I was slightly dubious about leaving my Capri for half an hour. Rafferty evidently didn't care—he probably had the vehicle insured for double its real value.

It had been Robert's idea to retain Rafferty as our British agent. I hadn't disputed his choice. We'd just started the business and not many people had taken us very seriously. Most of the agents we'd contacted simply hadn't been interested; others had wanted an arm or a leg as the price of their participation. Rafferty had been far more reasonable: the terms he'd proposed had been fair to both sides. Although I'd never liked him as a man, I couldn't fault his business acumen. It was Rafferty who had secured us our first major outlets in Britain. When we were established, it was Rafferty who pointed out how we could best exert pressure on our suppliers. He might have made money at our expense but we'd made money too. Inevitably, there had been differences, but none of them had posed a serious threat to the relationship. It had become more important than ever after I'd left the firm.

I locked the Capri and started across the road. My present interest in Rafferty wasn't directly connected with commerce. Rafferty was the man Robert had come to England to see. Although she hadn't known the purpose of the meeting, Angela had been adamant on this point. This was why I'd stopped off in Shepherd's Bush on my way to Heathrow.

Rafferty's office was on the top floor. Forewarned by his receptionist, Rafferty was waiting to greet me by the door. He was a big, florid man in his late fifties whose hooded eyes would have been the envy of many a Mafia don. For a few seconds we stood in the doorway and pumped hands vigorously.

"How long is it, Frank? It must be at least seven years now."

"Not quite that long."

My reply was irrelevant. Rafferty specialized in monologues.

"Isn't it terrible about Robert? I couldn't believe it when I first heard the news. According to the police, I was almost the last person to see him alive. And it was you who found the body, wasn't it?"

"That's right."

For the next couple of minutes I allowed Rafferty to maunder on.

Sooner or later I knew he'd run out of steam. Then I'd be able to stake a claim in the conversation. My opportunity finally came when he asked a question which wasn't rhetorical. By this time we were both seated.

"Who's going to run the business now Robert is gone? I suppose Sanchez will have to take over."

Sanchez was Robert's number two. Rafferty would be able to run rings round him.

"I think Mrs. Latimer might want to hold the reins herself."

"She's never shown much interest in the business before."

"There wasn't any real need while Robert was around. It's different now."

"She'll need help." Rafferty sounded dubious. It was in his own interests for Latimer SA to remain healthy.

"She'll be getting it. I'm going to stay in Lisbon for a few weeks. That should give her plenty of time to learn the ropes."

"The company has changed a lot since you left, Frank. There's been a lot of expansion these last few years."

"So Robert told me. It's one reason I dropped by to see you. I was hoping for a quick breakdown of what's been going on."

"Nothing simpler, old chap. You can look at the same résumé I prepared for Robert."

Rafferty took down a bulky box file from one of the shelves. The résumé itself ran to three typed pages. I read them through carefully while Rafferty smoked a cigar. When I'd finished, I was puzzled. As Rafferty had indicated, there had been a lot of changes. Robert had diversified. Ceramics remained the single most important trading item but the company had been given a much broader base. Exports of textiles, footwear and cork had all increased dramatically in volume. Lumped together, they now brought in more money than the ceramics. All the same, I couldn't find any explanation for Robert's excitement when he'd spoken to me. Considering the favourable exchange rate, the figures weren't that good. Volume might be up but so were the overheads; profits were almost static. The recession appeared to have hit Robert as hard as everybody else.

"May I have a photostat of the résumé?"

"Of course. My secretary will see to it before you leave."

"There's one thing it doesn't show. I gathered that Robert had some big new venture in the wind."

"Not that I know of." The answer came out pat. Perhaps it was a little too pat.

"Isn't that why he came to see you?"

"If he did, he must have changed his mind on the way." Rafferty sounded politely perplexed.

"What did he talk about then?"

"The usual. It was a normal six-monthly meeting. Basically we went through the résumé together. I made one or two suggestions. So did Robert. There was no question of any significant change in strategy."

"You surprise me. The way Robert was talking, he had some major coup in the pipeline."

"In what area?"

"That's what I'd like to know."

We sat in silence for a few seconds. This didn't get us anywhere.

"Do you know where Robert was going after he left you?"

"Back to Luton. We had lunch together. Then I dropped him off at the station."

"So he was with you all day."

"From eleven o'clock onwards, yes."

Rafferty sounded very convincing. I wondered what it was he had to hide. I also wondered if he was Pierce's mysterious Mr. Smith. Teague's recording hadn't been very good but it might have been Rafferty's voice I'd listened to. I'd definitely be seeing Rafferty again after I'd returned from Lisbon.

CHAPTER 6

"Are you feeling all right, sir?"

"I'm fine, thanks." My voice was hoarse and I could feel the sweat trickling down beside my eyes. The air hostess was looking worried. So was the middle-aged woman sitting beside me. It was probably she who had called the hostess.

"You don't look very well, if you don't mind me saying so. Can I bring you anything?"

"A glass of ice water would be nice."

The hostess swayed off down the aisle. The woman in the next seat was still looking at me.

"You were moaning in your sleep," she said.

"I'm sorry."

She was quite prepared to continue the conversation but I wasn't. I turned to look out of the window. There was a solid bank of stratus below us, and I guessed we must be over the Bay of Biscay by now.

"Here's your water, sir."

"Thank you. I apologize for being such a nuisance."

"That's perfectly all right. It helps to break the monotony. Just ring if you need anything else."

She made it sound like an invitation. I went back to looking out of the window. I felt ashamed of myself. The nightmare had crept up on me unawares, probably because I was overtired. For several years the dream had been a regular feature of my life. I couldn't begin to count the number of nights I'd spent drinking coffee in the small hours. At one stage it had been so bad I'd almost been afraid to go to sleep. Nowadays it troubled me much less frequently. Unfortunately, when it did come, it remained as vivid as ever.

There was only one sure way to get it out of my system. Sitting there, wide awake, I deliberately reran what had happened. This was painful therapy but it seemed to work. On occasions it brought me a whole month of undisturbed sleep.

It had been a Sunday afternoon in May. My father had been making one of his rare visits to Portugal, spending a long weekend with us. As it was sunny and hot, we'd agreed on an afternoon out. Robert and I had suggested driving north along the coast to Nazaré; Angela and Jane had wanted to go to Santarém for the big Ribatejo fair. Dad was quite content to fall in with the majority. This had left the casting vote with the twins, who'd sided with the women.

We travelled in two cars. Jane, Dad and the twins had used our Fiat, and I'd gone with Robert and Angela. There was a mystery knock under the bonnet of the Mercedes that Robert had wanted me to listen to. I could distinctly remember making a joke about Jane's driving before we set out. All I recalled of her reply was the laugh. She'd been in one of her sunniest moods. Jane and my father had always hit it off well together.

We were on the toll road north of Lisbon when it happened. Jane was in front, with us about fifty yards behind. The articulated lorry had been on the Madrid run. It ground past, klaxon blaring, and Robert gave the driver the finger. He thought the lorry was too close. So did Jane. I saw her glance up at the driver's cab. It was then that one of the lorry's tyres blew. The driver only lost control for a second. This was just long enough for the cab to sideswipe the Fiat. Jane spun twice. She was beginning a third spin when the car ploughed into the bridge support. Robert had only just started to brake as the petrol tank went.

By the time I reached it, the entire car was ablaze. Strangely, my brain remained icily calm. "Forget Jane," it instructed me. "She's dead." Even through the smoke and flames there could be no doubt about this. The whole bonnet had concertinaed, driving the engine back into the front seat. I only caught a glimpse but it was enough. Below the waist, it was impossible to tell where Jane ended and the jagged, razor-sharp metal began. "Leave Dad too. He's still alive but he's beyond help." With each breath, great gouts of blood were coming from his mouth, running down over his chin. "Go for the twins." I couldn't see them but they were both alive. I could hear their screams, a mixture of fear and pain. But the rear door had buckled. I attacked it with a ferocity I hadn't known I possessed. It still wouldn't budge.

"The glass," Robert shouted from beside me. "Go for the glass." Although I broke three fingers putting my fist through the window, I was beyond pain. Like the cuts and burns, my fingers didn't start hurting until later. For an instant, through the smoke, I could see one of the twins. It was impossible to tell whether it was Alison or Tracey. Her hair was ablaze, her face a bloody mess. I was reaching for her when the second explosion blew me backwards. After this, there were no more screams.

It took Robert and three other men who had come to our aid to hold me back. I was still ranting and raving when the first ambulance arrived on the scene nearly ten minutes later. By then the Fiat was no more than a smouldering heap of twisted metal. Just about everything I loved had died inside it. Part of me had died as well. Two days after the funeral I'd left Portugal to return to Luton.

Now I was going back for another funeral. By now the Boeing was over northern Portugal and we'd left the cloud behind at the coast. Whereas England was a green land, Portugal was predominantly brown. It was a harsh, proud country which had been forced into imperial expansion. There had been very little to keep the Portuguese men at home. The twentieth century had come later to Portugal than it had to the rest of western Europe—in some areas it still hadn't properly arrived. Portugal was a country which lived on memories of its past, with little to hope for in the future. In this context, Angela would fit in well. So, for that matter, would I.

The roads were wet from a recent shower. There had been a delay at the airport while we'd waited for Robert's coffin to clear customs, and, as a result, we caught the beginning of the evening traffic. For such a poor country, there were a hell of a lot of cars.

For most of the journey Angela didn't speak. She seldom did when she was driving. It was something she did really well. She was one of those rare people with a total understanding of the vehicle she controlled. And control it she did. The Alfa became a mechanical extension of her, responding to her slightest whim. Angela was completely aware of the patterns the traffic flow made around her. She found

space where lesser mortals would have been hemmed in. Her compe-
tence made me aware of the deficiencies of my own driving.

While Angela gave her virtuoso performance, I watched the buildings and people go by. The Lisbon area hadn't changed much since
I'd last been there. The buildings were more or less the same and the
people didn't look very different either. Even the slogans daubed on
the walls hadn't changed a great deal, although a lot of them were
beginning to fade. I suspected that this might be symptomatic of the
revolution. I'd never been entirely convinced that Portugal and democracy were compatible.

The house was in Monte Estoril, half a mile from the coast road. It
had been a gift from Angela's father. Before Caetano's overthrow the
area had been one of the bastions of privilege, and it remained so.
Some of the villas looked a little tatty. Paintwork was peeling and
gardens were overgrown. A few still remained unoccupied. For a
while it hadn't been safe to display too many outward manifestations
of wealth. Many of the wealthy had elected to sweat out the revolution abroad, and some had never come back. For all that, most of the
money had remained in the same few, privileged hands. For every
deserted villa, like the one across the road from Angela's, there were
ten which looked as substantial and prosperous as before.

Robert hadn't been one of the hypocrites. He'd seen no reason to
be ashamed of what he'd earned with his own sweat. He'd stayed in
Portugal and he hadn't hidden behind a façade. His boldness had
paid off—for the most part he'd been left alone. The white walls of
his villa looked as clean as they'd ever done.

It didn't take me long to unpack and freshen up. When I had, I
found Angela sitting out on the verandah with a pitcher of iced
lemonade on the table in front of her. I sat down opposite and
poured myself a glass. The house felt emptier than I remembered. I
wondered how it seemed to Angela. Robert had always expanded to
fill the space around him.

However, the view from the verandah remained as satisfying as
ever. The villa was right at the top of the hill and there was a clear
view down over the tiled rooftops to the graceful sweep of the bay.
The Algarve was for the tourists; most of the rest of Portugal had
been kept for the Portuguese. The tourists flocked to Estoril and
Cascais, of course, but they never swamped the native population.

The coastline hadn't been spoiled by a ribbon development of look-alike hotels.

"Do you want to eat out, Frank? Or shall I rustle something up for us?"

"That's entirely up to you."

Angela was looking much better than she had in England. The greyness had gone from her skin.

"I'd rather go out, I think. I don't seem to have much enthusiasm for cooking at the moment."

Or for being cooped up in the house, I suspected. Everywhere she looked there were reminders of Robert.

"O.K. Is it too late to get a table at Ferenc and Manuela's?"

"I doubt it. We may have to wait a little but they'll squeeze us in somehow."

The restaurant was on the Rua do Viveiro. People who didn't know it was there could walk right past without noticing it. The interior wasn't ostentatious either. There was simply a bar at the front and half a dozen tables at the back. Neither Ferenc nor Manuela was too interested in the passing trade. All the people who mattered in Estoril and the surrounding area knew about the restaurant, and many of them used it on a regular basis.

Ferenc was pleased to see us. So was Manuela when she was brought out from the kitchen. They'd heard about Robert and were tactfully sympathetic. The food, as usual, was superb. After we'd eaten, we chatted for a while at the bar. It was my suggestion that we should move to a quiet corner. Angela was in no hurry to return to the house and we had to talk.

"Have you had any second thoughts about what you asked me to do?" I enquired.

"None whatsoever." Angela sounded positive enough.

"Last time we talked I warned you there was no guarantee of success."

"I remember."

"There's something else to consider. If I am successful, you won't necessarily like what I find out."

"You mean the killer might be somebody I know."

"There might be more to it than that."

"In that case I don't follow you."

I poured myself some more of the dry cocktail port. The bottle felt pleasantly cold to the touch. It delayed what had to be said next. However carefully I phrased myself, Angela was likely to be upset.

"Robert was no chance victim," I said. "I know it's a possibility but it isn't very likely. At least I don't think so."

"Nor do I any longer. You and Inspector Teague managed to convince me."

"Fine. That leaves us with the question of motive. Unless Robert had an enemy neither of us knew about, I can see two main possibilities. Firstly, Robert might have had something in his possession which was important enough to kill for."

"What makes you think that?"

"The murderer searched Robert's room and luggage very thoroughly. He was obviously looking for something."

"It could have been money."

"No." I was very definite about this. "The killer went through Robert's wallet after he was dead. There was almost a hundred pounds in notes that he left behind. Besides, he only searched Robert's room. The rest of the house wasn't touched."

"But . . ."

I interrupted Angela before she had a chance to go any further. "Just let me finish. The second possibility is that Robert knew something that was important enough to kill for. Robert didn't die immediately. It looked as though he was questioned before he was killed."

"There could be plenty of other reasons." Angela was reluctant to accept what I was saying.

"Of course there could be. With what we know at the moment, I'm only guessing. You think about it, though. Can you think of another explanation which fits in with the facts? Can you explain why somebody would hire a private detective to keep an eye on me after Robert was dead?"

Angela started to speak. Then she changed her mind.

"I'm not closing my eyes to the other possibilities," I went on. "I'm simply saying these are the only explanations which make any sense to me. Later on, when I know more, I may have to change my mind."

Angela toyed with her glass while she considered what I'd said. I refilled it for her. So far she was bearing up remarkably well: she was managing to divorce theory from what had actually happened. "O.K., Frank," she conceded. "I can accept that. There's one thing I still don't understand. Why shouldn't I like what you find out?"

"Think about it. Let's assume I'm right. Robert didn't exactly advertise his visit to England in advance. His murder had to be arranged at pretty short notice. That immediately suggests something to me, especially if a hired killer was used."

"You're saying criminals were involved?" By now Angela was keeping step with me.

"Everything appears to point in that direction at the moment."

Although Angela was looking puzzled again, I left her to work it out for herself. I could tell the exact moment when the penny dropped. She actually stiffened in her seat.

"Let me get this straight, Frank MacAllister." Her voice was suddenly very tight and controlled. The hostility beamed across the table like a knife. "Are you seriously suggesting that Robert was involved in some kind of criminal activity?"

"I'm not suggesting anything. I'm trying to point out possibilities."

"But it's absolutely absurd. Robert never did anything dishonest in his life."

"That all depends on your interpretation of honesty. There were occasions when he bent the law a little to his own advantage. Both of us did."

"You're wrong, Frank. I know you are." Angela was shaking her head as she rose to her feet. "I want to go home."

We didn't speak on the short walk back to the villa. I knew I'd erected a barrier between us. I hoped it wouldn't last too long.

It was cool out on the verandah. There was a breeze blowing off the Atlantic which brought up goose bumps on my arms. I briefly considered going inside the house to fetch a pullover, but it didn't seem to be worth the effort. I'd finish off the Bacardi and lime I'd mixed myself, then I'd go to bed.

Angela had retired half an hour earlier. Although she'd been polite enough, she obviously hadn't forgiven me yet. Perhaps I ought to have left our discussion for later—it would have given Angela more time to adjust. Come to that, perhaps I shouldn't have brought the matter up at all. I'd been attempting to prepare Angela for the worst but the worst didn't always happen.

My mind drifted to what the following day would hold. I definitely wasn't looking forward to the morning. The funeral would be at the same church where Jane and the rest of my family were buried. I thought I could cope but I wasn't absolutely positive. On the credit side, there had been no real traumas about returning to Lisbon. In many ways it was nice to be back. The funeral would be different, though. Last time I'd broken down. It was a memory which still embarrassed me. I'd needed Robert to half carry me back to the car after the service. This time I'd be the one doing the carrying. Angela had asked me to be one of the pallbearers and I hoped I'd behave well. I didn't know quite what would happen when I saw the actual graves again. The last thing Angela needed was for me to act up. I was supposed to be a prop for her to lean on.

The click of the sliding door opening startled me out of my reverie. Angela wasn't tucked safely in bed after all. She remained standing by the door. I couldn't see her face properly in the dim light but she was wearing a long white robe over her nightdress. Like me, she found it cold on the verandah. She was clutching the robe tightly around her.

"I'm sorry, Frank." Her voice sounded very small.

"What about? I'd just decided I owe you an apology."

"No." She sounded very definite about this. "Can you mix me a drink?"

"Of course, but let's have it inside. It's chilly out here."

Angela perched on the leather sofa while I poured her drink. I deliberately made it a weak one. Both of us had been drinking too much. After I'd handed it to her, I dumped myself in an armchair on the far side of the fireplace. I'd successfully resisted the temptation to freshen my own drink.

"I've been lying in bed thinking about what you said."

"I didn't mean to keep you awake."

"I doubt whether I'd have slept much anyway. Besides, it was just the jolt I needed. I was beginning to turn Robert into a myth. You snapped me back to reality."

She was finding it hard going. Her pause allowed me to savour a sudden flash of insight. Wasn't this exactly what I'd done with Jane? Hadn't I constructed an idealized picture of what she'd been? The thought disturbed me.

"Robert changed a lot over this past year," Angela said. "He was very restless. I think he was becoming bored."

"With you?"

I hated myself for asking but it had to be done. The answer could be very important.

"Oh no." Angela was more surprised than offended. The idea obviously hadn't occurred to her. "There weren't any other women, if that's what you mean. We were as close as ever."

I believed her. Infidelity wasn't Robert's style. He'd found the woman he'd wanted, then he'd married her. I'd never believed anything other than death could have separated them.

"It was the company, I think. Robert seemed to have lost interest in it. He left Sanchez to do more and more of the work. Some days he didn't bother to go into the office for more than a couple of hours."

"Did you talk about it?"

"Once or twice. Robert felt he'd done everything he'd set out to do. The company had expanded almost as much as it was going to. He liked the money but it wasn't enough. He needed something more. There was no real challenge any longer."

I nodded. "When did Robert change again?"

"You know about it?" Angela was looking at me in surprise. The question had disconcerted her.

"If you remember, I talked to him. Robert wasn't acting bored then. He was excited. That's why he dragged me out on the town."

"I was forgetting." Angela smiled at me. The talking was doing her good. "That's what I was trying to work out in bed. When the excitement started."

"And?"

"It was just over a fortnight ago. Robert had been up to Caldas da Rainha for a couple of days. When he came back he was different. As soon as I saw him I knew he had something on the boil. He was like he used to be in the old days. I asked him about it but he wouldn't say. You know how Robert was, Frank. He wanted to have it all neatly wrapped up before he laid it out for me."

I nodded again. For the same reason Robert hadn't told me what he was doing in England. He'd simply dropped a few hints to keep me in suspense.

"Tell me something, Angela. Did Robert arrange his visit to Rafferty after he'd come back from Caldas?"

"Oh yes, but you didn't allow me to finish. When I thought about it some more, I realized it had started even before Robert went to Caldas. At least, the signs were there. I can't remember the exact date but it must have been about a week beforehand."

"What exactly happened?"

"Nothing much, really. It was just that Robert came home in a really good mood. He insisted that I get myself dressed up, then he dragged me into Lisbon for the night. We didn't get home until four in the morning."

"Was there any explanation?"

"Not that I can remember. Robert never was one to bring his work home with him. He simply said he'd had a good day at the office. I assumed he'd landed a big contract or something like that."

"You're sure Caldas and the evening out are connected?"

"I'm positive. It hadn't occurred to me before, mind you. Once you'd started me thinking, though, it was obvious. Is what I've said any help, Frank?"

"You know it is. Now you can help me some more. Go to bed and get yourself some sleep."

I stayed behind in the living room after Angela had gone. The motive for Robert's death was as much of a mystery as before but one thing was certain: now I had a definite starting point for my enquiries. Whether it led me anywhere was something only time would tell.

CHAPTER 7

The funeral was quiet and dignified. At Angela's insistence, only family and close friends had been invited. Robert had had no immediate family of his own, so there was only a handful of us at the graveside. Thankfully there were no painful, long-winded eulogies. The entire service lasted for less than half an hour. Angela herself was magnificent. Although she was pale and strained, she didn't waver once. I rather envied her inner strength.

Her father had handled all the funeral arrangements. Afterwards we all went back to his house near Sintra. Perhaps "house" wasn't the proper word to do it justice—in England people would have been paying admission to go inside and look around. Even Jane hadn't known exactly how many bedrooms there were.

I'd always seen the house as a symbol. Money alone wasn't important in Portugal, it was where it came from which mattered. A big landowner who was millions of escudos in debt enjoyed far more social prestige than any parvenu business tycoon. The Boulters represented old wealth, solidly based on the land. Their estates were dotted the length and breadth of Portugal. Until independence, they'd owned large chunks of Mozambique and Angola as well.

Essentially it was a patriarchal family. Anne Boulter, my mother-in-law, organized the servants, supervised social gatherings and bred children. Her great failure had been to produce two daughters and no sons. She was a charming, shallow woman who had once been a great beauty. I'd never, ever managed a meaningful conversation with her. There were too many clichés and conventions cluttering the way.

Adam, her husband, left nobody in any doubt about his position as head of the household. Towards family and employees alike, his attitude was positively feudal. It wouldn't have surprised me to learn he still exercised the right of deflowering the local virgins, and, if he did, I knew it would be for duty, not pleasure. Everything about him was patrician. He was tall, well over six feet, and there wasn't an ounce of surplus flesh anywhere. He had piercing blue eyes which seemed to look straight through you. His nose could have been fitted to the prow of an icebreaker. I'd never seen him other than immaculately dressed. Even his swimming shorts had creases in them.

Although this had never been voiced out loud, his daughters' marriages had been a grave disappointment to him. Robert and I weren't at all what he'd intended for them. They should have married into the aristocracy. However, Adam Boulter was a realist. While the issue had been in doubt, he'd raised every obstacle he could think of, but when it became inevitable, he'd handed over his daughters with the same grace he displayed when he later relinquished his estates in the Portuguese colonies. He had gone out of his way to be courteous and helpful. He was generous to a fault.

At the same time, the resentment had always been there, just below the surface. Robert and I were tolerated, not welcomed. There had never been any suggestion that Adam considered himself to have gained two sons. After Jane's death, there had been no further contact between us. With his daughter and grandchildren gone, I could be relegated to the status of a bad dream.

Consequently, I was rather surprised when he came over to where I was standing. Until this point I'd had to make do with a few rather perfunctory words of greeting.

"Can I speak with you for a few minutes, Frank? In private."

"Of course."

He led me through into the billiard room. This was the holy of holies. Apart from the maids who cleaned it, I doubted whether any woman had ever been invited in there. Both Angela and Jane swore their mother had never been inside, and they'd only been there on a handful of occasions themselves, sneaking in when their parents were busy.

"Do you want to play?" This was a command rather than a request.

"If you like."

"Snooker or billiards?"

"Snooker. It gives me more balls to aim at."

I was deliberately being plebeian. It was what Adam expected and I'd have hated him to be disappointed. While I was selecting a cue, I wondered what it was he wanted. There had to be some compelling reason for Adam to treat me like an honoured guest.

For a while we played in silence. Adam was good. In fact, he was very good. The only reason I could stay with him was that caution wasn't part of his game. He tried to pot every ball, however difficult it was. I lived off the shots he missed, and in between I played some sneaky safety shots, running the cue ball down into baulk. With five red balls left on the table, I was only half a dozen points behind.

"I wanted to thank you, Frank," Adam said abruptly, sinking a long red.

"For what?"

"It's been a very trying time for Angela. You've helped her a lot."

"She did the same for me when Jane died."

Adam had put too much side on the cue ball. This had left him out of position on the black. He went for it anyway, disdaining an easier shot on the blue. The black ended up hovering on the lip of the pocket. This meant it was as good as mine. There was an easy red into the opposite pocket.

"How long will you be staying in Portugal?"

"I'm not sure yet."

"Angela tells me you're going to help to run the company for a while."

"That's the general idea, yes."

"I could have done that for her. I've been trying to persuade Angela to live here for a while. I think she needs her family around her at a time like this."

There was nothing I could say, so I kept quiet. I'd already sunk the red and the black. Now there was another red which might go. Suddenly I very much wanted to win.

"Could you have a word with her, Frank? It really would be the best thing for Angela."

"I'll try."

But not very hard. Angela had already told me that she'd no intention of living with her parents, and this was an attitude I could sympathize with.

The second red had gone down. Unfortunately, there was no obvious colour to follow it with. I decided to play safe and take the cue ball down into baulk. More by luck than judgement, it ended tight behind the green. Adam went off three cushions and missed the red he'd been aiming at. It was another four points to me.

"There's another thing too." Adam was chalking the tip of his cue. "I understand that Angela has hired you to find out who killed Robert. I would have thought that was a job for the police."

"They'd undoubtedly agree with you."

"I'd like you to drop it, Frank."

"Why?"

Surprise made me miss the penultimate red. At least, that was my excuse. Adam didn't. He followed it with the black, then rolled the last red into one of the middle pockets.

"With all due respect, if the police fail to come up with anything, you're hardly likely to do any better. All you'll be doing is keeping the hurt alive for Angela."

"Angela doesn't see it quite like that. She says she needs to know what happened to Robert."

"She's wrong." Adam spoke with all the conviction of somebody who knew what was best for others. He should have gone into politics. "Angela is too close to the tragedy at the moment. In a week or two she'll have put it into perspective. She'll want to let it drop."

"When she gives me the word, I'll drop it."

This wasn't the answer Adam had wanted—I could tell by the way he crashed the black into a bottom pocket. He didn't have a hope in hell of getting the yellow but he went for it anyway. And he sank it. With all the other colours on their spots, the game was as good as over. I leaned on my cue and watched him pot them one by one.

"If it's a question of money, that's no problem. I'll match anything Angela is paying you."

"Money doesn't come into it." Now I was having trouble controlling my temper. "Robert was my friend. I want to know what happened as much as Angela does."

"All right, it's your decision." Adam closed his cue case with a snap which indicated the conversation was over. "I still believe you're making a mistake. For Angela's sake, let's hope it isn't a serious one."

On our way to rejoin the others, I reran parts of the conversation in my mind. There was something about it which didn't quite ring true, but I attached no particular significance to this. The same could be said of most of the conversations I'd had with my father-in-law.

I couldn't get to sleep. After half an hour of twisting and turning, I abandoned the struggle. I switched on the light, lit a cigarette and propped myself up on the pillows. Tomorrow I'd start work. The prospect pleased me. Too much time had been wasted already. There had been a large grain of truth in what Angela had said at the Strathmore. Unless the police came up with a solid lead in the first two or three days of an investigation, the chances of solving the case were drastically diminished. I knew Teague couldn't have made any significant progress at the English end. He'd promised to inform me of any developments.

My own first steps in Portugal would be the obvious ones. I'd have to go into the office to make sure everything was running smoothly. I was certain it would be: Sanchez had always been good middle-management material, reliable, conscientious and unimaginative. There shouldn't be too many problems of continuity.

While I was in the office, I'd take a look at the books. I wanted to compare them with the figures Rafferty had given me. If there were any discrepancies, these might give me some clue as to what Robert had been doing. I was equally interested in the contents of his desk diary. This should enable me to build up a picture of what Robert had been doing in the last few weeks of his life. Sooner or later I'd have to make the trip to Caldas da Rainha. Before I did, I wanted to have some idea why I was going there.

At first I thought I'd imagined the tap at the door. Then it came again and I swung my legs out of bed. Angela was outside the door. She was wearing the same robe as on the previous night. She also looked as wide awake as I felt.

"You weren't asleep, were you, Frank? I could see the light under the door." The words came out in a rush.

"No. I was awake."

"Can I come in?"

"Make yourself at home."

Angela took me literally. By the time I'd closed the door, she'd already dived under the covers of the double bed. She did this as though it was the most natural thing in the world. In a way it was. It was something Angela had often done before. The only difference was that Jane or Robert had always been around before. I wasn't sure that Angela was aware that there was a difference. There always had been a certain naïveté about her.

For a moment I was going to sit in one of the chairs. Then I realized that this might upset her and clambered in the other side of the bed. The implications were all in my own mind.

"What did Daddy have to say to you? I forgot to ask you earlier."

"He wants you to go back to live with him and your mother. I'm supposed to persuade you."

Angela pulled a face. "You might as well save your breath, Frank. I could never manage to be the daughter he wanted when I was young, and heaven knows how I'd cope now. I'm too old to be a gilded lily in a glass cage."

"I think you're mixing your metaphors."

Angela was laughing. She'd been very keyed up before the funeral; now she was much more relaxed, even if the tears were only just below the surface. "Anyway, you know what I mean."

"I get the general idea."

"Did Daddy have anything else to say?"

"He did, actually. He asked me not to investigate Robert's murder. He said it was better left to the police."

"Really?"

"Really."

"Did he give any other reason?"

"He thought it was best for you."

"The bloody old hypocrite. Now Robert's dead and buried, he wants to go back to moulding me in his image."

For a while our conversation was desultory. On my part it was rather uncomfortable. Although our bodies weren't touching I was acutely aware of Angela's proximity. It was a long time since a woman had been in my bed. I'd always envisioned it happening in a very different context.

It was almost two in the morning before Angela's eyelids began to droop. I allowed her five minutes after they'd finally closed. Then I began to edge out of bed. I didn't get very far before a hand seized hold of my arm.

"Hey," Angela said sleepily. "Where are you going?"

"Next door. I thought you were asleep."

"Don't go." I hesitated. "Please, Frank. I don't want to be alone tonight."

Reluctantly I slid back under the sheets and switched off the light. Within a few minutes Angela's deep even breathing indicated that she was asleep again. For a long time I lay beside her, staring into the darkness. I didn't dare move, in case I disturbed her. It must have been nearly dawn before I eventually drifted off myself.

Angela was already up and about by the time I awoke the next morning. There was only the dent in the pillow and the lingering smell of her perfume to remind me where she'd passed the night. While I was shaving, I could hear her banging around in the kitchen. However, when I went down to join her, she was no longer there.

"I'm out here, Frank." She was calling from the verandah. "I thought we could have breakfast outside."

"That suits me. I'm on my way."

This was precisely what the sniper had been waiting for. He was in the deserted villa on the far side of the road. The first I knew of his presence was when the patio door beside me exploded into a thousand shards of glass. For an instant I was frozen to the spot. My conscious brain was still in shock as my subconscious took over. It could remember being shot at before.

I pushed off from a standing start. The second stride took me level with Angela. As I scooped her from her chair, the fruit bowl in front of her disintegrated, showering us with a mush of orange and apple. Then I was diving for the protection of the waist-high verandah wall. On the way I somehow managed to twist my body. This meant I hit the concrete with my left shoulder instead of my head. It still hurt like merry hell.

Angela still had no real appreciation of the danger. I had to forcibly drag her legs into the lee of the wall. As I did so a third bullet gouged a hunk from the tiled floor.

"What are you doing, Frank? What's happening?"

She was struggling to free herself from me.

"For God's sake lie still. We're being shot at."

Angela lay very still. Now she was beginning to piece it together for herself. She could see the shattered patio door. There was also the devastation on the breakfast table.

"I didn't hear any shots." Her voice was commendably calm. I could only detect the faintest tremble in it.

"The gunman is using a silencer."

"Oh."

There were a lot of other questions Angela would have liked to ask, and most of them would have been seeking a reassurance I couldn't give her. It said a great deal for her character that she managed to keep them to herself.

I was thinking furiously. The possibility of outside assistance was something I'd already discounted. The house was at the very top of the hill. Apart from the deserted villa, no other buildings overlooked us. Thanks to the silencer, there had been no shots to hear. For the moment we were pinned down. We might be safe, but huddling behind the wall was no permanent answer. Our friend with the rifle might cross the road for a closer shot. Come to that, he might not be on his own.

"Does your maid come in to work this morning?"

"No. She isn't due until this afternoon."

Angela had wriggled round to face me.

"O.K. You stay here. Keep as close to the wall as you possibly can."

"What are you going to do?"

"Find out whether the gunman is still around."

After we'd disentangled ourselves, I started crawling on my hands and knees. When I reached the angle where the front and side walls met, I stopped. No more than a couple of minutes had passed since the first shot. Another minute passed while I plucked up my nerve. I was very careful not to look in Angela's direction. I didn't want her to see how frightened I was.

A jack-in-the-box couldn't have done any better. For a microsecond my head popped up above the level of the balustrade. Then it was on its way down again. Nobody had shot at me but this didn't mean a thing. The sniper hadn't had a chance to react. Next time around he'd be ready and waiting for me. For a few seconds I sat and listened to my ragged breathing. This was a sound I hoped to continue hearing for a long, long time.

"Has he gone, Frank?" Angela was speaking in a whisper.

"I don't know. Let's give him another chance."

I moved a couple of metres back along the wall before I tried again. I offered my head as a target for another microsecond. There was still no shot. I spotted no movement in the villa across the road. Once again this proved absolutely nothing. I was left facing the same big question mark. Had the bastard really gone? Or did he want me to think he'd gone? I'd have to find the answer the hard way.

"I'm going to try for the telephone." Now I was the one doing the whispering.

"What do I do?"

"You sit tight and keep your fingers crossed. If I am hit, you start screaming. Make as much noise as you possibly can."

"I could scream now."

"No. Save your breath for when it's needed."

This was our last resort. The best we could hope for was that the noise might scare the gunman off. I didn't think there would be anybody else to hear Angela. The nearest neighbours were the Borges, who were both in their seventies, and their villa was nearly a hundred metres away. Although they weren't actually deaf, they were the next-best thing. With the wind off the sea, there wasn't much hope of them hearing. We could forget about passers-by as well. There was no through road. It ended at the top of the hill. Besides, in this part of Monte Estoril, there was no such thing as a pedestrian. Everybody travelled in Mercedes-Benzes, Ferraris and Jaguars. Even the servants arrived by taxi. We had to do it on our own.

I reminded myself that it wasn't too far to the patio doors. When I made my run, I'd have the advantage of surprise. I could pick my own moment. Telling myself this did something to boost my confidence. My morale sagged again when I added the other element in the equation. If the gunman was still around, he'd know I only had the one place to run to. He'd have had his rifle zeroed in on what remained of the patio doors ever since I started playing jack-in-the-box. However fast I ran, he'd have time for at least one shot.

In fact he managed two. The first bullet plucked at the shoulder of my shirt while I was still stretching into full stride. The second followed me in through the doors, removing a sizable hunk of plaster from the wall at the far end of the room. I didn't give the gunman an opportunity to try again. I simply grabbed hold of the telephone as I passed and dived over the back of the sofa. Sheer spite made him fire twice more. The bullets dimpled the leather at the back of the sofa but they didn't come through. The horsehair was wadded too tightly.

It was so ludicrous I nearly laughed out loud. Now I had the phone, I didn't know what number to dial for the police. I decided to try the operator instead. As soon as I picked up the receiver, I knew I was wasting my time. The phone was completely dead, and this wasn't because Robert hadn't paid his bills.

"Are you all right, Frank?" Angela was unable to restrain herself any longer.

"I'm fine but the phone isn't working."

"Oh." There was a brief silence. "What do we do now?"

"I'm not sure. Did Robert keep a gun in the house?"

"He used to but that was years ago. I don't know where it is now."

I thought I did. It was probably in the hidey-hole in Robert's office. It might just as well have been on the moon. I didn't have the time to travel the twenty-odd miles to Lisbon and back.

Our situation wasn't improving. Keeping my head low, I risked a peep around the end of the sofa. The gunman had to be using one of two windows in the villa opposite. Both of them were on the first floor. I thought the shutters of the one to my left were slightly ajar. If they were, this was where he had to be.

Back behind the sofa, I tried to visualize the terrain. Provided I went the long way round, cover shouldn't be a problem. The only real danger spot was likely to be the road. Even there I suspected the palm and acacia trees should be a fairly effective screen. I hoped I wasn't deluding myself.

"Angela." I pitched my voice low.

"Yes."

"I'm going for help. I want you to stay exactly where you are."

"All right."

My heart went out to her. Angela hadn't allowed any of her doubts to show through. She didn't have to. Out there alone on the verandah, she must feel the way I had in a gun pit in Oman. I knew how she must hate the idea of being left entirely on her own.

"I shan't be long," I promised her. "Whatever you do, don't move until I'm back."

"I won't."

I couldn't think of anything else to say, so I started crawling. Once I was out in the hall I was able to stand up. Now I could move faster. The knife rack in the kitchen was a temptation but I resisted it. I preferred to use the door into the garage. Robert had always kept a good selection of tools, and I settled for a chisel and a flashlight. The help I'd mentioned to Angela was self-help. I didn't want the gunman scared off. I wanted him caught.

It helped to know that Angela was probably safe enough. The sniper had ignored her while she had been sitting alone on the verandah. He'd waited until I'd put in an appearance before he'd started shooting. Now I was going to give him another chance at me. This time it would be at close quarters.

The side door from the garage led into the garden. The house was between me and the gunman. To begin with, I was moving away from him. Once I reached the laurel hedge which split the two levels of the garden, I angled to the right. The hedge concealed me nearly all the way to the wall separating the garden from the street.

Crouched in its shadow, I peered across at the villa. From where I was, I could only see the red tiles of the roof. The gunman couldn't possibly see me, but it would be different on top of the wall. The trees might conceal me but I couldn't be sure. By now the gunman should be wondering where I was. He could calculate the routes available to me as well as I could. He only needed to catch a flash of movement as I went over the wall and I'd be in real trouble. There would be plenty of time for him to plan my reception.

I went anyway. The hours I'd sweated away on the commando obstacle course hadn't been wasted after all. The wall was about two metres high. I went over it in one continuous movement, landing in a crouch on the pavement below. There was nobody in sight as I ran across the road. The wall on the far side was higher. Fortunately there was a useful ledge a quarter of the way up. It caused me no more problems than the other wall had.

As soon as I was concealed in the overgrown shrubbery, I paused to take stock. All I'd ever seen of this garden had been from the verandah. This was probably more helpful than my survey from ground level. For the last five or six years there had been no gardener to keep the vegetation under control. Even if I couldn't see very far, shortage of cover certainly wasn't going to be a problem. At least, not until I reached the last stretch. There was a wide strip of gravel which went all the way round the house. When I crossed it, I'd be completely exposed.

To begin with, I did a complete circuit of the villa, keeping under cover. It all looked peaceful enough. There was no indication as to whether or not the gunman was still inside. I could only think of one way to find out. I elected to cross the gravel at the side of the house. All the windows overlooking me were tightly shuttered but I made more noise than I liked on the loose stones. With my back pressed against the wall, I began to edge my way towards the rear of the villa. I held the chisel in my right hand. At the corner I stopped. There was nothing to hear apart from the rustling of the breeze in the trees. When I looked around the corner, there was nothing to see either. I started along the back wall. I was uncomfortably aware that the gunman would have had plenty of time to change his position. He might have moved into the shrubbery bordering the gravel path. If he had, he must have run out of ammunition. Either that or he'd changed his mind about killing me.

He'd entered the house by forcing the locks on the back door. I stood beside it, peering in through the gap. It was very dark inside. When I went through the door, I couldn't avoid being silhouetted against the light. It belatedly occurred to me that I might have been a trifle foolhardy.

The house was empty. It had taken me less than ten minutes to check and there could be no doubt about it. Over the years the dust had accumulated into a thick carpet on the floor. I could clearly see the double set of footprints leading to and from the bedroom the gunman had used. Unless he'd sprouted wings, he hadn't been inside any of the other rooms. I guessed that he must have left immediately after I'd escaped from the verandah. It made my heroics of the last few minutes seem rather futile. I was also left wondering what might have happened if he hadn't decided to go.

I stood in the window and looked across at the verandah. The gunman had definitely selected a perfect vantage point. Because Angela's house was slightly higher up the hill, he'd been shooting at an angle of no more than twenty degrees. The range was less than fifty metres. A chair had been positioned in front of the window to support the barrel of the rifle. I knelt on the cushion he'd put on the floor and mimed the action of shooting at the patio doors. Even if the sniper hadn't had a telescopic sight, I failed to understand how he could have missed.

I poked around on the floor for a few seconds. I even hunted under the nearest pieces of furniture. The cartridge cases weren't anywhere to be seen. They had all been collected before the gunman had left. The only clues to his identity were the footprints in the dust. There couldn't be more than a quarter of million people in the Lisbon area who had the same shoe size.

I returned to the window again. The gunman couldn't possibly have missed me. He'd fired four times at what amounted to point-blank range. A child of ten could have done better throwing rocks. There was only one explanation I could see. The gunman hadn't intended to kill me. My mock heroics were seeming more futile by the minute.

Suddenly I remembered my promise to Angela. She still had no idea she was safe. I went back at a run, only slowing down when I was inside the house. Her nerves had already had enough to put up with for one day. If I came crashing unannounced through the house, this might be the final straw. As it was, she heard me as I entered the living room.

"Who is it?"

It must have been a long, long wait for her. There was a note of hysteria in her voice.

"It's me, Frank. You can come out now."

"Thank God for that."

Angela must have been very cramped lying against the wall. She walked with a pronounced limp as she started across the verandah towards me.

"Watch out for the glass, Angela."

I'd only just noticed that her feet were bare. Angela didn't appear to hear me. Fortunately, most of the shards of glass were inside the patio doors. I didn't think she trod on any before I stepped forward to intercept her. When we met, she simply leaned into me. It was as though her legs had given way beneath her. With one arm supporting her, I could feel her whole body trembling.

"Oh, Frank." The words were almost a moan. "I was so scared."

"So was I but it's all over now. Put one of your arms round my neck. I'm going to carry you over the broken glass."

She felt surprisingly light as I carried her across to the sofa. It took time to calm her down. Although she was soon talking coherently enough, the trembling wouldn't stop. A cup of coffee and a large brandy seemed to help. Even so, it was almost half an hour before I could deliver the little speech I had prepared.

Part of it she accepted without any argument. Angela could understand why I didn't want to involve the Portuguese police. There was very little point, as there was nothing for them to find in the villa across the road. Equally important, the link between the attack and Robert's death was an obvious one. The police would be able to see it as clearly as we did. Unfortunately it wouldn't take them any closer to a motive. All police involvement was likely to do was remove my freedom of action. The police would have to be told what I was doing in Portugal, and their inevitable reaction would be to impose restrictions. This would effectively remove the one advantage I had.

Angela found this easy enough to swallow. Other aspects stuck in her craw. It was the implications of what had happened which disturbed her.

"You say it was intended as a warning, Frank. What's going to happen if you ignore it?"

"I don't know."

"But you can guess. Next time they might really try to kill you."

"Maybe."

There was no point in lying to her. My response made Angela start shaking her head.

"I won't have it." There was a kind of desperation in her voice. "There's been enough blood spilled already. I don't want you to end up dead like Robert. I'd rather you forgot all about it and went back to England."

"No. That's precisely what the killer wants me to do. Besides, there wouldn't be any need for a warning unless there was something for me to find."

"Whatever it is, it's not worth your life. I'm unhiring you."

"It won't make any difference, Angela. I was aware of the dangers when I agreed to come here. And there's another thing you're forgetting. I'm not simply in Portugal because you asked me to come. Robert was the best friend I'm ever likely to have. I couldn't just turn my back. I couldn't live with the knowledge that his murderer was still walking free. If the police can't find him, I will. Or at least, I'll know I've done my honest best."

Angela was about to object again. Then she changed her mind. She knew me too well. My stubborn streak was just as wide as hers.

"How do I help?"

"You don't. At least, not actively. I'd like you to go and stay with your parents until it's all over."

"Why should I?"

She was all set to start arguing again. I took both of her hands in mine.

"Listen to me. I need to know you're safe. At the moment you're my Achilles' heel. I think I can look after myself. I'm not so sure I can manage both of us. Worrying about your safety makes me more vulnerable. It might even get me killed."

"That doesn't leave me with much choice."

The admission cost her a lot. I knew how much she hated the idea of returning to the opulent mausoleum her parents lived in. This was why I'd spelled it out so bluntly. Presenting her as a danger to me was the only hope I'd had of persuading Angela.

"Tell your father what happened here today." I was pressing home my advantage. "Make it clear that you might be in danger. Ask him to hire you a bodyguard. It will make things much easier for me."

Once again, there were no serious objections. When Angela went off to dress, I poured myself a brandy. I was more excited than apprehensive about what might lie ahead. The gloves were off now. After the shooting, I knew I'd been correct in assuming that the trail to Robert's murderer must start in Portugal. All I had to do now was discover what it was which made me such a threat.

CHAPTER 8

I drove the Alfa into Lisbon. Angela had loaned it to me for the duration of my stay. If she needed transport herself, she could use one of her father's fleet.

The offices of Latimer SA were on the 24 de Julho, almost opposite the Cais do Sodre Station. It was a good location. The docks, the warehouse and the commercial heart of Lisbon were all close to hand. The only real disadvantage was the lack of parking spaces: it took me almost ten minutes to find somewhere to leave the Alfa.

I caught Sanchez sitting at Robert's desk. He didn't look particularly comfortable there, but this didn't necessarily mean a thing. Looking harried was a way of life with Sanchez. At his happiest he resembled somebody suffering from acute depression. I'd always attributed this to his wife. She was a mountainous, domineering woman who rigorously controlled every aspect of his private life. She was the reason Sanchez put in so many hours at the office.

Although Sanchez was in his early forties, his worry wrinkles and baldness made him seem a good fifteen years older. He was a short, thin man with sloping shoulders who had never looked young. I'd seen snapshots of him as a child. Even then Sanchez had looked like a mini-adult. He was somebody I'd always liked a lot.

"Frank." There was genuine warmth in his voice. "It's really good to see you."

"You too, Antonio. It's a shame it couldn't be under happier circumstances."

"I know. It's been a terrible shock to all of us. How is Sra. Latimer?"

"She's bearing up pretty well."

"I'm glad to hear it. The last few days must have been very difficult for her."

While we'd been talking, Sanchez had been manoeuvring me around the office. I ended up in Robert's chair as he'd intended. Sanchez sat on the other side of the desk. He preferred it this way. Sanchez's only ambition in life was to keep it as tranquil as possible. Although he wasn't afraid of responsibility, he never sought it out. This was what made him such an ideal number two. There was never any need to check for knives in your back.

"Sra. Latimer told me you'd be taking charge for a while."

"Not exactly. I'll be available if I'm needed but it's purely an advisory capacity. You're the one who knows what's going on. You'll still be doing all the hard work."

"It's not so hard."

Sanchez almost sounded embarrassed. Self-depreciation was another of his characteristics.

"Is there anything that needs my attention at the moment?"

"There's nothing urgent. There is a minor problem with our suppliers in Caldas."

"What's that?"

I was very interested in anything to do with Caldas da Rainha.

"It's the usual story. There's been a slump in the domestic market. Their sales are down."

"How does that affect us?"

"The suppliers want us to help out by taking up some of the slack."

"What would you do?"

Sanchez was far more in touch with the market than I was.

"I'd help them a little. If nothing else, it will stop them looking elsewhere."

"So you'd increase our orders from them."

"Slightly but I'd make our assistance conditional. I'd negotiate completely new contracts with all of them. I'd make sure they're tied to us for the next few years."

"I assume you've done some projections. How would we come out of it?"

"Initially we'd probably lose a little. It's nothing we can't absorb.

Once the market picks up again, we'll be in a much stronger position."

"Is it going to pick up?"

The years of Thatcherism had made me cynical.

"I think so. All the indications point that way."

"How will the suppliers feel about it?"

"Grateful. Sr. Latimer had already tested the water, so to speak."

"Do it then. Prepare some draft contracts. When they're ready, I'll tout them around the suppliers."

"I can arrange for them to come into Lisbon if you like."

"No. They'll need reassurance now Sr. Latimer is dead. It will look better if I go to Caldas."

I should have plenty of opportunity to do some poking and prying while I was there.

Bookwork had never been my forte. Pages full of figures did nothing to set my pulses racing. They either gave me a headache or made me yawn. I did an awful lot of yawning over the next few hours. Once Sanchez had dug out the ledgers for me, he left me in peace. Apart from the girl who brought in the coffee in mid-afternoon, I saw nobody. It was just me and the figures.

There was nothing significant about them I could see. On a couple of occasions I thought I might have found something, but further investigation proved me wrong. I could find no obvious discrepancies. There were no bold ventures which might account for Robert's excitement.

It all seemed depressingly straightforward. Despite the expansion in the years since I'd left, the basic structure of the company hadn't altered a great deal. Robert had discovered a successful formula and he'd stuck to it. There was nothing at all in the books for me to latch on to. Later, if all else failed, I might have to go back to them in greater detail, but I sincerely hoped this wouldn't be necessary.

When I'd finished working through the ledgers, I examined a few of the individual files. I concentrated exclusively on the suppliers in Caldas. Queen's Hot Springs was the English translation of Caldas da Rainha. One of the Portuguese queens had established a hospital there in the fifteenth century, and it had gradually developed into a popular spa. Nowadays it was far better known for its glazed ceramic pottery, the maiolica.

There were scores of producers in and around the town. All of them made high-quality decorative pottery, and it was some of these producers who had formed the nucleus of Robert's original company. They'd made the pottery; Robert had marketed it for them abroad. Both parties had done well out of the arrangement. Proof of this was that most of the suppliers' names were familiar to me. Nearly all of them had been with Robert from the very beginning, and there was nothing in any of the files to suggest that the basic relationship had changed. The files appeared to be another dead end.

This left the desk diary. Robert had always been meticulous about keeping it up to date. His habits evidently hadn't changed. Although I was only really interested in the last three weeks of his life, there were scores of names for me to check. There were also a couple of weekdays which had been left completely blank. They interested me almost as much as the names did.

What I needed to do was sit down with Robert's secretary so we could go through the diary day by day. Unfortunately, she wasn't at work. According to Sanchez, she was suffering from grippe. Taken literally, this meant she had influenza. On the other hand, it could as easily be menstrual pains. The Portuguese often used grippe as an all-purpose catchword for any non-specific ailment. Whatever it was, the diary would have to be left until she returned.

In any case, it was getting late. Even Sanchez had gone for the night. I was on the point of leaving when I remembered what else I'd come for. The incident that morning had shown how vulnerable I was. Next time somebody shot at me, he might not be aiming to miss. In this eventuality, I didn't want to have to rely on a chisel, however sharp it was. I wanted to be able to shoot back. Angela might not know where Robert's gun had vanished to but I was pretty sure I did. I certainly knew why it had been removed from the house.

The years 1974 and 1975 had been very nervous ones in Portugal. It had been one thing to overthrow the Caetano regime, but establishing a stable democracy was quite another. Government had succeeded government with kaleidoscopic speed. At times nobody appeared to be governing at all. In Lisbon, mass demonstrations by the rival factions had been an almost daily occurrence. Many of the most violent were organized by the Communist-dominated labour unions, and all too often their target had been private enterprise. Although successive governments were busily nationalizing everything from banking to brewing, the process wasn't speedy enough for some elements on the extreme left. Frequently they attempted to take matters into their own hands.

While Robert and I had elected to remain in Portugal throughout these upheavals, we hadn't been blind to the dangers. Estoril might be relatively safe but Lisbon was where we had to work. As foreigners we were especially vulnerable. We'd both realized that events might force us out of the country, and that if we did have to go, speed might be vital. The escape fund had been my idea; Robert had contributed the gun. The hidey-hole had been a joint effort. The necessity for an escape fund had long since passed but I hoped the gun was still where we'd cached it.

I went into the washroom attached to Robert's office and looked up at the ceiling. We'd made a good job of the hidey-hole. Simply looking wasn't enough. I had to count the tiles before I was sure. Then I stood on a chair and removed the one which concealed the opening.

The gun was still there, wrapped in an oily piece of cloth. So was the box of ammunition. I took them out and placed them on the floor beside the chair. As an afterthought, I felt around in the cavity to see whether there was anything else concealed inside. My subconscious was having a good day. It was only as my fingers touched the second box that I realized this was where I should have looked first. If Robert had had any secrets, the hidey-hole was the obvious place for him to protect them. The office safe was far too public.

It took a great deal of restraint to prevent myself from tearing the box open immediately. I had to force myself to carry it through into the office, along with the gun and the ammunition. Lying there on the desk, it looked innocuous enough. It was a perfectly ordinary shoe box. Judging by the weight, the shoes could still be inside. Except that there was no reason to hide a pair of shoes above the ceiling of an executive loo. The lid was held firmly in place by two thick rubber bands. My fingers were trembling slightly as I removed them and lifted the lid.

My initial reaction was one of disappointment. I wasn't quite sure what I'd expected to discover but it definitely wasn't money. Apparently Robert had still maintained an escape fund after all. The disappointment faded slightly when I realized just how much money there was. There were five bundles of English £20 notes. I selected one of them and started counting. There were fifty notes in the bundle. All the others seemed to be as thick. Five bundles, each containing £1,000. This was a tidy sum to have tucked away in a shoe box. Not excessive maybe, but definitely interesting.

For the moment, there was something which interested me far more than the money. Now that the bundles had been moved, I could see that there was more in the box than money. In the bottom were two cassette tapes, some broken pieces of pottery and a small bottle full of capsules.

The tapes I put to one side. They were useless until I had access to a cassette recorder. The pieces of pottery were a different matter. In fact, I'd recognized them immediately. Fitted together they would have comprised one of the company's most popular lines. They came from a honey pot. The pot itself was designed to represent a section of log with bees crawling over the bark. On one side was a yellow circle, supposedly where a branch had been sawn from the log. Up in Caldas da Rainha, MEL would have been inscribed inside the circle. The one in the box had HONEY written there instead. This marked it as one of the pots Robert had exported. They were produced especially for the British market.

I carefully fitted all the pieces together. When I'd finished, I could see that the pot in the box wasn't quite complete. There should have been a circular lid. On top of it there should have been a handle in the shape of a queen bee with her wings extended skywards. None of the fragments of the lid or handle were in the box. Whether or not this was significant was something I might find out later.

On closer examination, there was something else missing as well. There was no manufacturer's mark on the bottom of the pot. This wasn't unusual but it was a nuisance. MADE IN PORTUGAL was no help at all. It meant the pot could have come from any one of half a dozen suppliers. Pots produced for the domestic market would have carried the mark of the individual factory.

I'd deliberately saved the capsules until last. Ever since I'd first seen them, my brain had been making the obvious connection, but

obvious didn't necessarily mean right. This was one occasion when I
desperately wanted to be wrong. As I'd said to Angela, bending the
law a little was part of Robert's style; outright dishonesty most definitely wasn't. Any involvement by him in drug trafficking was absolutely unthinkable. At least, it had been until I'd seen the contents of
the shoe box. Then it had become a terrifying possibility.

The outside of the bottle told me very little. According to the
label, it contained Lomotil. This was a favourite drug amongst tourists, especially those whose stomachs had been upset by their increased alcohol consumption. The capsules had been purchased in a
farmacia in Nazaré. When I removed the cap, I could see the bottle
was almost full. As far as I could tell, none of the capsules had been
used.

I put a piece of notepaper on the desk and carefully broke open
one of the capsules. Looking at the contents didn't tell me a thing.
What I knew about drugs could have been written on the head of a
pin. And there would have been room left over. I wasn't tempted to
test by taste. About all I could identify was aspirin. This was a job
for a qualified analyst. Or it was until I tipped the rest of the capsules
into my hand. This was when I discovered what else was in the
bottle. The obvious had been wrong after all.

"Yes?"

It was a very poor connection. I could hardly hear Angela's voice.

"It's Frank. I'm at the house."

"You're all right?"

"I'm fine. So are your patio doors, by the way. They've been fixed
as good as new. How are you?"

"Still trembling. Every time I think about what happened this
morning, I turn into instant jelly."

The very fact that Angela could joke about it was a good sign. It
meant she was getting the shock out of her system. Her resilience
continued to surprise me.

"What did your father have to say?"

"He seemed to agree with you. He thought it advisable not to
involve the police."

"He did, did he?"

This was the last thing I'd expected.

"It surprised me too. I was ready for a lecture on civic responsibility."

"How about protection? Is he arranging that for you?"

"There's a full-time bodyguard starting work in the morning. Until then he's mobilized the male staff. They're all traipsing about the estate with shotguns."

"Let's hope they don't start shooting each other by mistake. Listen, the reason I rang you was to say I won't be staying at the house after all. It looks as though I'll be spending most of my time in Lisbon. It makes more sense to move into a hotel in town."

"Well, remember to send me the bill."

"We'll discuss that later. I'll give you another ring once I'm booked in. O.K.?"

"Of course. Look after yourself, Frank."

"I will. Goodbye for now."

"Goodbye."

The phone call had been an exercise in self-discipline. Only half my mind had been on what I'd been discussing with Angela. As soon as I'd hung up, I headed for the kitchen. Robert's cassette recorder was already on the table, and the first of the two tapes was in the holder. I lit myself a cigarette and made sure there was an ashtray near to hand before I pressed the PLAY button.

"Maria? It's Cristovão here."

"Let me guess. You've rung to say you're going to be late."

Both people were speaking in Portuguese. The woman's voice sounded shrewish.

"I'm afraid so. I'm sorry."

"You always are. What is it this time?"

"I have to see Alfredo. It's urgent. He can't make it before five. I tried to put the meeting off until tomorrow but he couldn't manage it. He's off to Porto in the morning. He won't be back before the end of the week."

"Isn't it amazing how these things always seem to crop up when my parents have arranged to come over? Exactly how late do you expect to be?"

"I can't really say yet. With any luck it won't be any later than eight."

"It had better not be. I've . . ."

I switched off and ran the tape forwards. Domestic disputes weren't what I'd been hoping to listen to. About a quarter of the way through the tape, I tried again. This time I cut into the middle of a conversation. Both of the speakers were men. One of them had featured as the apologetic husband earlier.

". . . Fifteen thousand escudos. That's the best I can do, I'm afraid."

"I don't know, Cristovão. It's expensive."

"It only sounds expensive. When you consider what you'll be getting for your money, it's really very reasonable. Remember, we'll have to make a special mould. And it's a one-off job. There won't be any repeat orders."

"I realize that but . . ."

This seemed to be a good point to switch off again. A couple more random selections were no more informative. The miniaturized transmitter had obviously been attached to a phone. It was probably only activated when the phone was in use. In order to sort out the deadwood, I'd have to go all the way through both tapes. This would be a lengthy process, much better left until I was at my hotel. I knew Angela wouldn't mind me borrowing the recorder.

York House seemed as good a place as any to spend a few nights in Lisbon. Strictly speaking, it wasn't a hotel any more than York House was its real name. Its proper title was Albergaria Residencia Inglesa but I'd never yet heard anybody call it this. The main block of the *albergaria* had once been a private mansion which stood in its own grounds. Because I'd made my reservation so late, I had to make do with a room in the annexe along the street. This suited me fine.

The *albergaria's* main advantage to me was its proximity to the offices of Latimer SA. It stood on the Rua Janelas Verdes, no more than an easy walk away. The Tavares restaurant in the Rua da Misericórdia was almost as close and this was where I elected to dine. The bill was hefty but I didn't have any complaints. Neither the cuisine nor the service had deteriorated since I'd last been there. Nor had the atmosphere. Eating there was a return to the stately, civilized days of the turn of the century. It was as far removed from a fast-food eatery as Concorde was from a kite.

The food and the wine put me in a suitable frame of mind for what I had to do afterwards. Back at York House I lay on my bed and played both of the tapes all the way through. When I'd finished, I played them through again. They made for compulsive listening if you were at all interested in the trivia of a small ceramics company. Unfortunately, I wasn't. Even the occasional interludes of domestic drama did nothing to enliven the tapes. There were no obvious clues as to why Robert had gone to the bother of recording them. If, in fact, he had. Although a picture was emerging, it was rather like a photographic puzzle on a television quiz game. The parts which did emerge did little to illuminate the whole. The best I could do was make some educated guesses.

Only part of the second cassette had been used; the rest was blank. I played it through a third time. Even then I couldn't be absolutely sure. Perhaps I was reading more into the recording than was actually there. A fourth attempt was no more help. All I was left with was an impression.

For most of both tapes, the conversations sounded perfectly normal. They were a record of ordinary people discussing everyday matters. Towards the end I thought I could detect a subtle change. The content didn't change appreciably but the language seemed to be a little more stilted. Once again I turned to television for an analogy. It reminded me of the reaction of people who suddenly realized they were being filmed. Although they tried to continue behaving normally, they couldn't quite bring it off. They couldn't hide their new self-consciousness. If I was correct, this suggested that the bug on the telephone must have been discovered.

It was getting very late by now. There was nothing more I could do before morning. Even so, I couldn't settle down to sleep. I was too excited. In a few hours I'd come a long way, far further than I could reasonably have expected. There was an even longer distance to go. Now I had to put in the hard work. Hopefully, when I'd finished, I'd know who had killed Robert. I already thought I knew why.

CHAPTER 9

I spent most of the morning in the Municipal Library on the corner of the Arcado Cego and the Praça de Touros. I went into the building with high hopes. Several hours later I emerged confused and disappointed. Originally I'd only expected to have to go back a few months in the newspaper files. I ended up going back two years and I still didn't find what I'd been searching for. So much for my powers of deduction.

The frustration was building up inside me. I knew I must possess most of the key pieces in the jigsaw, but for some reason they refused to fit together. A plate of king prawns in garlic butter and a couple of drinks in the Cervejaria Portugalia did something to restore my sense of proportion. I was trying to go too far too fast. It was too early to throw in the towel. After another three hours in the library I did anyway. I tried reminding myself that there were still plenty of other leads for me to follow up; the failure of one line of enquiry was no real cause for despondency. This didn't stop me feeling despondent.

It was late afternoon when I reached the office. Robert's secretary still hadn't returned to work—perhaps her grippe was the genuine article. I went looking for Sanchez and found he was busy with the new contracts. There was nothing for me to do except make a nuisance of myself. I made a phone call instead. Joaquim Targa was at home. I was welcome to come right over.

Before I left, I put the tapes back in the shoe box with the money. This seemed as good a place as any to keep them safe. The bottle of Lomotil I put in my pocket. It immediately made me feel uneasy. It reminded me that I might be following the same path Robert had trodden before me.

All the way to Estoril I kept one eye on the driving mirror. If there was anybody on my tail, I couldn't spot them. I wasn't particularly reassured. Not everybody was as inept as Pierce had been. A good tail wouldn't allow himself to be seen. Reaction was setting in to the events of the previous day. I was visualizing myself in the eye of the hurricane. All around me the storm clouds were building up. I was glad I had Robert's gun in the glove compartment.

Joaquim lived in the less fashionable part of Estoril. His house stood on one of the quiet side streets leading up the hill from the coast road, in the middle of a short terrace. He must have been watching for me, because he had the front door open before I'd clambered out of the Alfa. His smile of welcome virtually split his wrinkled face in half. Mine was almost as broad. I'd no real idea how old Joaquim was. He had to be in his seventies but there was no easy point of reference. He'd looked exactly the same when I'd first been introduced to him. He'd been a good friend to both Robert and me, and I'd have come to visit him even if I hadn't needed his help.

We met halfway up the path. Joaquim held my hand in both of his as he pumped it up and down. His grip was surprisingly firm.

"I see you've managed to stay one step ahead of the firing squad."

"Of course." Joaquim was grinning. "Nobody would want to harm a nice old man like me."

"Don't you believe it. They're bound to catch up with you one day."

It was a long-standing joke between us. Joaquim had spent his entire working life in the police. He'd gained promotions under both Salazar and Caetano. By the time I'd met him, he'd already progressed beyond conventional police work. Even Robert hadn't been certain of his exact rank or function. Joaquim never discussed his work and we'd been careful not to ask awkward questions. The general consensus was that he had some connection with the PIDE, the Policia Internacional e de Defensa do Estado. This had been the notorious Portuguese secret police.

If this had been the case, the revolution should have proved fatal for Joaquim. However, he'd carried on as though nothing had happened. He was never forced into hiding, and he was never arrested, not even when the hostility to the old regime's security forces had been at its height. Instead he'd been allowed to retire on what appeared to be a comfortable pension. This had only added to the aura of mystery which Joaquim seemed to relish.

There was no such mystery about his private life. Joaquim was a confirmed bachelor. The living room of his home said a lot about his character. It was a self-indulgence which was entirely selfish. None of the furniture matched but it was old, comfortable and well used. In this it was a reflection of Joaquim himself. Nearly all the wall space was given over to bookshelves. There were hundreds of books on every conceivable subject, so many that they'd overflowed from the shelves to the chairs and table. The titles were a mixture of Portuguese, Spanish, French, Italian and English.

"I'm sorry about the mess."

As he spoke, Joaquim moved a pile of magazines from one of the armchairs.

"Like hell you are. You enjoy it."

"True." He was returning my smile. "At my advanced age I can afford to be eccentric. People have to take me as they find me."

He spoke in English. It wasn't as fluent as my Portuguese but addressing me in my own language was one of Joaquim's little vanities.

"I've been expecting you, Frank."

"I'd have visited you sooner if I'd been able to. To be honest, I thought I'd see you at the funeral. I know Angela expected you to be there."

Joaquim shrugged. "It was a family affair. I didn't want to intrude."

For a while our conversation was relaxed and general. It was Joaquim who did most of the talking. His latest enthusiasm was for the eighteenth century. In particular, he'd become an ardent admirer of the Marquês de Pombal. It was his contention that Portugal needed another Pombal now to reforge her destiny. I wasn't sure I agreed with him but I didn't know enough history to argue.

In any case, I enjoyed listening to the old man. He managed to be interesting and informative at the same time. I'd always considered him better suited for work in a university than with the police. It was almost half an hour before I began to think of steering the conversation back to Robert. Joaquim saved me the trouble. Perhaps he'd sensed that my attention was wandering.

"I'm talking too much," he announced. "You didn't come here to listen to a lecture on Portuguese history. You came here to talk about Robert. You have come back to Portugal to find his assassin, haven't you?"

"That is one of the reasons, yes."

I wasn't really surprised. Joaquim had always been very perceptive.

"Have you made any progress?"

"Some."

I took the bottle of Lomotil from my pocket and handed it to him. Joaquim only wasted a few seconds on the label. Then he did what I'd done, tipped the capsules out into the palm of his hand. There was sufficient sunlight coming in through the window to make the two diamonds glint and sparkle. They had a cold, icy beauty to them. If Joaquim was at all surprised, it didn't register on his face. He'd reached an age where life had very few surprises left.

"Where did you find these?"

"In Robert's office."

I told Joaquim about the shoe box and its contents. There was no point in holding anything back. If I couldn't trust Joaquim, I was truly on my own. He listened attentively without interrupting. Occasionally he nodded his head. It was as though what I was saying fitted in with information he already possessed.

"Does Angela know about the diamonds?" he asked when I'd finished.

"Not yet."

He nodded again.

"I wouldn't mention them to her until you have to. The knowledge might be dangerous to her. These diamonds have caused one death already."

"You mean Robert?"

"Oh yes." It hadn't occurred to Joaquim that I'd think he was referring to anybody else. "Robert wanted to talk about diamonds the last time I saw him. Like you, he came to me for information."

Although Joaquim was very matter-of-fact, I was suddenly tense. I'd come to him hoping for advice. Now it seemed he might be able to offer a lot more.

"Were you able to help him?"

"Obviously not. Otherwise Robert wouldn't be dead. Unfortunately I had no idea what he was doing. I should have realized from what he said. It was very stupid of me."

The old man fell silent. He seemed to be brooding. It was almost as though he felt Robert's death was some fault of his. He was leaving me way behind.

"Do you know where the diamonds came from, Joaquim?"

"Don't you?" Now Joaquim really was surprised.

"I assumed they must be stolen. That's why I spent most of the day at the Municipal Library. I was searching the newspaper files for any recent jewel thefts. I went back about four years and I couldn't find a thing."

Joaquim allowed himself a small smile.

"You wouldn't," he told me. "If I'm correct, the diamonds came from Angola."

"They were stolen there?"

"For lack of any evidence, it might be more accurate to say they were lost."

Having roused my curiosity to fever pitch, Joaquim refused to satisfy it immediately. He enjoyed nothing more than prolonging suspense. Before he answered my questions, he insisted on brewing both of us a cup of the sludge he called coffee. I had to contain my impatience as best I could.

Joaquim's knowledge of diamonds appeared to be as comprehensive as it was on most other topics. Some of what he had to say I already knew, but most of it I didn't. He didn't simply talk about the two diamonds on the table. He insisted on giving me a potted history of the diamond as a gemstone.

He began by explaining that diamonds were a form of pure carbon. They were also the hardest naturally occurring substance known to man. So far he hadn't told me anything new. After this brief introduction, however, he led me into uncharted territory.

Diamonds only occurred in kimberlite pipes or in alluvial or glacial gravels. The theory appeared to be that they were formed in kimberlite some seventy to eighty miles under the ground. The semi-liquid kimberlite was then intruded into the earth's upper crust, where it cooled. Sometimes, as in the area around Kimberley in

South Africa, the diamonds remained locked in the kimberlite. Sometimes they were washed out by erosion or glaciation. In this case the diamonds were redeposited in rivers, streams and glacial tills. Although I had only the haziest idea of what kimberlite or a glacial till might be, I didn't ask for enlightenment. Joaquim was assuming I did know and I didn't want to reveal my ignorance. Besides, this was the least interesting aspect of what he had to say.

Broadly speaking, diamonds could be divided into two categories. By far the more widespread were industrial diamonds, and they were also the more important. Industrial diamonds comprised all those which were too small, flawed or irregularly coloured to have any value as a gem. Joaquim maintained that any serious shortage of industrial diamonds would devastate most forms of mass production, and might well undermine the whole industrial base. I'd no idea whether Joaquim was exaggerating or not but he made a very convincing case.

However, it was the gemstones which interested him most. Natural diamonds varied from colourless to black. They might be opaque, translucent or transparent. Most of the diamonds used for jewellery were transparent and as nearly colourless as possible. It was these colourless or pale blue stones which were the most highly valued, mainly because of their rarity. The majority of diamonds were tinged with yellow, which detracted from their value. This was a distinction which was usually only apparent to an expert. Apparently, there was also a strong market for "fancies." These were diamonds with a distinctive colouring. Of these, red, blue and green were the rarest— consequently, they commanded the highest prices.

The diamonds mined in Angola were almost exclusively alluvial in origin. Production was centred in the northeast, around Dundo in Lunda province. It was an extension of the larger Kasai field in neighbouring Zaire. However, there was one very significant difference. Whereas nearly all the Zairian diamonds were destined for industrial use, three-quarters of those found in Angola were of gem quality. In fact, Angola accounted for a healthy 15 percent of the world's gem diamond output. Although the centre of diamond production was based around the Chicapa River, there were also important deposits of alluvial diamonds in the Luachimo, Chiumbe and Luembe river basins. This factor was important to Joaquim's story.

Traditionally, the diamonds had been mined under concession by the Angola Diamond Company, which controlled all the most lucrative fields. However, it was known that other significant deposits must exist.

It was a shift in emphasis in the Portuguese attitude towards Angola which speeded up their exploitation. For many years the colony had been the richest of Portugal's overseas possessions. It was regarded as the country's African garden, with a heavy emphasis on agricultural products. This was the attitude which led to Angola becoming one of the world's largest producers of coffee.

Exploitation of the colony's mineral wealth had to wait until much later. Once it had started, though, the process soon acquired a momentum of its own. As well as diamonds, there was iron ore and oil in abundance. With Portugal's own domestic economy stagnating, Lisbon saw the development of Angolan industries and minerals as some kind of panacea. Expansion became the order of the day. In keeping with this, the Angola Diamond Company's stranglehold was effectively broken. Other companies were granted licences to prospect for diamonds. Many of these sank without trace but there were others which prospered.

All the while this was happening, a large black cloud was looming just over the horizon. The Portuguese tendency to live in the past had finally caught up with them. Portugal had become the last great colonial power. While the British and French empires were breaking up, the Portuguese grimly hung on to their African territories. Their leaders stuck resolutely to the myth that the colonies were an integral part of Portugal. They persevered with administrations which effectively prevented black Africans from having any say in the government of their own countries. Nationalist movements, such as Frelimo in Mozambique, were opposed by the Portuguese armed forces. Only the Portuguese themselves were blind to the fact that this state of affairs couldn't possibly last.

It was the 1974 revolution in Portugal itself which finally made the dam walls burst. One by one the colonies tore themselves free. In Angola there had been sporadic guerrilla warfare for the past fourteen years. Within eighteen months of the mutiny in Caldas, the country had descended into virtual anarchy. Lisbon offered Angola self-determination, but the nationalist groups demanded total independence immediately. Once their demands had been accepted, they turned to fighting amongst themselves. Very soon UNITA, the MPLA and the FNLA were making headlines across the world. Angola had suddenly become a very dangerous place to be. The foreign-based companies were racing each other to extricate themselves from the mess with what few assets they could salvage.

The diamond interests had been no exception. Indeed, they'd been in the front line longer than most. For years, the north and east had been the main areas of MPLA guerrilla activity. The diamond concerns had realized that the colonial dream was about to end long before most of the other white settlers.

Of course, the Angola Diamond Company had made its own preparations for disaster. The smaller companies were far more vulnerable. Although they'd wanted to continue production until the last possible moment, they had been acutely aware of the risks. In order to minimize them, a group of the smaller producers had banded together. In effect, they formed a diamond cooperative. All their production was pooled at a central collecting point. They maintained a light plane in full readiness for the evil day.

When it came, a small fortune in diamonds was loaded aboard and the plane flew out. Unfortunately, it never reached its destination. A hundred miles short of Cabinda, the aircraft plunged into the trees below. It happened so suddenly that the pilot had no chance to radio his exact location.

This wasn't quite the end of the saga. The plane had come down in the Ile de Mateba, northeast of Banana. This was the narrow strip of Zaire which separated the Cabinda enclave from the rest of Angola. It was possible for the diamond companies concerned to mount a search party. Although it had crashed in dense jungle, the wreckage of the plane was eventually located. Unfortunately, there were no diamonds to be found. The aircraft appeared to have been destroyed by an explosion. Pieces of the fuselage were scattered over about a square mile of forest.

"So that was the end of it."

I knew it couldn't be. Otherwise Joaquim wouldn't have spent so much time filling in the background. For the moment, though, he appeared to have dried up.

"Very nearly. For a while there were all manner of rumours flying around. The most persistent one was that the diamonds never actually went aboard the plane. A bomb was substituted for them."

"And?"

"Nothing. There was no proof to back up the rumours. No formal accusation was ever made. In a few weeks the whole affair had blown over. Too many other things were happening at the time. The authorities weren't particularly interested."

"Were you one of the authorities involved?"

Joaquim shrugged.

"Not really. It was sheer chance I heard about it at all. One of the men who lost most in the crash happened to be an acquaintance of mine. He discussed the matter with me unofficially. He was quite bitter about the whole business."

"I can imagine. How much did he lose?"

"I'm not sure. I doubt whether he knew the exact figure himself. You see, they were all uncut stones. I did hear that the total consignment was supposed to be worth several million English pounds. I've no way of knowing how accurate an estimate this was, but I suspect it may have been rather inflated."

For a few seconds neither of us said anything. Outside the sky had clouded over. It was getting dark in the room. Even so, I could see the quizzical expression on Joaquim's face. He knew I had questions to ask.

"O.K.," I said. "You've told me an interesting story. How is it connected with those diamonds on the table?"

"I don't know that it is. I'm simply making an educated guess."

"There must be more to it than that."

"There is." Joaquim was nodding his head in agreement. "I'd forgotten all about the incident until Robert came to see me. I've already told you that he wanted to talk about diamonds. What I didn't mention was that it was those missing diamonds which interested him most. Apparently he'd heard the same rumours I talked about. The story evidently intrigued him. At the time I didn't think anything of it. With the benefit of hindsight, his interest becomes more significant. He seemed remarkably well informed."

"How long ago was it that you saw Robert?"

"It was five days before he came to England. I checked the date."

This was almost a week after Robert's trip to Caldas da Rainha. The date fitted well enough into the framework I was constructing. "There's one thing which doesn't make any kind of sense to me, Joaquim. Why would these diamonds suddenly surface now? It's almost eight years since the plane crashed."

"Who knows? Haven't we engaged in enough speculation for one afternoon?"

"Indulge me. You must have some theory."

Joaquim shrugged again. The gesture was more Gallic than Portuguese.

"There are any number of possible explanations. The most probable one concerns the nature of the diamond business itself. It's a very close-knit community. There are all manner of controls and restrictions. It would be very difficult to feed such a large number of stones into the system without their being noticed. My guess is that they're being released a few at a time, and somehow or other Robert must have stumbled across these."

Joaquim had picked up the two diamonds. He was holding them in the palm of his hand. Without any light to refract, they looked like two pieces of glass. They didn't appear to be worth anybody's life.

"Those stones have been cut," I pointed out. "You said the ones on the plane weren't. Exactly how do you account for that?"

"Antwerp isn't the only home for diamond cutters. There have been cutters in Lisbon almost since the first diamond was discovered in Angola. It would be easy enough to arrange."

Although I accepted almost everything Joaquim had said, I felt vaguely dissatisfied. The picture was slowly emerging but some of the pieces still didn't fit. I was sure I must be missing something.

"I have a friend in Lisbon who is a diamond cutter," Joaquim said suddenly. "He might be able to help us. Have you made any plans for the evening?"

"None at all."

"In that case I'll find out whether he can see us. Excuse me while I make a phone call."

He was only out of the room for a couple of minutes. When he returned Joaquim was rubbing his hands with satisfaction.

"He'll see us later tonight at his house. There will be a price to pay, though."

"Oh?"

His puckish smile gave me some warning.

"If I'm going into Lisbon, I shall need feeding. That will be your responsibility, Frank MacAllister."

"All right." Now I could understand the smile. Joaquim was renowned as a great trencherman. "Where would you like to eat?"

"I think I shall allow you to take me to the Aviz. The kitchen there should be able to cater to my simple tastes."

I guessed it might at that. The Aviz was arguably the best restaurant in Lisbon.

"What do you make of them?" Joaquim enquired.

"They're diamonds."

We all laughed. José Figeira wasn't at all what I'd imagined a diamond cutter would be like. I'd visualized somebody old, wizened and Jewish. José certainly wasn't young. He was probably in his late fifties. However, this was the only part of the image he adhered to. He reminded me more of an ex-wrestler than anything else. His face was all angles and bumps and he had forearms like Popeye's. His enormous hands didn't look at all suited for the delicacy and dexterity of his trade.

He was an immensely cheerful man. You could tell he enjoyed life simply by looking at him. One reason for this was probably his wife, Rosita. She was Spanish and at least twenty years his junior. Even in an apron she emitted an aura of dark Andalusian sensuality. It wouldn't have surprised me to learn she glowed in the dark.

"Come on, José. You can do better than that."

"If you insist. They're fine whites cut from the same stone. Both of them are I.F.—internally flawless. I don't have my scales with me but I can give you approximate weights. The smaller stone is about two and three-quarter carats. The other is just over three. They're very nice stones."

"How much are they worth?"

"That all depends where you're selling them. And who's doing the buying. Anything less than three million and you're being robbed. Over three and a half million and you're the robbers."

He was referring to escudos. José didn't speak English, so we were talking in Portuguese. It seemed ridiculous that two little pieces of rock could be worth £35,000.

"Can you tell who did the cutting?"

My question amused him.

"It definitely wasn't me. I do know that."

"Doesn't each cutter have his own trademark?"

"Not on stones of this size. With a diamond the size of the Cullinan I might be able to help you. All I can say about these are that they're standard brilliant cut. That means there are fifty-eight facets on each stone. It's far and away the most popular cut. It makes even a poor-quality diamond look quite good."

I couldn't think of anything else to ask. It seemed that our visit had been wasted. However, Joaquim hadn't finished yet.

"Presumably most of your work is with accredited dealers."

"Oh, yes. Nearly all of it is."

"So if somebody you didn't know asked to have some diamonds cut, you'd ask questions."

José laughed. "The policeman in you is showing through, Joaquim. You know perfectly well I'd ask questions. I wouldn't run the risk of handling stolen goods."

"Are there any other cutters you know of who would be less particular?"

The smile faded from José's face. He thought for a few seconds before he answered.

"Is this official? I thought you'd retired."

"It isn't and I have."

"But you think the diamonds might be stolen?"

"Yes."

José hesitated again. "This is entirely between the three of us?"

"You have my word on it. I'm asking you as a friend."

"Manuel Breyner." José had come to a decision. "There's nothing definite, you understand, but he does have a certain reputation."

"I understand."

We left shortly afterwards. For a while we drove in silence. I knew something was troubling Joaquim. We'd reached Monsanto Park before he brought it into the open.

"I don't want to interfere, Frank, but there's something I have to ask you. Are you planning to take all this to the police?"

"No. Not yet, at any rate."

This was a question I'd been expecting.

"Strictly speaking, you ought to."

"Why? What could I tell them? What crime am I supposed to report? All I have is bits and pieces. As far as I know, I don't have any information relating to a police investigation here in Portugal."

"That's true." Joaquim conceded the point. "At the same time, there's more than enough circumstantial evidence to start an enquiry. I'm not arguing with you. I want to know why you're so intent on keeping it to yourself."

"O.K." I paused a moment to put my thoughts in order. "All the evidence I have points in the wrong direction. I'm here in Portugal to find Robert's killer, nothing else. The diamonds are purely incidental as far as I'm concerned. All they do is provide me with a motive for Robert's death. The police attitude would be the other way round. If I went to them, the diamonds would be their main interest. Robert was killed in England. His murder wouldn't directly concern them."

"Good." Joaquim sounded pleased. "Even though I was a policeman myself, I tend to agree with you. All the same, you'll have to tread carefully. The Portuguese police make very bad enemies. They certainly wouldn't approve of what you're doing."

"I'll bear it in mind."

"Please do. It's important. I think it's probably best if you leave this Manuel Breyner to me. It would avoid any unpleasant repercussions. Besides, I may get more from him than you would."

I was sure of it. I saw Joaquim's qualified approval of what I was doing as an important bonus. If anything did go wrong, I'd need him to pull a few strings on my behalf. Retired or not, Joaquim would still have a lot of influential friends.

"There's one question I've been meaning to ask, Joaquim."

"I know. It's about the plane crash, isn't it?"

"Sort of. When all the rumours were flying around, were any names mentioned? Was the finger ever pointed at anybody?"

"There were never any direct accusations. However, if a crime was committed, there was one obvious suspect. A man called Francisco da Silva was in charge of all the arrangements for flying the diamonds out. He was the one who saw them on board the plane."

"I see. Do you know where da Silva is now?"

"I believe he lives near Nazaré. It won't be difficult to find out. Until the troubles in Angola, he used to be a very wealthy man. He probably still is. I can check easily enough."

"Thanks. I haven't said so before but your help means a lot to me."

"It's the least I can do. Remember, Robert was my friend too."

Joaquim didn't speak again until we reached the outskirts of Estoril.

"There's something you ought to know about this da Silva. He was a business associate of your father-in-law. They were partners in several enterprises in Angola."

"Including the diamond business?"

"So I believe."

Suddenly there was a nasty taste in my mouth. I didn't want to ask the next question but there was no avoiding it.

"Did you tell Robert about the connection?"

"No. But that doesn't necessarily mean he didn't know about it."

For the rest of the journey we drove in silence.

CHAPTER 10

"May I know the purpose of this, Sr. MacAllister?"

"Of course not."

"I'm sorry I asked."

Two spots of red had flamed on Sofia's cheeks. I smiled at her to remove any possible offense.

"Don't be. I was only teasing you. How's the grippe? I meant to ask before."

"I'm fully recovered, thank you."

To me, she still looked a little feverish. Sofia was almost as dedicated to her work as Sanchez. She was that rarest of all breeds in

Portugal, a professional spinster. Sofia wasn't a feminist. She was simply afraid of her own femininity. While other women dressed to make the best of themselves, Sofia did exactly the opposite. Ugly spectacles and shapeless, unfashionable clothes had been her uniform for as long as I could remember. She didn't want to be noticed as a woman. Any attempt at flirtation would have sent her into a paroxysm of embarrassment.

"To answer your question, I'm simply being nosey. I was going through Sr. Latimer's desk diary and there were one or two entries I didn't understand. I hoped you might be able to clear them up for me."

"I'll certainly do my best."

Sofia treated me to a thin-lipped smile. Any more and I might have noticed what a nice mouth and teeth she had.

"Fine. Most of it seems straightforward enough." I had the desk diary open in front of me. "There's only a couple of points. On the 13th here you simply entered, 'Warehouse.' What does that mean?"

"Sr. Latimer spent the day at the warehouse with Sanchez. It was their regular quarterly check. If you remember, you used to do them when you were still with the company."

I nodded. The only reason I'd asked was that the 13th had a special significance. It was the date when Robert had taken Angela out on the town in Lisbon.

"I thought as much. Now, Sr. Latimer went to Caldas da Rainha on the afternoon of the 19th. He didn't return until late on the 21st. I see there were several appointments on the 20th but the 21st is completely blank. What happened there? Is it anything I should know about?"

"I'm not sure. Perhaps Sr. Latimer left the 21st clear in case there was any business carried over from the previous day."

For some reason Sofia was blushing again. She also looked distinctly uncomfortable. I couldn't begin to think why.

"I wondered whether Sr. Latimer might have gone on somewhere else from Caldas. You've made a note that you booked him in at the Pensão Portugal for the night of the 19th. There's no reservation for the night of the 20th."

"There isn't, is there?"

Now Sofia was being evasive.

"Did you make a reservation for him for the 20th?"

"No. Only for the 19th."

"But Sr. Latimer knew in advance that he'd be gone for at least two nights. He told Sra. Latimer that he wouldn't be back until the 21st."

"That's what he told me too."

By now Sofia's entire face was a fiery red. For some reason she was refusing to look me in the eye. The penny dropped so suddenly I couldn't quite suppress a smile.

"Tell me something, Sofia. Why did you think Sr. Latimer had only booked in for one night?"

"I'd rather not say."

She was still refusing to meet my eye.

"Did you think he might be doing something he didn't want Sra. Latimer to know about?"

There was no immediate answer. Sofia might be meek but she was also loyal.

"Please, Sofia. You can't hurt Sr. Latimer now. Is that what you thought?"

"Yes."

She spoke in a whisper. I had to strain my ears to hear what she said.

"Did you think he might be seeing another woman?"

"Yes."

"Was there any reason for thinking this?"

"No." Sofia's head suddenly came up. Now the words poured out in a rush. "Sr. and Sra. Latimer always seemed so happy together. It was the last thing I'd have expected. But it was so unusual. I mean, I always made his hotel reservations for him. I always have done. When I asked him about the 20th he said it was none of my concern. He was quite snappy about it. It wasn't like Sr. Latimer at all. And I know he didn't stay at the *pensão* for a second night. I had to phone him there to leave a message for him on the 20th. They said he'd already booked out."

The torrent of words dried up almost as abruptly as they'd begun.

"Is that all? Was there anything else which made you suspicious?"

"Oh, yes." Now Sofia had decided to talk, she was going to say it all. "Sr. Latimer was different when he came back. He seemed excited about something. And the following Monday he was out of the office all day. He cancelled all his appointments. I think he went to Caldas again."

"When did he decide to go to England?"

"It was a couple of days after that. I think it was the Thursday or Friday."

So that was it. I toyed with a pencil while I considered what Sofia had told me. It slotted in nicely with what I already knew. However, Sofia deserved a little reassurance. She obviously thought she'd been helping Robert to deceive Angela.

"Sofia," I said. "Sr. Latimer didn't have a mistress in Caldas or anywhere else. I can promise you that. He would have told me if he had."

"I didn't really believe it could be true." Sofia was clearly relieved. "It was just so strange."

"Well, you can push the idea right out of your mind. While we're talking about Caldas, though, I'll have to go there myself. Did Sanchez tell you anything about the new contracts?"

"He mentioned it when I came in."

"Fine. He says the contracts are almost ready, so book me into the Portugal for tomorrow night. Then warn the suppliers I'm on my way."

"It's very short notice."

Sofia sounded dubious.

"From what Sanchez told me, the suppliers are in a hurry themselves. I'm sure they'll make time to see me."

At least, one of them would. Of this I was absolutely positive.

The bodyguard certainly looked the part. He was tall for a Portuguese, with broad shoulders and dark, watchful eyes. There was a pump-action shotgun on the table beside his coffee cup. The handgun was in a shoulder holster. He seemed very tough and equally competent. I definitely approved of the way he checked me for concealed weapons. Angela had told him it wasn't necessary but he checked anyway. Good bodyguards didn't take anything on trust.

Angela was sitting at another table with her father. She was wearing jeans and a white T-shirt. There was a certain tension between them, as though I'd interrupted an argument.

I accepted a coffee and waited for Adam to leave us alone. He didn't, so we chatted about the weather and the latest political upheavals in Lisbon. From where I sat, I could look out over the gardens. They'd been laid down when formal elegance had been the style, and the years hadn't changed them much. No weeds dared to show themselves in the formal flower beds. It was difficult to remember that outside the walls the common herd were hustling to earn a daily crust.

After a quarter of an hour, Adam was still with us. He was evidently prepared to sit there as long as I did. It was up to me to make some kind of a move.

"How about a walk?" I suggested to Angela. "I seem to have been sitting around all day."

"All right."

The bodyguard rose to his feet when we did. He picked up his shotgun and followed us down the steps. Ahead of us a gardener was trimming the edge of a lawn with a pair of shears. It was probably like painting the Forth Bridge. By the time all the edges had been trimmed, it would be time to start all over again.

"How's it going?" I asked.

"It's a barrel of fun. Couldn't you tell?"

"Relations did appear to be a tiny bit strained."

"That's the understatement of the year. What have you been doing for the past couple of days, Frank?"

"Poking and prying."

"Has it helped?"

"Some. I'm going to Caldas tomorrow. I should know more when I get back."

Angela stopped suddenly, disengaging her arm from mine. This meant I had to stop too. So did the bodyguard behind us.

"You're being shifty again, Frank. I recognize the signs. What have you found out that you don't want to tell me about?"

"Can't it wait?" I made no attempt to deny the accusation. "There's no point in sharing half-baked theories. I'd rather give you something definite."

"You're as bad as Daddy." Like Jane, Angela's temper burned on a short fuse. "Can't any of you accept that I'm grown up now? I'm not a child, I don't have to be cocooned from what's happening in the big, bad world."

Despite myself, I couldn't hide my grin. Angela was positively bristling.

"Hush now, lady." I was quite pleased with my American accent. "There's no call for you to worry your pretty little head. This is man's business. You be a good girl now and I'll bring you some pretties when I come back."

"Frank MacAllister." Angela was caught midway between anger and laughter. "Either you stop playing the fool or I'll show you just how much of a lady I really am."

"But, honey child, it's for your own good."

Fists clenched, Angela advanced threateningly. I backed off, raising my hands.

"All right, all right. I surrender."

There was a bench in the shadow of one of the hedges. We sat on it while I gave Angela a résumé of what I'd learned. Although I hadn't wanted to tell her so soon, there was no denying her right to know. Theoretically at least, I was being retained by her.

While I was talking, the bodyguard hovered in the background. The way he clutched the shotgun suggested he was perfectly prepared to use it. He wasn't somebody I'd have liked to tangle with.

"Let me get this straight." Angela was perplexed. "Somebody has been using Latimer SA to smuggle stolen diamonds out of the country?"

"That's what it looks like to me."

"How did Robert find out about the smuggling?"

"Purely by accident, as far as I can tell. He went to the warehouse with Sanchez for an inspection. According to Sanchez, one of the crates was dropped and broke open. Sanchez wasn't with Robert at the time but I'm assuming that's when he found the diamonds."

"And this was why Robert was killed?"

"Probably. That's one of the things I'm hoping to find out in Caldas da Rainha. I think Robert went there to force a confrontation."

Angela shivered. This had nothing at all to do with the temperature.

"Where do the Lomotil capsules fit in?"

"I don't know that they do. I think Robert simply wanted somewhere he could conceal the diamonds while they were on his person."

"How about the honey pot? Do you know which factory it came from?"

"Not yet."

This was my first direct lie. Otherwise my only sins were those of omission. I'd kept my interpretation of the money in the shoe box to myself. In the same way, I hadn't mentioned everything Joaquim had told me.

Angela was right. I was doing exactly what she'd accused me of, cocooning her from reality. Robert hadn't been killed simply because he'd uncovered the diamond smuggling. At least, I didn't think so. He'd died because he'd tried to cut himself in on the action. But I'd have to be very sure of my facts before I hinted at this to Angela.

We didn't talk much on our way back to the house. After our conversation, neither of us was in a particularly jocular frame of mind. I left Angela on the terrace with the bodyguard and walked around the house. Adam was waiting for me by the Alfa. I'd half expected him to collar me before I left.

"I gather that you've chosen to ignore my advice."

"What advice was that?" I knew exactly what he was talking about but I hadn't liked his tone.

"About stirring up dead ashes. It's not good for her, you know."

"Surely that's something Angela has to decide for herself."

We seemed to be going over the same ground as before. Adam lit himself a cheroot. He neglected to offer one to me. This was just one small indication of his disapproval.

"However she might appear to you, Frank, Angela is still in a highly emotional condition," he said. "I'm not sure she's in any fit state to judge what's best for her."

"But you are."

"Yes, I think I am."

For a few seconds we simply stared at each other, measuring our hostility. I fully expected Adam to say something more but he didn't. He simply turned on his heel and started to walk away. I didn't bother to shout a farewell after him before I drove away.

There was something wrong with Joaquim's telephone. I'd tried to contact him three times during the late afternoon and early evening. On each occasion I'd been answered by a demented, high-pitched buzzing. This was a nuisance. I needed to talk to Joaquim before I left for Caldas.

Now the time had come, I wasn't sure what strategy to adopt. Direct confrontation seemed unadvisable. I had no official authority. I didn't even know all the questions to ask. A degree of subtlety was called for. This was where Joaquim could have helped. I'd have liked to discuss my approach with him. Quite apart from this, there was the matter of the diamond cutter José had referred us to. Joaquim might have learned something I could use.

Just after eight I made my fourth and final attempt to phone him. The buzzing hadn't stopped. On the spur of the moment I decided to drive out to Estoril. I didn't have anything else to do. Besides, sitting around in my room at York House was making me edgy. If nothing else, an hour or two in Joaquim's company would help to calm me down.

Traffic was light and I made good time. It had only just turned a quarter to nine when I pulled up outside his house. I knew immediately that it had been a wasted journey. There were no lights anywhere in the house. But having come this far, it was as well to make certain.

I was halfway up the path before I noticed that the front door was ajar. This was sufficient to stop me in my tracks. Joaquim didn't leave doors open behind him, especially not outside doors.

I could feel the goose bumps breaking out on my arms. In the darkness, the pleasant, terraced house had suddenly become forbidding. I could clearly remember walking into an empty house in Luton—and what I'd discovered inside. I was frightened of what might be waiting for me now.

I went back to the Alfa. Robert's gun was in the glove compartment. It was a clumsy weapon, one of the old Savage 7.65-mm. M/915 automatics. The barrel was four inches long and the weapon weighed well over a pound. On the credit side, Robert had kept it in good working order. There were also ten rounds in the magazine. It gave me some confidence as I walked up the path again.

Before I ventured inside, I rang the bell. There was an outside chance that Joaquim was at home. He could be having an early night. But I didn't really believe this for a moment. What I was doing was giving any intruder ample opportunity to get clear. I'd purged all the foolhardiness from my system the other morning. The Savage was purely for insurance. I had no desire to use it.

Nobody answered the bell. The house was so quiet I could hear the ticking of the clock in the hall. I could also hear my own ragged breathing. I didn't want to find any more dead bodies. Almost anything was preferable to that. The light switch was just inside the door. I depressed it before I pushed the door fully open. The hall was empty. I eased myself inside, closing the door behind me. The ticking of the clock still sounded monstrously loud. In one of the neighbouring houses I could hear the murmur of a television or radio. By now my breathing was under control.

The stairs were to my left. At the top, the landing was in darkness. After I'd turned on the light on the stairs, I felt much better. I took the downstairs rooms first, switching on the lights as I went. All of them were empty. There was absolutely nothing to suggest that anything was amiss. Instinct still insisted otherwise, and this was what I listened to. I was equally cautious when I checked the rooms upstairs. There was nothing out of the ordinary in any of the bedrooms. The same was true of the bathroom.

I switched off a few lights and seated myself on the top stair. The Savage remained in my hand. Despite all the evidence to the contrary, I wasn't reassured. Something was wrong. Joaquim wasn't the sloppy type. I couldn't imagine any normal circumstances where he'd go out and leave the front door open. It just wasn't in character. This train of thought prompted me to go downstairs to take a closer look at the door. It definitely hadn't been forced. Nor were there any scratches around the lock. So much for that.

Another thought occurred to me. It led me to the alcove where Joaquim kept his telephone. The receiver was off its hook, lying on the table. This explained why I hadn't been able to get through to Joaquim. Other questions remained unanswered. I tried to tell myself I was building mountains out of molehills, but this didn't work. I was sure I was lying.

There was nothing more I could do inside the house. I switched off the rest of the lights and closed the door behind me. Without a key I couldn't lock it. I tried the house on the right-hand side first. A teen-aged girl answered the door. Despite the hour, she was neither sur-prised nor alarmed to find a strange man on the doorstep. Portugal was one of the last European countries where innocence had been able to survive.

"May I have a word with your parents, please?"

"They're out at the moment. Perhaps I can help you."

"Possibly." The girl had a nice smile and I'd responded with one of my own. "I've driven out from Lisbon to see Sr. Targa but he isn't in. I wondered whether you had any idea where I might find him."

She hadn't. Apparently she hadn't been home long herself. I apol-ogized for disturbing her, earning myself another pleasant smile. Then I went to disturb the neighbours on the other side. The middle-aged lady I spoke to proved far more helpful. She'd no idea where Joaquim might be but she had seen him go out.

"What time was that?"

"It must have been about five, I suppose. He left with his friend."

"He wasn't alone, then."

"Oh, no. His friend must have arrived about a quarter of an hour earlier. I noticed him because he was driving one of those big Ameri-can cars."

"It was probably Manuel." I'd selected the name at random. "Did you happen to notice what he looked like?"

"Not really." She gave an embarrassed little laugh. "To be honest, I was more interested in the car. He was youngish, I do know that. And he was wearing a smart suit. I think he was dark-haired."

"That sounds like Manuel. Thanks a lot for your help. The only reason I disturbed you was that I was a bit worried. Joaquim wasn't at home but he'd left the front door open."

"That's not like him at all. Is it shut now?"

"It's closed but not locked. Perhaps you'd keep an eye on the house until Joaquim gets back."

She promised she would and I returned to the Alfa. The Savage was ruining the shape of my pocket, so I put it back in the glove compartment. I was still worried about Joaquim. I'd have very much liked to know who his friend was, and where they'd gone in the big American car. Perhaps I was mistaken but I had the feeling that events were slipping out of my control.

CHAPTER 11

As far as Latimer SA was concerned, there was no real need for my trip to Caldas da Rainha. Sanchez had known this but he'd been far too polite to say so. The suppliers had already been consulted about the terms of the new contracts, and none of them had raised any serious objections. They were between a rock and a hard place. If we'd insisted on it, they'd probably have crawled to Lisbon on their hands and knees to sign on the dotted line.

Their basic problem was that Caldas wasn't on the main tourist route, and very few visitors used the town as a base for their holidays. This was why the Pensão Portugal and the Central were the only real hotels. Nor did the tourists flock to Caldas for the day. It was no Obidos or Nazaré. Caldas da Rainha was a place where tourists stretched their legs for a few minutes on their way to somewhere else. Apart from the Manueline church, Nossa Senhora do Pópulo, and a statue of Queen Léonor, there was little to see. Pleasant little market towns were ten a penny in Portugal.

Admittedly, the calcium sulphide waters, which stank of decaying cabbage, still attracted visitors. Unfortunately, the ceramics industry couldn't survive on the trade of invalids suffering from respiratory ailments and rheumatism. Less than a century before, Caldas had been one of the most popular resorts in the country. It had been a favourite meeting place for writers, artists and musicians. However, it had been a caricaturist, Rafael Bordalo Pinheiro, who had given pottery its biggest boost. His profession was reflected in the style he had created. Glazed ceramic reproductions of fruits, vegetables and animals were certainly guaranteed to set Caldas pottery apart.

There had been one major built-in flaw. Nobody actually needed ceramic cauliflowers or strawberries. People might like them but they were strictly luxury items. Consequently, whenever times were hard, the ceramics industry suffered badly. This was a basic truth which Robert had recognized immediately. It had formed the basis of his company and not much had changed since.

The current recession had brought hard times to Caldas again. The number of tourists and day-trippers had dwindled to a trickle. Unless they cut back drastically on production our suppliers had to sell far more outside the immediate locality. Effectively, this meant outside Portugal. It meant they had to turn to Latimer SA.

All this made for quite a pleasant morning. Everybody I visited welcomed me with open arms. It was simply a question of doing the rounds and collecting signatures. I'd have been enjoying myself if I hadn't been so worried about Joaquim. I'd tried to contact him again before I'd left for Caldas. Although I'd allowed the phone to ring for almost five minutes, there had been no reply. At eight o'clock in the morning Joaquim should have been at home. I tried again before lunch. Once more there was no answer. I couldn't afford to leave it much longer. If I couldn't reach Joaquim by the next morning, I was going to the police. Exactly what I could say to them was something I'd have to sort out when the time came.

For the moment, I had to sort out what I intended to say to Cristovão Pomar. I'd deliberately kept him to last on my visiting list. Pomar was the man who had starred in Robert's recording. His firm also made honey pots like the one I'd found in the shoe box. In the end I reached no firm decision. I still wasn't sure what I was going to say when I was shown into his tiny office. I'd simply have to play it by ear.

Pomar was a tall, lean man with dark hair which was brushed straight back. This tended to emphasize his high forehead and rather protuberant eyes. He had a gaunt, cadaverous face which would never win any prizes in beauty contests. More important, Pomar was clearly very nervous. This was sufficient to remove most of my doubts. In his condition he was almost asking to be leaned on.

We disposed of the contract very quickly indeed. Although he was polite enough, Pomar was evidently intent on getting rid of me as fast as possible. All the while we were talking he never once looked me in the eye. He couldn't keep his hands still any more than he could control the nervous tic in one cheek. The more I watched him, the more confident I became. Subtlety wouldn't be necessary. I could tackle him head on.

"Is there anything else, Sr. MacAllister?"

Pomar wasn't using subtlety either. He wanted me gone and he didn't mind me knowing it.

"There is, actually. Cigarette?"

"I don't smoke."

Perhaps this accounted for his nerves. I took my time lighting up. Pomar hunted out an ashtray from beneath a pile of invoices.

"I gather Sr. Latimer came to see you recently."

"That is correct. He was here about three weeks ago."

"Was there any particular reason for the visit?"

Pomar shook his head. "He was simply doing the rounds. All of us in ceramics have been in trouble these past few months. He came here to discuss what Latimer SA could do to help. In fact, he suggested a new contract rather like the one you brought with you today."

"There wasn't anything else?"

"Not that I can remember."

He was a terrible liar. Although Pomar tried to meet my eyes, he couldn't quite bring it off. At the last moment his own eyes slid away from the contact.

"That's strange."

An uncomfortable silence developed. At least, it was uncomfortable for Pomar. After a few seconds he couldn't stand it any more.

"What's strange?"

"I was thinking out loud. Sr. Latimer went to considerable trouble to obtain some tape recordings. They were made here in your office."

"I don't understand." His smile was a mere rictus. "What tape recordings?"

"I thought you knew about them. He bugged your telephone. He was recording all the calls you made."

"You're joking with me."

Pomar's attempt at a carefree laugh was no more convincing than his smile had been. He'd started sweating heavily. The meeting was obviously going far worse than he'd anticipated. For my part, I'd already given away far more than I'd originally intended. Now wasn't the time to stop.

"I listened to the tapes, Cristovão."

"I don't believe you."

He did, beyond any shadow of a doubt.

"Parts of them are quite intriguing. Why are you always late home when your in-laws come visiting? Don't you get on with them?"

"You're mad. I don't know what you're talking about."

We settled into another uncomfortable silence. I was pleased with the way it was going. Pomar wasn't going to confess to anything. That would be too much to hope for. However, I might provoke him into doing something stupid. He was so shaken anything was possible. Once again it was Pomar who broke first.

"I don't want to hurry you, Sr. MacAllister, but I have work to do. I have another appointment in a few minutes."

"I'd cancel it if I were you. This is far more important. We haven't discussed the diamonds yet."

"The diamonds?"

"That's what I said."

I'd read about people turning as white as a sheet. Pomar turned grey. All the colour simply drained from his face. For a moment I thought I'd gone too far. He seemed to be having trouble with his breathing. When he stood up, he had to lean on his desk for support.

"I think it's time you left. The contracts are signed and I'm a busy man. Good day, Sr. MacAllister."

"Honey pots," I said. "Diamonds in honey pots."

Pomar almost fell back into his seat. If he'd been grey before, he was positively ashen now.

"Get out. Now."

"As you wish. But I'll be back. Perhaps we can discuss it sensibly then."

I'd reached the point of diminishing returns. Pomar clearly didn't intend to tell me anything. He didn't need to. Despite his repeated denials, he had guilt stamped all over him. But he was small fry. I was relying on his panic to lead me to the next link in the chain.

After a quarter of an hour I was sure I'd miscalculated. I was still sitting in the Alfa across from the factory. So far there had been no sign of Pomar. Perhaps I'd been wrong, although I couldn't fault my reasoning.

Pomar's panic had been genuine—there could be no doubt about this. I'd gambled that he'd seek advice and reassurance. He'd want to get in touch with his fellow smugglers. I'd also gambled that he wouldn't trust the telephone. This was why I'd been so heavy-handed about the tape recordings. It seemed I'd been mistaken. I hadn't been nearly as clever as I'd thought. All I'd managed was to show Pomar nearly all my cards without receiving anything in return.

I lit myself a cigarette and decided to wait a few more minutes. After all, I didn't have anything else to do. There was still half of my cigarette left when Pomar scuttled out of his office. I immediately ducked down in my seat but I needn't have bothered. Apparently it didn't even occur to him that he might be watched. He simply clambered into his tan Volkswagen beetle and drove off.

After I'd allowed him a hundred-metre head start, I set off in pursuit. This wasn't particularly demanding. There was hardly any traffic about and Pomar wasn't driving fast. The only real surprise was that he was heading into Caldas da Rainha itself. My guess had been that he'd be going north, towards Nazaré.

Pomar parked almost outside the hospice in the centre of town. I found myself a space on the opposite side of the square, over by the park. Following him on foot was as easy as it had been by car. His height meant there was no problem about keeping him in sight. He was going up the hill towards the market. I drifted along behind, ready to duck into a doorway if he should look back. He didn't.

We didn't have far to go. Without any warning, Pomar turned into a café. The sign above the doorway proclaimed it to be the Cozinha d'el Rey. This was probably an example of Portuguese understatement. I crossed the road and entered the pottery shop on the far side. There were more than enough items on display in the window to conceal me. Equally important, I had a good view of the café.

When I saw what Pomar was doing, I swore under my breath. I'd obviously underestimated him. He might not have trusted the phone in his office but he had no such qualms about the one in the café. I was no lip reader. In any case, Pomar spent most of the time with his back to me. He gesticulated a lot as he talked. This was no help to me at all.

After a couple of minutes, Pomar put down the phone and went up to the counter. He appeared to be upset. While he drank his coffee, I pretended an interest in the earthenware around me. In fact, some of it was very nice. There were one or two lines which could profitably be added to the Latimer SA export range. I made a mental note to have a word with Sanchez about them.

Then we were off again, walking back down the hill towards our cars. By now I was convinced that I'd blown it. My pessimism seemed to be confirmed when Pomar began driving back in the direction of the factory. I was wondering what my next step should be when my interest suddenly revived. Pomar had taken a left turn and the factory was to the right. There was still the possibility that he was going home. It was only after we had left Caldas well behind that I dared to congratulate myself. It appeared we were going to Nazaré after all.

I was very nearly right. Our destination wasn't in Nazaré itself. The house Pomar was heading for stood just outside the town. As far as I could see from the road, it was completely enclosed by the pale blue stucco walls. On the top, shards of glass were set in the cement. I could see them glistening in the sun. This was about all I could see. The house itself was almost completely obscured apart from the pink tiles of the roof.

Fortunately, I had plenty of warning when Pomar turned into the drive. I was about two hundred metres behind him. There was no question of my stopping outside the house. It was a long, straight section of road with no other houses nearby. Unless I wanted to advertise my interest, I had to drive on. As I passed, I could read the nameplate on one of the entrance pillars. It said Francisco da Silva. All I caught of the house was a quick glimpse. It was pale blue, like the walls, and seemed to be enormous.

The road I was on was narrow and full of potholes. This made it similar to most country roads in Portugal. I had to continue for almost a quarter of a mile before a bend hid me from the house.

Where I parked, there were plantations of eucalyptus trees on either side of the road. The trees perfumed the air with a distinctive scent.

I'd taken bearings well before I stopped. I knew exactly where I needed to go. The belt of eucalyptus trees only extended for fifty metres or so. Then I was out among the carefully tended vines. None of them came higher than my waist. There was a small hill between me and the house. I started up it, climbing the terraces. The dry, crumbly soil didn't make for easy climbing, and quite a lot of it found its way into my shoes. It was very hot out in the sun, and I was sweating profusely by the time I reached the top of the hill. I sat down on a convenient pile of stones while I mopped my brow.

From the hill I had plenty of elevation to see over the walls. Well over an acre of ground was enclosed within them, and almost half of the area was covered by a complex of buildings. The main house was all on one level. It spread in every direction, without apparent rhyme or reason. In the centre of the jumble, there was a small interior courtyard. To the rear of the main building there was a much smaller one, which I guessed must house the servants. There were two other small buildings beside the kidney-shaped swimming pool. One of these would be for changing in; the other looked as though it might be a bar.

Facing me, beside the main house, was a large, paved patio, slightly above the level of the surrounding lawn. To provide it with shade, there was a lattice of pillars and beams covered with climbing plants. Three men were sitting round a table on the patio. Although I was too far away to be certain, one of them looked like Pomar. Presumably, one of the others was Francisco da Silva.

They all appeared to be intent on their conversation. It wouldn't have surprised me at all to learn I was the main topic under discussion. I'd deliberately put myself out on a limb, and it was up to me to move fast before it was sawn away from beneath me.

The garage was at the front of the house. Apart from Pomar's Volkswagen, I could see two other vehicles. One of these was a black Mercedes. One of the servants was busy polishing the bodywork, and judging by the way it gleamed, he was making a good job of it. The other vehicle was big and unmistakably American. It looked like a Cadillac.

This was the vehicle which interested me most. There were plenty of big American cars in Portugal but I was no great believer in coincidences. I wondered whether Joaquim might be somewhere inside the house. It was certainly big enough to accommodate the odd house guest. And it was remote enough for it not to matter if the house guest was an unwilling one.

Half an hour later, Pomar drove off. I sat on the hill and watched him go. He was heading back in the direction of Nazaré and Caldas. Once he was out of sight, I pushed myself to my feet and started down the hill. Although I was returning to my car, I'd no intention of following him any longer. Pomar had served his purpose. He'd established the link Joaquim had suggested. Now I had other matters to attend to.

Nazaré had used to be my favourite place in Portugal. Now I wasn't so sure. Of course, the town was as picturesque as ever. Nothing could destroy the long sweep of golden beach or the massive cliff towering above it. It was the character of the town which had changed. The round-bottomed boats and the fishing nets still adorned the beach but the men who used them had been forced away. Now the beach area belonged to the tourists. The long line of restaurants and gift shops were for them, not the fishermen who risked their lives off the coast.

Most of the fishermen had moved up the cliff to Sitio, and I hoped they looked down on what was happening to Nazaré with contempt. Change had been inevitable but this didn't mean I had to like it. When I'd first come to Nazaré with Jane, oxen had pulled the fishing boats from the sea. Now the work was done by tractors. This was progress but the cost had been high.

I booked myself into the Dom Henrique just off the beach. Caldas was too far away to be a base for my night's work. At the latest count, I was paying for three separate hotel rooms. I was well on the way to becoming a one-man tourist boom.

Before I went out, I made two phone calls. The first was to the Pensão Portugal in Caldas, asking them to relay any messages to Nazaré. The other was to Joaquim. Although I allowed the phone to ring for several minutes, there was no answer. I hadn't really expected one.

It was early evening now. Most of the tourist coaches had set out for home. So had the resident pickpockets. I was hungry but I had no trouble resisting the lure of the larger restaurants. The best food was to be found in the places the local people used. They were much cheaper too. I'd been promising myself fresh, grilled sardines with a salad of tomatoes and peppers. When I stepped inside the small restaurant, I abruptly changed my mind. There was *caldeiradas* on the menu, and the rich smell of the fish stew started me salivating at once. When I tried it, it tasted as good as it smelled. The local wine I drank with it would have put many a famous vintage to shame.

By the time I finished eating, it was almost dark. I continued along the front, the cliff looming behind me. On the beach side of the road, an old man was sitting on a box, gazing out to sea. I crossed to stand beside him. At first he didn't acknowledge my presence. He was staring out towards the barrier reef, which created a treacherous swell that had to be coped with on every voyage in or out of Nazaré. Over the years, hundreds of the local menfolk had been drowned there.

When I offered him a cigarette, the old man accepted it without comment. He hadn't asked for it, so he owed me no thanks.

"How is the fishing?"

"Costly." The old man spat on the sand at his feet. "Two boats have been lost already this year."

"Were there deaths?"

"No. We were fortunate."

He was speaking on behalf of the community as a whole. We puffed at our cigarettes in silence. I knew better than to hurry him. I'd asked my questions. Now it was his turn.

"You're a foreigner." This was more of an accusation than a statement.

"Yes."

"Are you German?"

"No. I'm English."

"I don't like the Germans. English are better. You speak Portuguese well for a foreigner."

"Thank you."

This was acceptance of a kind.

"What do you want with me? You didn't come to talk about the fishing."

"I need a grapnel. I shall also need a length of rope to go with it. I was hoping that you might be able to help me find them."

"There are shops which sell such things."

"All of them are closed."

He nodded to acknowledge the point. I was glad he didn't question me further. It would be difficult to explain that a shop would remember if things went wrong. Of course, the old man would remember me too. However, he was far less likely to take his knowledge to the police.

"What use is a grapnel without a boat?"

"Surely that is my concern."

"Undoubtedly."

"I would pay well. And I would return the grapnel and rope in the morning."

The old man considered my request for a few seconds longer. I was sure that the implications of what I'd said hadn't passed him by.

"Five thousand escudos," he said.

"That would be fair," I agreed.

It would be outright extortion.

"Come with me."

I followed him as he set off across the road. For somebody of his age he was remarkably spry. I hoped I found Joaquim in the same condition.

CHAPTER 12

It was very dark standing beside the wall. Although the moon was out, it was partially obscured by cloud. I stood in the shadows and listened. I could faintly hear music coming from the direction of the house; otherwise it was quiet. I uncoiled the rope and hefted the grapnel in my hand. It was much heavier than I'd expected. I was glad that I didn't have to throw it far.

My first attempt was unsuccessful. The grapnel went over the wall easily enough but the hooks didn't catch. As soon as I put my weight on the rope, it slid back over the wall. I had to move out of the way to avoid being hit. A shower of glass came with the grapnel. I could feel some of it sprinkling on my hair. My only cause for satisfaction was that there was hardly any noise. The sacking I'd wrapped around the hooks appeared to be effective. A second attempt didn't fare any better. The grapnel was sliding on the stucco.

Inside the house, the record had been changed. The plaintive wail of a *fado* singer had replaced an Italian love song. It didn't help me to concentrate on the problem. There were no trees inside the wall I could use. I decided to try again in the corner. The angle formed by the two walls should give more purchase.

This time the grapnel held. All I had to worry about now was the glass fraying the rope. I walked up the wall, holding the rope with both hands. Once my head was above the level of wall, I stopped. Lights were shining from several windows in the main house; there were more in the servants' quarters. It all seemed peaceful enough.

I pulled myself the rest of the way up. The top of the wall was slightly rounded. This made it difficult for me to retain my balance while I tried to clear away some of the glass. I didn't try for very long. I was making too much noise. In any case, the glass was well embedded in the cement. I should really have brought more sacking with me.

Repositioning the grapnel on the outside of the wall wasn't much easier. The darkness was affecting my sense of balance. The longer I spent on top of the wall, the more I wobbled. It was a distinct relief when I had the rope down the inside of the wall and I could slide into the garden.

For a few seconds I remained where I'd landed. Guard dogs were my most immediate fear. This was why I'd purchased the fish-gutting knife to go with the grapnel. Although I hadn't seen any dogs while I'd been watching from the hill, I hadn't been high enough to see the entire enclosed area. There could be a dog pen on the far side of the house. Twelve-foot walls topped with glass suggested a certain preoccupation with security. Dogs would be a logical back-up.

After a minute or two, I began to relax. If any of man's best friends were on duty, they should have reached me by now. Da Silva must have put all his faith in the walls. I wasn't sufficiently confident about this to return the knife to its sheath.

While I'd been on the hill, I'd had plenty of opportunity to plot my route across the garden. Although the darkness didn't help, I had the swimming pool as a point of reference. What moonlight there was reflected from the water. I went forwards carefully, keeping in the shadows. There were no trees but there were plenty of bushes and shrubs. As I went, I took note of my surroundings. When I left, speed might be more important than stealth. If I did have to run for it, I wanted to know about potential obstacles in advance.

The buildings beside the pool were my first staging post. I leaned against the wall of one of them while I examined the main house. Close to, it seemed larger than ever. It was big enough to house a small army. I wondered how many people were actually inside. Excluding Pomar, I'd counted half a dozen that afternoon. There were undoubtedly more. These weren't the kind of odds I relished.

The patio itself was deserted. Now the sun had gone down, it was quite chilly. The mosquitoes and other night insects had long since driven everybody indoors. Lights were shining behind the glass doors which led out onto the paved area. As the drapes were drawn, I couldn't see inside. Further along the side of the house, two other rooms were lit. Only one of the windows was curtained. The music I'd heard was coming from the servants' quarters. Somebody inside was laughing. I'd no intention of discovering why. This was an area I intended to keep well away from.

I decided to try the patio first. Although some light was coming through the doors, there were plenty of deep shadows. Besides, I'd come to the house to have a look around. I wanted to know if Joaquim was there. Cowering beside the swimming pool wouldn't tell me a thing.

There was no cover at all on the lawn. I crossed the grass in a crouching run. It formed a lush carpet beneath my feet, deadening any sound. Once I was on the flagstones, I used the pillars. I went from one to another until I was pressed against the wall of the house. It took a few seconds for me to get my breathing under control. My exertions weren't the problem. I was frightened and tense; I had to consciously force myself to relax. Knowing what to do was very different from putting it into practice. My Army days were a long, long way behind me.

The glass doors were no more than five metres from where I was standing. No sounds came from inside. I dropped down and bellied forwards across the flagstones. The curtains were slightly rucked up at the bottom, and there was a small gap I should be able to see through. This meant going out into the open but it was a risk I had to accept. If I'd been playing safe, I'd never have climbed the wall in the first place.

The gap in the curtains wasn't big enough for me to see more than a part of the room. It was very large. The floor was of polished pine. Over to my right was a huge stone fireplace. The section of the far wall that I could see was covered with bookshelves.

An elderly man was sitting in an armchair to one side of the fireplace. He was reading. I knew at once that this must be da Silva. He was one of the two men Pomar had been talking to that afternoon. Besides, money and power left distinctive marks. Even in repose, there was a certain arrogance about him. He looked like somebody who was accustomed to being served. There was far more of the aristocrat about him than the criminal. He managed to look distinguished and pleasant at the same time. There was character in his face and a definite hint of humour. It was the face of somebody I could like. I'd have preferred otherwise.

There was a bell push set in the wall beside the fireplace. Da Silva reached out to press it. Seconds later a servant appeared. He was smartly liveried in a white jacket and a bow tie. Before he left again he mixed his master a whisky and soda. I didn't stay to watch da Silva drink it.

I started off along the side of the house. The first window I came to was in darkness. As the curtains weren't drawn, I peered inside. It looked as though it was a study or office. Beneath the window I could distinguish a desk. Further back were bookshelves and what seemed to be a filing cabinet. While I was there, I tested the bars which protected the window. They were depressingly solid, firmly anchored in the brickwork. I couldn't move them at all. This was probably why there were no dogs. All the windows in the house were similarly protected. At a rough guess, the bars were made of hardened steel. It would need an awful lot of work with a hacksaw to get past them.

The next room along was occupied. Unfortunately, there were no chinks for me to peep through. Straining my ears, I could just distinguish the quiet murmur of voices from inside. It sounded as though a man and a woman were talking. I didn't pause for long.

A great pool of light was flooding from the window of the neighbouring room. The curtains hadn't been drawn at all. The thorns of a rosebush had snagged in my trousers. I had to stop to disentangle myself. I knew I must be leaving a trail of footprints behind me in the soft soil of the flower bed. This couldn't be helped. By the time the footprints were noticed, I hoped to be long gone. If I wasn't, they wouldn't matter anyway.

Despite the lights, the room was quiet. I still hesitated before I looked in. Once I did, I'd be completely exposed. Unfortunately, there was no alternative. My first glance inside was a quick one. Then I was back in the shadows again. All I had time to see was that it was a bedroom. And that there was somebody asleep in the bed.

It wasn't until I looked again that I recognized the occupant of the bed. Even then I wasn't sure I believed my eyes. I'd come searching for Joaquim. I'd hoped to find him but I hadn't really expected to. Logic had suggested that he was almost certainly dead. So much for logic. I'd seldom seen anybody sleeping quite so peacefully. There was even a little smile on his lips.

It was shortly after midnight when the last light in the house went out. I waited for another hour, crouched behind the poolside changing rooms. For a while I'd had my doubts. What I'd discovered just didn't tally with what I'd been anticipating. Joaquim wasn't dead. He wasn't being held in durance vile. He seemed considerably more comfortable than I was in my hotel. There were no indications of any ill-treatment. I began to harbour dark suspicions of some form of collusion between Joaquim and da Silva.

My paranoia took time to master. It wasn't until the initial shock had died away that I started to think straight again. Joaquim could no more have harmed Robert than Angela could have done. This was completely unthinkable. Besides, I knew Joaquim hadn't left home willingly. The open front door must have been intended as a

message. It had been an appeal for help. There was no other explanation for it. Perhaps there was a more sinister reason for his peaceful
slumbers. I'd realized this when I'd taken a longer look at Joaquim.
He wasn't moving at all. Even when I tapped on the window, he
didn't stir. He could well be sedated.

The last shreds of doubt had been dispelled just after eleven
o'clock. One of the servants came into the bedroom to pull the curtains and switch off the light. Although I'd retreated deeper into the
garden by then, I could clearly see the key on the outside of the door.
There were also a couple of bolts. Comfortable or not, Joaquim was a
prisoner. He was being held in the house against his will. Somehow
or other, I had to get him out. I wasn't sure this was possible but I
owed it to Joaquim to try.

The windows I dismissed at once. They could be forgotten as a
possible means of entry. After a complete circuit of the house, I'd
ruled out most of the doors as well. They all had double locks fitted
on them, and it was reasonable to assume that there were also bolts
inside. In any case, lock-picking wasn't one of my specialities. Anything more complicated than a simple Yale and I was in trouble. This
left me with a severely limited range of choices.

Nothing at all could be done until everybody had settled down for
the night. Once I was satisfied on this score, I headed for the patio
again. The sliding doors ran in aluminium tracks. Like all the other
doors, they were locked. When I tested, there was very little give in
the handle. I'd read somewhere that sufficient pressure on the handle
of a sliding door could break the locking mechanism. This wasn't
applicable to the doors in front of me. All I managed to do was give
myself a pain in the arm. I consoled myself with the thought that the
sliding doors were probably fitted with some kind of alarm anyway.
The rest of the house had been designed like a fortress. It was hardly
likely that the sliding doors would have been overlooked.

There was only one other alternative. I selected the downpipe between the patio doors and the study. It was square and sturdy. The
brackets which fastened it to the wall made reasonable footholds.
More important, I knew there was nobody sleeping in the neighbouring rooms.

The only awkward part came when I encountered the overhang of
the roof. Fortunately, the guttering was as strong as the drainpipe.

After a little scrabbling, I managed to heave myself up onto the tiles. The roof itself wasn't steeply pitched, and none of the tiles seemed to be loose. I wriggled up on my stomach until I could grip the ridge tiles. As far as I could tell, I'd made very little noise. No lights had come on in the house below.

The interior courtyard was almost directly in front of me. After a moment's reflection, I crawled down the slope headfirst. I wanted to see where I was going. The moon had come out from behind the clouds by now. With my head stuck out over the guttering, I had a clear view into the courtyard. There were two doors, one at either end. Both of them were closed, and my money was on them being locked as well.

It was high time I took stock again. I might be able to get inside. I might be able to find my way in the dark through a strange house to where Joaquim was sleeping. I might even discover he wasn't sedated after all. Then, still in the dark, I'd have to find us another way out. Fit as he undoubtedly was, Joaquim was an old man. He was well past the age for shinning up drainpipes and crawling across roofs. I doubted whether he was any better fitted for balancing on top of twelve-foot walls. An attempt to rescue Joaquim might well be the death of him.

There was a much easier way. One call to the police and they'd be out at da Silva's house in force. Then, again, they might not. They'd think twice before they hassled somebody as rich and influential as da Silva. Threatening him with the police might be far more effective. In the morning I'd find out how well this worked. For the time being, I started backing carefully up the roof. If nothing else, the night had taught me one important lesson. Breaking and entering should be left to the professionals.

There were roadworks in progress outside the Dom Henrique. A pneumatic drill woke me shortly after eight. I felt sluggish and tired. Even with the window open, the hotel room was hot and oppressive. I guessed that a thunderstorm must be on the way.

A shower did nothing to make me feel appreciably better. I was paying the price for the previous night. It wasn't so much the physical exertion. I'd been drained by the constant nervous tension. And the new day didn't promise to be any less demanding.

Before I did anything else, my clothes had to be cleaned up. They hadn't stood up to the previous night's adventures much better than I had. My trousers still looked distinctly scruffy after I'd finished with them. All the same, they'd have to do. My suitcase was still in Caldas da Rainha. Going to fetch it was very low on my list of priorities.

Once I'd breakfasted, I appropriated some of the hotel stationery. It took me almost an hour to compose the letter. However clear the facts were in my own mind, it was difficult to present them coherently. There were still several flaws in the final version. Although I wasn't completely satisfied, it was good enough. I sealed the letter in an envelope, addressed it and went downstairs.

The young receptionist would go far in the hotel trade. He was polite and good-looking and he had a great smile. He looked as though he was genuinely anxious to be of service. Underneath, though, he remained his own man. Being a guest in the hotel didn't necessarily make me any better than he was. It simply meant I had more money. I could read what he was thinking in his eyes. Quite probably, his assessment was correct.

"Yes, senhor. What can I do for you?"

"You can keep this letter for me, please." I slid a banknote across the counter with the envelope. The money might not be necessary but it wouldn't do any harm. "Hang on to it until midday. If I haven't reclaimed it by then, could you please post it? Have you got that?"

"Of course, senhor."

The receptionist dutifully repeated my instructions. He'd already noticed that the envelope was addressed to the police. If he drew any conclusions from this, he was keeping them to himself.

"Excellent. Please make sure it is midday, though. No sooner and no later. That's very important."

"I understand, senhor."

I sincerely hoped he didn't. There was a public telephone on the far side of the lobby. This was far more secure than the one in my room which went through the hotel switchboard. I'd looked up da Silva's number in the directory before I'd come downstairs. When I rang it, I was answered almost immediately. The man who picked up the telephone proclaimed himself to be da Silva's secretary.

"Is Sr. da Silva at home?"

"Who is that, please?"

"MacAllister. Frank MacAllister."

"I'm not quite sure where Sr. da Silva is at the moment, Sr. Mac-Allister. Perhaps you could wait a minute while I check."

"Of course. Please tell him it's urgent."

I had to wait for almost five minutes. While I did, I swapped glances with the receptionist. He wasn't doing very well at disguising his curiosity.

"Mr. MacAllister?"

"That's right."

"I'm so glad you called." Da Silva's English was good. He had a low-pitched, soothing voice which went well with his appearance. "I was hoping for an opportunity to speak with you."

"I'll be doing the talking. All you have to do is listen."

My rudeness was calculated. I didn't want a dialogue. More important, I didn't want to allow da Silva an opportunity to think.

"I don't understand."

"That's why you have to listen. Do you have a pencil and paper handy?"

"Yes, but . . ."

"There aren't any 'buts.' I expect you to do exactly as I say. Otherwise I'm handing over everything I know about you and Pomar to the police. The arrangements have already been made. I've written down where the diamonds came from, how they are smuggled out of Portugal and how they're connected with Robert Latimer's death. I've also explained where to find the physical evidence I have in my possession. The only way you can prevent this information reaching the police today is by releasing Joaquim Targa."

"And if I do?"

There was no attempt at a denial.

"In that case, I shan't go to the police for twenty-four hours. Incidentally, if I should suffer any unfortunate accidents, the information will go to the police automatically."

"Mr. MacAllister, I can assure you that there's no need for . . ."

"Listen." I almost barked the word out. "My terms aren't negotiable. You're to deliver Joaquim to the church in the plaza at Sitio. You drive him there yourself in your Mercedes. Nobody else is to accompany you. You have until eleven to get to the plaza."

"That's impossible. I'll need more time."

"You'll manage. Tell Joaquim to take the cable car down into Nazaré. Once he's there, he's to go directly to the Tofa restaurant on the front. He's to take an outside table and remain there until I contact him. You're to stay in the Mercedes outside the church until half past eleven. Then you can return home. Sr. Targa will be under observation from the moment he leaves you. If there's any indication that he's being followed, the whole deal is off. Is that clearly understood?"

"Yes, but . . ."

"You have until eleven, Sr. da Silva. I'd make sure you aren't late."

As I hung up, I could feel the beads of sweat trickling down my face. There were several gaping holes in my presentation but I thought the plan would work. I hadn't allowed da Silva time to spot the flaws. Or to take any countermeasures. I didn't think he could afford not to comply with my instructions. In any case, the die was cast. In a little under three-quarters of an hour, I should know how right I'd been.

I'd once heard a climber say that standing on a mountain peak made him feel closer to God. At the time it had struck me as incredibly arrogant. Since I'd been coming to Nazaré, I was no longer so sure. Whenever I looked down from the Pederneira cliff, I could understand how the mountaineer had felt.

The panorama below was breathtaking. Awesome wasn't too strong a word for it. The cliff fell sheer, descending almost three hundred feet to the turbulent Atlantic swell. Nestled at its base, the town of Nazaré was like a collection of toy houses. The people in the street were like two-legged ants. At the top of the cliff, you were completely removed from the world below.

I only allowed myself a minute or so to admire the view. Then I turned to face the plaza behind me. It was huge, on a scale to match the cliff. From where I was standing, the church was almost a hundred metres away. It had been built in dedication to a local miracle. According to legend, a Portuguese nobleman, Fouas Roupinho, had been in the area for a day's hunting. He'd been in hot pursuit of a white deer when one of the characteristic sea mists had descended around him. The mist had been so thick that he'd lost all sense of direction. The best he could do was spur his horse in what he took to be the right direction. Suddenly, a vision of Our Lady had appeared in front of him. Not surprisingly, the startled horse had stopped in its tracks. As Roupinho dismounted to kneel before the apparition, the mist lifted again. To his horror, Roupinho found himself on the very brink of the cliff. The vision had saved him from plunging to his death.

At least, this was the story Roupinho had related when he'd re-joined his companions, and none of them were about to call some-body of his importance a liar. Instead the church was built to cele-brate the miracle. A shrine was also constructed on the edge of the cliff. Inside, the hoofprint was preserved, showing where the horse had stopped. Cynics might scoff at all this but it made a nice story. Besides, the shrine was going to be useful to me. I intended to use it as my observation post. From there I could keep an eye on the plaza without anybody being able to see me.

It was still only a quarter to eleven. I'd deliberately arrived early, before da Silva could possibly reach Sitio. I wanted to see what other vehicles came into the plaza apart from the Mercedes. For the mo-ment, there was only a van outside one of the shops. Two men were leisurely unloading fruit from it. An old beggar woman, dressed en-tirely in black, was sitting on the steps to my right. She was making a long day of it. I hoped both of us would be lucky.

On the opposite side of the plaza, directly in front of the church, a group of men were talking together. The amount of gesticulation gave a clue to the topic under discussion. It must be either sex, football or the price of fish. Nothing else was likely to get them so steamed up. Otherwise the plaza was empty.

At ten to eleven the first tourist coach of the day arrived from Leiria. The sign at the front proclaimed that it was visiting Nazaré, Obidos and Fatima before its return to base. This should make for a busy day. The tourists disembarked and fanned out across the plaza. I wished they'd delayed their arrival by about half an hour. There were approximately forty of them, all Portuguese. The plaza was beginning to seem crowded.

In the next ten minutes there were two more arrivals. One of these was a woman leading a donkey. I felt I could dismiss her as a potential threat. The other I wasn't so sure about. He was driving a battered Renault and he parked on the left-hand side of the square. This in itself wasn't suspicious, but the way he stayed behind the wheel with the engine running most definitely was. I only relaxed when a young woman came running out of one of the buildings to join him in the car. They were just driving off when da Silva's Mercedes appeared.

I drew further back into the shadows of the shrine's doorway. There were only two people in the Mercedes—at least, there were only two I could see. I'd no way of telling whether there was anybody crouched down in the back. There were no other vehicles following behind.

I ran another quick check of the people in the plaza. Everything seemed normal enough. It appeared as though da Silva had followed my instructions to the letter. My one slight cause for concern was that Joaquim didn't leave the car immediately. The Mercedes had pulled up outside the church but none of the doors had opened. The two men were still in the front seats. I'd have liked to know what they were discussing. I kept one eye on the Mercedes and the other on the plaza itself. Although there was absolutely nothing to arouse my suspicions, I was very much on edge. Da Silva had a lot to lose. So, for that matter, did I.

I breathed a little easier when Joaquim emerged from the car. Now he was free, I thought I could cope with any attempt at a double cross. Joaquim started off around the plaza without a backwards glance. Apart from me, nobody appeared to be paying any attention to him. If he had suffered any maltreatment, this certainly wasn't evident in his walk. Although he wasn't hurrying, he seemed to be moving easily enough. Da Silva had stayed in his Mercedes in front of the church.

Until Joaquim was out of sight, I remained where I was. As far as I could tell from a distance, there was nobody tailing him. This wasn't necessarily significant. Da Silva knew the itinerary I'd laid down. He could have arranged for one of his men to travel with Joaquim in the cable car. There could be somebody waiting to pick him up at the bottom of the cliff in Nazaré itself. This was something I'd have to check. Nothing could be taken for granted.

The first of the day-trippers had already entered the shrine. When they started to leave, I drifted out with them. The Alfa wasn't in the plaza. I'd parked it in a side street. Once I'd reached the car, I didn't waste any time. I wanted to be down in Nazaré before Joaquim's cable car arrived. This meant I had to break one or two of the local traffic regulations. Fortunately, there weren't many other cars on the road. And it was all downhill.

The cable car still hadn't completed more than half of the descent when I reached the station at the bottom. Apparently the timetable had been accurate after all. I parked about a hundred metres from the terminal. From where I was I had an unobstructed view. There was a small group of people waiting for the return journey up the cliff. There were also several cars parked beside the road. None of those I could see had drivers sitting at the wheel. I was beginning to relax slightly. This was something I'd have to watch.

Joaquim was among the last of the passengers to emerge. There was only a middle-aged couple behind him. I guessed that he was deliberately dawdling. He'd want to make it as easy for me as he possibly could. I sank lower in my seat and watched Joaquim come towards me. Nobody was following him on foot. Nor were any of the other parked cars a threat.

It was a simple decision to make. Waiting for Joaquim to reach the restaurant wasn't necessary. I switched on the ignition as I rolled down the window. Joaquim was almost level with me, on the far side of the road. I checked my mirror one last time. It was still clear.

"Joaquim," I called. "Over here."

He might almost have been expecting me. There was only the slightest of hesitations. Then he recognized me and started across the road. He was smiling as he came. I pushed the passenger door open for him while I checked the mirror yet again. There was still no apparent cause for alarm.

The Alfa was already rolling forwards as Joaquim slid into the seat beside me. For the next few minutes he didn't attempt to speak. He realized I had other things on my mind. I ducked in and out of half a dozen side streets before I was satisfied. Only then did I find us a space in a line of parked cars. We were about a quarter of a mile from the front.

"Are you all right?" I asked.

"I'm very well. And thank you for all your efforts on my behalf."

"It was the least I could do. I dragged you into this mess. I owed it to you to get you out again."

"Noble sentiments indeed." Joaquim sounded gently ironic. "There's something you must tell me, Frank. Were you prowling around da Silva's house last night?"

"I was."

"I thought as much. There was considerable consternation this morning when the footprints were discovered. Da Silva doesn't like the thought of prowlers."

"I'll bet." I allowed myself a small smile of satisfaction. "I doubt whether my phone call was any more popular."

"It did come as something of a bombshell."

There was something wrong. I couldn't put my finger on what it was but it was definitely there between us. Although I knew that effusiveness wasn't Joaquim's style, he wasn't behaving the way I'd expected. He didn't appear to be either relieved or apprehensive.

"Are you sure you're not hurt?"

"Not a single grey hair has been harmed."

This wasn't the answer I'd wanted. I could sense the irony again.

"Exactly why did da Silva kidnap you?"

"It wasn't really a kidnapping. It was more of a forceful invitation. I'm speaking with the benefit of hindsight, of course. At first I was afraid for my life."

"So was I."

"In that case, both of us were worrying ourselves unnecessarily."

I was still uneasy. For the life of me, I couldn't think what I'd missed.

"How did you trace me?" Joaquim continued. "Was it through Pomar?"

"That's right. I squeezed him a little. When he ran to da Silva for advice, I followed him."

Joaquim laughed.

"You must squeeze very hard, Frank. From what I can gather, Pomar was ready to flee the country after you'd finished with him.

You were far more successful with him than I was with the diamond cutter. He didn't tell me a thing. All he did was ask da Silva to get me off his back."

I lit myself a cigarette. I'd have liked Joaquim to say more but he didn't. He sat half turned in his seat. He still looked as though something was amusing him. Perhaps he could sense some of my doubts.

"Why did da Silva have you brought to Nazaré?"

"He wanted to talk."

"And that's all?"

Joaquim shrugged. "He would have liked to negotiate with me as well. He was after some kind of a deal. I had to explain to him that this wasn't possible. I told him he'd have to speak to you."

By now I was completely out of my depth. The best I could manage was to return to my original theme. Even to my ears it sounded like an accusation.

"You weren't badly treated, then?"

"I was forced to leave my home. Once I reached Nazaré, there was some restriction on my freedom of movement. Otherwise it wasn't too bad. To be honest, I quite enjoyed myself. It was all very civilized."

"Murder isn't a civilized pastime."

"Da Silva had nothing to do with Robert's death. I'm sure of that."

I wasn't. I shook my head in perplexity as much as anything else.

"What's been happening to you, Joaquim? You used to be a policeman. You know that da Silva must have been involved. Robert died because of those diamonds he discovered."

"Maybe he did. Then again, maybe he didn't. I was a policeman long enough to know it isn't always wise to grab at the obvious. I'd like you to talk to da Silva yourself. He'd welcome the opportunity."

"No way." I was shaking my head more vigorously now. "Whatever you might say, I don't trust him."

"But you're mistaken, Frank. You do trust me, don't you?"

"I used to. Now I'm not so sure."

"Why is that? Do you think I might be in league with da Silva?"

I nodded. This was precisely what I was thinking.

"I suppose that's understandable." Joaquim was almost talking to himself. "After all, my behaviour must seem very strange to you." He fell silent for a few moments while he thought. I kept an eye on the road while I did the same. I was badly confused. Half an hour previously, I'd known exactly what I was doing. The facts had all been clear in my mind. I'd been positive that Robert's murder was all but solved. Now, everything was crumbling about my ears. Despite the apparent contradictions, I did trust Joaquim. At least, I very much wanted to.

"Listen to me, Frank." Suddenly Joaquim's voice was crisp and authoritative. "Set up safeguards. Take any precautions you think necessary. Robert apart, there are powerful threats you can hold over da Silva's head. You have more than enough evidence now to start a police investigation. Use this leverage any way you see fit. But go and see da Silva. It's important to you and Angela."

"You have to give me more, Joaquim."

This was almost a plea. Joaquim recognized it as such. He promptly went for my weakest point.

"Please, Frank. I'm asking you as a friend. I promise you that you'll be perfectly safe. Will you do it?"

"I'll think about it."

And while I was thinking, I'd be driving back towards my hotel. Otherwise, the receptionist would very shortly be posting the letter I'd entrusted to him. It appeared that there might be more flaws in it than I'd originally imagined.

CHAPTER 13

Large mansions obviously had their disadvantages after all. The servant took much longer to locate Angela than I'd expected. I sat on the bed and stared out of the window. Although the sun was shining brightly, the cumulus was building up in the distance. There was no breeze at all. It helped to make the hotel room oppressively humid. I felt no better than I had first thing in the morning. It would be a relief when the storm eventually broke. I was wiping sweat from my face when somebody eventually picked up the receiver at the far end of the line. To my surprise, it was Adam.

"Angela isn't here at the moment," he explained. "She's out shopping. Do you want me to take a message for her?"

"That all depends. Do you have any idea when she'll be back?"

"She shouldn't be too long. She promised that she'd be back for lunch."

I hesitated for a second. I'd really wanted to talk to Angela herself. On the other hand, I didn't have anything particularly important to say to her.

"Perhaps you would take a message to save me ringing back. I originally told Angela I'd be back in Lisbon by tonight. Since then there's been a change of plan. Tell her I'll probably be staying in Nazaré tonight. If everything goes according to plan, I should be back late tomorrow morning."

"You're in Nazaré now?" Adam sounded surprised. "I thought Angela said you were going to Caldas da Rainha."

"That was yesterday," I told him. "I've moved on since then."

"Does that mean you're making progress with your investigations?"

"Of a kind. Hopefully, I'll know more by tomorrow."

"You really think you might be on the right track?"

"It looks like that at the moment."

It was unusual for Adam to be so chatty. He normally ended his conversations with me as rapidly as possible. Perhaps he was mellowing with age.

"So I may have to eat my words."

"I hope so. If it's necessary, I'll come and remind you in person."

Adam laughed. "You do that, Frank. I'll pass on your message to Angela."

"Thanks. You can tell her I'll be in touch as soon as I'm back in Lisbon."

"I'll tell her. Goodbye."

"Goodbye."

I changed into the new shirt I'd bought myself, then went downstairs to join Joaquim. I found him sitting at the horseshoe-shaped bar. He was sipping Vimeiro water. I slid onto the stool next to him and ordered a beer. We were the only customers in the bar. The majority of the other guests seemed to be lounging around the swimming pool outside. Most of the bodies on display were pale and slack-muscled. Nazaré didn't attract many youngsters. They preferred the bars and discos of Estoril and Cascais.

"I phoned da Silva," Joaquim told me.

"And?"

"He'll be at home all afternoon. I said we'd be out at about three."

I drank half of my beer. It tasted cold and sharp.

"Are you sure it's wise? Going to da Silva's house, I mean."

"I wouldn't have recommended going otherwise."

Joaquim obviously didn't have any doubts at all.

"I'd feel much happier if you gave me some kind of an explanation."

"It's best left to da Silva himself. I'm sure you'll agree with me, Frank, once you've heard what he has to say."

"We'll see." I still had reservations. "What exactly happened with the crooked diamond cutter? That's something else you haven't told me about."

"There's very little to tell. Breyner flatly denied ever handling any illicit diamonds. He way lying, of course, but nothing I said could shake him. He knew I didn't have any real proof. As soon as I'd gone, he must have telephoned da Silva. The first I knew of it was when Alexis turned up on my doorstep."

"Alexis?"

"He's da Silva's chauffeur and bodyguard. I think he's a Pole. Anyway, he was very polite at first. He simply said da Silva would like to talk to me. When I refused, he took me just the same. He had a gun although I don't think he would have used it."

"I suppose you left the front door open on purpose."

Joaquim shrugged. "It was all I could think of. At the time I didn't realize the gun was simply for show."

What Joaquim had said tied everything up neatly. There were no loose ends. Except that Robert had been killed. If Joaquim was right

and da Silva really was innocent, who the hell had been responsible?
The trail I'd been following only went as far as Nazaré.

From where I was sitting on the patio, I had a clear view of the
hill. I could even pinpoint the spot where I'd been the previous
afternoon. Today somebody was working up there among the vines. I
very much doubted whether he had any interest in what was happening at da Silva's house.

There were three of us at the table, da Silva, Joaquim and myself.
Da Silva was doing his best to be hospitable. He possessed a stately,
Old World charm which it was difficult not to respond to. I worked
at it nevertheless. Despite what Joaquim had said, da Silva had to
remain a prime suspect. Everything I'd learned so far indicated that
he must be implicated in Robert's death. This was why I had the
Savage in my pocket. So far the conversation had been general. Da
Silva had been attempting to thaw some of the ice. However, I hadn't
come for social chitchat.

"You had something you wanted to tell me."

I was deliberately being blunt.

"Yes." Da Silva's smile revealed a set of perfect teeth, which
looked as though they were his own. "It's simply that I'm not quite
sure where to begin."

"I think Frank is primarily interested in Robert Latimer's murder."

Joaquim had appointed himself linkman.

"So you mentioned before. Unfortunately, there's very little I can
say. I simply have to repeat that I had no part in it."

"You'll have to do much better than that. Robert was killed because of the diamonds. It seems to me that you had most to gain
from his death."

"On the contrary. I had most to lose. Besides, murder isn't a crime
I want any part of. I never have done and I never will."

Da Silva had spoken with a certain dignity. It hadn't impressed me
very much.

"You must have a very poor memory. You've killed before when it
suited you."

"What do you mean?"

He seemed genuinely taken aback.

"Surely you can't have forgotten. I was referring to the pilot. The one who was supposed to fly the diamonds out of Angola for you."

"But he's still alive. As far as I know, he lives in Rio de Janeiro now."

"That's easy enough to say. What proof do you have?"

He didn't have any. Da Silva admitted this readily enough. However, he did have an explanation which appeared to make sense. According to da Silva, the pilot had been a part of the conspiracy from the very beginning. The diamonds had, in fact, gone aboard the aeroplane. They had also left with the pilot. Before he'd taken to his parachute, the pilot had primed the device which had destroyed the plane so thoroughly. This was why no body had ever been found among the wreckage.

"Is that true?" I was addressing Joaquim.

"No body was ever found."

"O.K." For want of anything better I was prepared to accept da Silva's version of events. "That still leaves us with Robert. How could his death possibly be to your disadvantage?"

"It's sent you and Sr. Targa after me, hasn't it?" Da Silva was smiling again. "Perhaps it would be best if I told you the whole story, right from the very beginning."

"Suit yourself. We have plenty of time."

Da Silva was refreshingly frank. At least, that was the way he sounded. There was no apparent attempt to distort events to show himself in a better light. The diamonds had been stolen. Da Silva admitted this, together with his part in planning the robbery.

He even explained his motives. Nearly all of da Silva's holdings had been in Angola. He'd known that independence would inevitably lead to their expropriation. Although he'd managed to transfer most of his liquid assets to Lisbon, his losses would be tremendous. Hijacking the diamonds had seemed to be the only way of minimizing them. This obviously wasn't something he was proud of. He admitted that there was no real justification for what he'd done. As he said, his motives had been entirely selfish. He'd been too old to relish starting afresh in Portugal. The diamonds had meant the difference between a comfortable retirement and a luxurious one. Da Silva had preferred the latter. He'd wanted to continue living in the manner to which he'd become accustomed.

Obtaining possession of the diamonds had been the easy part. Disposing of them had been a different matter. Despite his careful planning, not everybody had been prepared to accept the crash at face value. Da Silva himself had come under suspicion. The word was out in the diamond community to keep an eye open for the missing stones.

Da Silva's choice had been a simple one. Either he held on to the diamonds until the fuss had died down or he could dump them on the black market. Da Silva had elected to hold on to them. He'd had more than sufficient money for his immediate needs. Besides, any sale on the black market would realize only a fraction of the diamonds' true value.

It was almost three years before da Silva considered it safe to begin unloading the diamonds. While he was waiting, he'd been working out ways and means of moving the diamonds out of Portugal. Although it hadn't been difficult to recruit Breyner to do the cutting, this was only a small part of the problem. Because of their size, diamonds were relatively easy to smuggle. However, da Silva had been reluctant to use couriers. He'd had over two hundred gemstones to dispose of. There was no question of dumping them on the market in one large shipment. To avoid detection they'd have to go in small packages spread over a considerable length of time. He'd need either a hell of a lot of couriers making a few trips each or a few couriers making a hell of a lot of trips each. Neither option had appealed to da Silva.

He needed a system which was more secure. Da Silva had used the three years to take a careful look at those companies exporting goods to London, Amsterdam or Antwerp. Pomar had been an acquaintance of his. At the time Pomar had been in severe financial difficulties. There was even a possibility that his factory might have to close down. When da Silva had approached him with his proposition, Pomar had jumped at the opportunity. The risks weren't too great and the financial rewards would be considerable.

Recruiting Pomar had just about wrapped up the Portuguese end of the operation. It was nice and tight with only a small number of people involved. Equally important, the honey pots Pomar manufactured were an ideal vehicle for transporting the diamonds.

The main remaining problem was at the English end. Here da

Silva was deliberately vague. His account omitted any details of the arrangements he'd made. He probably thought I knew too much about his operation already. Even so, I could read quite a lot between the lines. If there was a weak link in the chain da Silva had established, it was definitely in England.

Nevertheless, it had worked well enough. To begin with, there had been some test runs. The package of stones da Silva had acquired included some industrial diamonds, which were sent along the pipeline first. There were no hitches, so da Silva had started dispatching the more valuable gemstones. From what I could gather, no more than three or four diamonds were sent each month. Until Robert had appeared on the scene, there were no real problems.

When he reached this stage in his narrative, da Silva stopped. He'd filled in all the background. Now it was up to me.

"What exactly did Robert do?" I enquired.

"You've heard about the accident at the warehouse?"

"Yes. Robert found a couple of your diamonds in one of the honey pots."

"That's right. Well, Sr. Latimer knew who had manufactured the honey pot. He went to Caldas da Rainha and confronted Pomar with what he'd found. Poor Pomar was in a terrible spot. Either he told your friend everything about the diamond smuggling or the police would be brought in."

"So Pomar referred Robert to you."

"Not exactly. He tried to stall until he discovered Sr. Latimer had bugged his telephone. That really panicked him. That's when he contacted me to ask for advice. I told him to send Sr. Latimer to see me."

"Why?"

Da Silva shrugged. "Why not? It was fairly obvious that Sr. Latimer wanted some kind of a deal. Otherwise he would have gone directly to the police when he discovered the diamonds."

"And was that what he wanted?"

"Oh, yes. He didn't make any bones about it. If his company was being used to smuggle diamonds, he wanted part of the action."

"What was your attitude? Didn't you object to Robert trying to cut himself in?"

"Of course I did. Unfortunately, there was no real alternative."

"Except to have him killed."

"True."

Da Silva was silent for a moment. When he spoke again, he looked me straight in the eye.

"I considered it very seriously," he admitted. "I even discussed ways and means with Alexis. In the end, I decided against. I wasn't very proud of being a thief. I didn't intend to become a murderer as well."

"Was all this before you actually met Robert?"

"Yes."

"And you didn't change your mind afterwards?"

This time da Silva laughed.

"You still haven't seen it, have you? O.K., Sr. Latimer wanted his ten percent. He didn't expect it for nothing, though. He had an awful lot to offer in return. For one thing, with his active participation, we wouldn't be restricted to Pomar's ceramics any more. The diamonds could go in tins of sardines or heels of shoes. There was a whole range of possibilities. Better still, Latimer was confident he could provide us with a really reliable contact at the English end of the operation."

"Rafferty."

The penny had just dropped.

"Rafferty," da Silva agreed. "That's why Latimer went to England. It also explains why I wouldn't have dreamed of killing him. I still have over half of the diamonds in my possession. It's by far the most valuable half because it includes the largest stones. With Latimer and Rafferty's help I'd have had a totally secure pipeline all the way to Hatton Garden. Believe me, I'd have been absolutely delighted to pay Latimer his commission. In fact, one payment had already been made. His death was almost as much of a blow to me as it must have been to you."

I did believe him. Much as it went against the grain, I really did. Da Silva sounded sincere. What's more, his story made sense. It fitted in with the Robert I'd known. He would have seen the diamond smuggling as a game. Outwitting the authorities would have been a challenge to him. The excitement would far have outweighed the dubious morality of the enterprise. The Robert I'd known wouldn't have had too much difficulty squaring it with his conscience. I wouldn't have done myself.

"What do you think, Joaquim?"

"You know already, Frank. With one or two minor reservations, I can believe Francisco."

"Do you, Sr. MacAllister?"

Da Silva was still looking me straight in the eye. I avoided his stare. I preferred to gaze up at the hill while I put my thoughts in order. A sudden flash of light near the top had caught my eye. I couldn't see what had caused it. Although the man was no longer working in the vineyard, he might have left a bottle behind.

"Well?" For the first time da Silva sounded anxious. "What do you intend to do?"

"What I've intended to do all along. Find out who killed Robert."

"And am I still a suspect?"

"No. At least, not unless I find some reason to reinstate you."

"There is no reason. I promise you that. I had no part in your friend's death."

I nodded wearily and lit myself a cigarette. Although Joaquim had done something to prepare me in advance, I was still depressed. I hadn't been looking any further than da Silva for the killer. Now I'd have to think again. I really couldn't see da Silva in the role of murderer. Equally important, nor could Joaquim. And he had a lifetime in the police to back up his judgement.

"There's one thing I want clearly understood," I said. "No more diamonds are shipped out of Portugal by Latimer SA."

"Of course not. You have my word on it."

"I assume you're not going to the police with what you know."

The query came from Joaquim.

"Not unless you insist on it. I don't give a damn about the diamonds. Besides, it would mean dragging Robert's name through the mud. I don't want to inflict that on Angela."

"I'm inclined to agree with you. Francisco and I will have to come to some private arrangement about the rest of the diamonds. There should be some element of justice."

I wasn't entirely sure what Joaquim meant. Da Silva evidently was. His grimace suggested he wasn't in wholehearted agreement.

Up on the hill there was another flash of light. I still couldn't see

what had caused it. There was something vaguely disturbing about it
but I didn't attempt to analyze what this was. Other things were
disturbing me more. I'd been wrong about da Silva. This was a fact
I'd already accepted. Did this necessarily mean all the rest of my
thinking had been wrong too? I thought not. I still couldn't believe
that Robert had died at the hands of a passing maniac.

"The diamonds must have had something to do with Robert's
death." This was a stubborn affirmation of faith. "Nothing else
makes sense."

"I tend to agree with you, Frank. Coincidences do happen, of
course, but . . ."

Joaquim tailed off into a shrug. Da Silva responded with one of his
own.

"I won't attempt to argue with you. All I can do is reiterate my
own innocence. The first I knew of Sr. Latimer's murder was when I
read about it in the newspaper. I only wish I could be more helpful."

I was still believing him. Who else was there, though? Pomar
could be discounted immediately. He wouldn't act independently of
da Silva. Besides, he didn't have the guts for murder. I couldn't see
why Rafferty should be involved either. Like da Silva, he benefited
from Robert staying alive. He wouldn't even have heard about the
diamonds before Robert had visited him in London. I was fairly
certain that Rafferty had put Pierce on my tail but this was easily
explained. Rafferty must have wanted to know what the hell was
going on.

However, there was one other possibility. It had been festering at
the back of my mind for the past day or two. I suspected that I'd
deliberately avoided considering it previously. Now I had to. It was
still very difficult to take it seriously.

"Tell me something," I said to da Silva. "Whose idea was it to
steal the diamonds in the first place?"

"Mine, I'm afraid. I have to accept full responsibility."

"You didn't take anybody else into your confidence?"

"You know I did. I've already explained that the pilot was working for me."

For the first time that afternoon, da Silva didn't ring completely
true. I didn't think he was lying to me. He was simply being evasive.

"I'm talking about principals, not employees."

Da Silva hesitated for a few seconds before he replied.

"Funnily enough, your friend Latimer asked me almost the same question. I'll give you the answer I gave to him. I can't deny my own part in what has happened. However, I do refuse to implicate others unnecessarily. Call it honour among thieves if you like."

"So you did have an associate?"

"If I did, he'd no more be implicated in Latimer's death than I am." He was still picking his words carefully.

"How can you be so sure?"

Da Silva's laugh was devoid of humour. "I know, I assure you. The very idea is unthinkable."

"That isn't good enough." I refused to let him off the hook so easily. "I need a name. I think you have to give it to us."

"We need to satisfy ourselves."

Joaquim was lending me his support. He'd probably guessed what I was after.

"No." Da Silva's shake of the head was final. "No names. Please believe me when I say they wouldn't help you."

"Surely that's something we have the right to decide for ourselves."

"I'm sorry."

He sounded adamant. I wanted to avoid direct confrontation for as long as possible. This was why I tried a slightly different approach.

"If I mention a name to you, can you manage a simple yes or no?"

There was a noticeable pause before da Silva nodded. He was reluctant to concede even this much.

"All right."

"Adam Boulter," I said. "Was he in it with you?"

Da Silva never did answer me. As he opened his mouth, the top of his head simply disintegrated.

For an instant I was frozen in my chair. I could actually see the bone, flesh and tufts of hair in a grisly halo around da Silva's head. Then everything began to happen very fast. Da Silva folded at the waist and toppled forwards across the table. At almost the same moment, a gaping, bloody hole appeared in Joaquim's throat. Without a sound, he tipped backwards in his chair. I dived out of mine, rolling frantically across the flagstones. This time I'd seen the tiny puff of smoke from the top of the hill. This time the man with the silenced rifle was playing for keeps.

The third bullet whined off the flagstones while I was still rolling. I couldn't suppress a high-pitched whinny of fear. The nearest cover was an ornamental flower tub. It was the bottom half of a port barrel which had been filled with earth and plants. I scrambled behind it as yet another bullet kicked up concrete chippings by my right leg. I felt one of them gouge a strip of flesh from my ankle. This made me the lucky one. When I looked over my shoulder, I could see Joaquim was sprawled on his back. He was staring sightlessly up at the sky from a spreading pool of blood. Da Silva was face downwards across the table. The cloth beneath his head was already stained red. Neither of them was even twitching.

Although there were at least half a dozen other people in the house, there had been nothing for them to hear. Apart from the clatter of Joaquim's chair, there had been no noise. None of them had any idea that anything was wrong. A radio was playing in the servants' quarters. In the house, one of the maids was using a vacuum cleaner. Away from the patio, life was continuing as normal.

I knew the flower tub was no permanent answer. I had my knees up against my chest and my head between my knees. Even so, I felt dangerously exposed. I had the uneasy feeling that parts of me must be visible from the hill.

The gunman did nothing to make me feel more secure. His next attempt showered me with splinters from the tub. I could hear a trickle of earth coming from the hole the bullet had made. The next two bullets converted the trickle into a flood. The man on the hill knew there was no hurry. He was systematically shooting the barrel to pieces.

This left me with a straight choice. I could stay where I was until I was shot. Or I could make a run for it and be shot. Neither course of action held any great appeal for me. I was very, very frightened.

"Alexis."

I shouted as loud as I possibly could. Alexis was da Silva's bodyguard. He should be somewhere nearby. The last time I'd seen him, he'd been in the study. If he was still there, he wasn't answering.

Another bullet hit the tub. I couldn't turn my head but it sounded

as though the tub was falling apart. The only real safety was offered
by the swimming pool or the patio doors. Both of them were too far
away. Two clean kills with two shots was impressive marksmanship.
The sniper would pick me off long before I reached either of them.
The only alternatives were the pillars on the patio. The nearest of
them was a mere five metres away. Unfortunately, it would offer
even less protection than the flower tub.

"Alexis."

Fear had added a few more decibels to my voice. This time the
bodyguard heard me. I saw his reflection in the mirror above the
fireplace as he hurried into the living room. He still had no idea of
what was happening. It wouldn't help me at all to have him killed.

"For Christ's sake," I yelled. "There's a gunman out here. Keep
away from the doors."

Although he was no longer in my line of vision, Alexis must have
heeded my warning. Either my panic had communicated itself to
him or he could see the two bodies. Another bullet thudded into the
tub. There couldn't be much earth left by now. Very soon the bullets
would be coming right through the wood.

"Where is he shooting from?"

Alexis's voice sounded reassuringly calm.

"He's up on the hill behind a pile of rocks."

"O.K. I have him. Stay where you are, Sr. MacAllister. I won't be
a minute."

I caught his reflection in the mirror again as he went out of the
room. As there was nowhere for me to run to, I did as he said. Two
more bullets had hit the flower tub before Alexis reappeared. He kept
himself pressed against the wall as he approached the sliding doors. I
was relieved to see the gun he was carrying. It looked suspiciously
like an M-16 but I couldn't be sure. Another bullet struck the tub. I
felt the wood against my back jar with the impact but it didn't come
through.

"Are you ready to run? Head for the doors when I start shooting."

Alexis allowed me no opportunity to reply. He simply stepped into
the doorway and opened fire. He obviously had the carbine on automatic. The spent cartridges were spewing out in an almost continuous stream. Nobody could possibly be unaware of what was happening any longer. The noise was deafening.

It didn't interfere with my running. I came out from behind the barrel like a sprinter out of his blocks. I ran with my head down, my arms and legs pumping like pistons. My attention was reserved exclusively for the sliding doors ahead of me. If any more shots came from the hill, I wasn't aware of them. I certainly wasn't hit.

The last metre or so I covered with a dive which sent me sliding on my stomach across the highly polished floor. Alexis stopped shooting as soon as I was inside. He'd fitted a new magazine before I'd pushed myself to my feet. The smell of cordite was very strong.

"O.K.?"

"I think so."

"Good."

He stuck the M-16 out of the doors and hosed the top of the hill again. There was no answering fire. This time Alexis only continued for a few seconds. Then he withdrew behind the protection of the wall. After a minute or so he stuck his head out into the open. It stayed firmly on his shoulders. From the back of the house I could hear a lot of excited shouting.

"Stay where you are, Sr. MacAllister," Alexis instructed. "I think the bastard has gone but I can't be sure."

Alexis slipped out of the doors onto the patio. He headed directly for the table. Even at a crouching run, he must have presented an easy target. There were no shots from the hill. Alexis only spent a few seconds examining da Silva and Joaquim. When he rose to his feet again, he shouted orders to one of the other servants. They didn't include anything about telephoning the police. His face was grim when he rejoined me in the room.

"They're both dead."

"I thought they were."

Reaction to my narrow escape was beginning to set in. Various parts of me were already shaking.

"Perhaps it would have been better if you had died too, Sr. MacAllister. If you had, there would be far less complications."

Until I looked across at Alexis, I thought I must have misheard him. Then I realized that he was deadly serious. The M-16 wasn't actually aimed at me but it was definitely pointing in my general direction. The safety was off and Alexis's finger was on the trigger. Several more parts of me started to shake.

"Why do you say that?" Even to me, my voice sounded unnatural.

"Diamonds," Alexis answered succinctly.

"What diamonds?" Under pressure, I could think very fast indeed. "I don't want to discuss them with the police any more than you do."

"What will you say, then?"

"Sr. Targa was an old friend of mine. For the past couple of days he'd been staying here as a house guest of Sr. da Silva. As I happened to be in Nazaré, I was invited over for the afternoon."

"How about the shooting?"

I shrugged. "What can I say? We were just sitting around talking together when some maniac started shooting at me. I don't know who he was any more than I know why he wanted to kill Sr. da Silva. That's my story."

Alexis nodded thoughtfully. Although I'd made the right noises, I could tell that he still wasn't entirely convinced. He still thought it might save a lot of trouble to put a bullet in my head.

"There's the ballistics to consider as well," I pointed out. "Our friend on the hill wasn't using an M-16. That might make for a few awkward questions."

"True." Alexis flashed me a wintry smile. "I was forgetting that."

Suddenly the carbine wasn't pointing in my direction any longer. I felt even better after Alexis had picked up the telephone and contacted the police.

CHAPTER 14

Cabral was the detective in charge. Fortunately, he wasn't in Teague's league as a policeman. As he didn't ask me any of the right questions, I wasn't forced to tell him many lies.

Being a foreigner probably worked to my advantage. So did being shot at. As far as Cabral was concerned, my sole value was as an eyewitness. I wasn't a suspect and I'd only met da Silva a couple of hours before he was shot. It didn't even occur to him that I might have anything more to contribute. Without any prompting from me, Cabral cast me as the innocent bystander.

I was careful not to say anything which might shatter his illusions. Once I'd finished my account of what had happened, the rest of the interrogation was perfunctory. However, I knew I'd only bought myself a reprieve. The really awkward questions would come after Cabral had been in touch with the Luton police. Teague would fill in a lot of the details I'd omitted. Hopefully, I'd have decided exactly what to say by then.

Perfunctory or not, the questioning took time. It was after seven in the evening before Cabral told me I was free to leave. I drove slowly on the way back to Nazaré, putting my thoughts in order. This wasn't easy. I needed more time. What was more, I had to drop out of sight for a while because something was painfully obvious. Somebody very much wanted me dead. Regardless of what Cabral might have assumed, I was no bystander. I'd been as much of a target as da Silva or poor Joaquim. I remained a target now. Wherever I went I was likely to be at risk.

This was very much on my mind. It encouraged me to use the driving mirror far more than usual. It made me look with suspicion at every car I saw on the road. From choice, I'd have kept well clear of Nazaré. The town was somewhere I'd been pinpointed. It would be the starting point for any search. Unfortunately, my passport was in my room at the Dom Henrique. There was also the question of my unpaid bill. I had enough problems already without having the police after me for fraud.

The hotel was an obvious danger spot. There weren't that many hotels in Nazaré. It would only take somebody with a telephone five minutes to discover I was resident at the Dom Henrique. Before I went into the hotel, I drove past a couple of times. I checked the street thoroughly. Everything seemed normal enough. Even so, I parked the Alfa in a side street and went back on foot. On the way, I didn't pass a soul carrying a silenced rifle. Nor were there any in the hotel lobby. It was deserted apart from a receptionist. This one was female. She welcomed me with a pleasant smile.

"Room 312, please."

"Certainly, senhor."

She handed me the key with her smile intact.

"Have there been any messages for me while I've been out? The name is MacAllister."

It only took her a second to check.

"None at all, Sr. MacAllister."

"No phone calls or visitors?"

"Apparently not."

"That's what popularity does for you. Perhaps you could prepare my bill for me. I'm going up to collect my things from my room, then I'll be leaving."

"You're leaving now, senhor?"

The receptionist was clearly perplexed. Most Portuguese were naturally thrifty. It was so late by now, I'd have to pay for the room whether I used it or not. She clearly couldn't understand why I'd want to waste my money. I didn't enlighten her. Although it would have been simple enough to invent a plausible explanation, I couldn't be bothered. Perplexed receptionists were the least of my problems.

It only took me a minute or two to gather together the few things in my room. My bill was waiting for me when I returned downstairs. The receptionist hoped I'd be visiting the hotel again. I hoped I'd be alive to do so.

The street outside was still quiet apart from the occasional rumble of distant thunder. By now the lowering storm clouds covered the sky. Everybody with any sense was staying indoors.

I still wasn't sure where I was going when I reached the Alfa. It needed to be somewhere quiet and off the beaten track. Somewhere I couldn't easily be traced. This would allow me an opportunity to replan my strategy. Or what remained of a strategy. It could well prove that going to the police was the only safe option available to me. Whether it was or not, I had to reach a decision quickly.

The decision wasn't mine to make. I realized this when I felt the hard metal digging into the nape of my neck. It was one of those dreadful moments when my heart seemed to miss a beat or two. I was having considerable difficulty with my breathing as well.

"Surprise, surprise," the mocking voice said from behind me.

This was the understatement of the year. Shock kept me rooted woodenly in my seat. Part of my brain was reminding me that I had a gun in the glove compartment. The rest was advising me to forget about it. Suicide wasn't my style.

The man who had been concealed in the back pushed himself up onto the seat. His gun didn't leave the back of my neck for an instant. Once he was upright, I had a clear view of his face in the driving mirror. It belonged to Angela's bodyguard, the man Adam had supposedly hired to protect his daughter. I didn't find the irony at all amusing. For the moment nothing was likely to amuse me.

"What do you want?"

This had to rank among the most stupid questions of the century. I could already see the answer in his eyes.

"It's what you want that counts, Frank." His voice was very soft for such a big man. "I should imagine that you'd like to live for as long as possible. You manage that by doing exactly as I say. Understood?"

He added emphasis to his question by pressing harder with the gun.

"Understood."

My mouth was dry and my bladder seemed full to bursting. This was another of life's little ironies which failed to amuse me.

"Here's what you have to do. You drive slowly and smoothly. I'll tell you where. Both of your hands remain on the wheel where I can see them. I'll have the gun held against the back of your seat. You won't be able to see it but I promise you it will be there. The slightest hint of trouble and you're dead. O.K.?"

"O.K."

I'd have made a great parrot.

"That's very good. Try to remember that your life isn't nearly important to me as it is to you. We'll be taking the Leiria road out of town. Do you know the way?"

"I think so."

Like the man said, we took the Leiria road. And I drove slowly and smoothly. At least, I drove as smoothly as the road allowed me to. Every pothole made me wince in anticipation. I sincerely hoped that the gun an inch or two from my spine didn't have a hair trigger.

We didn't travel very far towards Leiria. We were only a mile or so out of Nazaré when I was instructed to turn off the main road. Now we were heading in the general direction of Marinha Grande. The road we were on was little more than a track. Bumps separated potholes from other bumps. I was sweating so much that I found it difficult to see. I daren't remove a hand from the wheel to brush the perspiration away. Although I only caught an occasional glimpse of the sea, I knew we were travelling parallel to the coast.

"What's your name?" I asked. "I heard Sra. Latimer call you Toni."

It had taken time before I dared to speak.

"That will do."

"I thought you might use the name Oliveira."

"Did you now? You have been busy."

Toni was grinning at me in the driving mirror. He was young, good-looking and tough. He also seemed to be depressingly competent. As he appeared to be in a good humour, I tried another question.

"It was you who killed Robert Latimer, wasn't it?"

"Among others. Why don't you forget the questions and concentrate on your driving?"

I did as he suggested. However hard I worked at it, anger couldn't displace fear as my dominant emotion. Very soon I was going to die. I didn't think there was anything I could do to save myself. Nor could I place any reliance on outside assistance. The houses we passed were becoming further and further apart. Many of them appeared to be deserted. I hadn't seen another living soul for almost five minutes. Away to our left was the sea. To our right were trees and rocky hills. There wasn't anybody around to help me.

"Turn right here."

I turned right. It was little more than a track running between the pine trees. In places, it was barely wide enough for the car. After a couple of hundred metres, the track widened into a clearing. There was a small stone cottage to one side of it. It looked desolate and deserted. This was the way I felt.

"Stop here."

I parked virtually outside the door. It was now or never, I decided. This was probably the last chance I'd have to try to save my life. I was wrong. My muscles were still tensing when Toni hit me hard with his gun. He didn't intend to allow me any chance at all.

My head felt as though it didn't belong to me. I almost wished it
hadn't. Then I could have had a new one which didn't hurt so much.
The throbbing pain went all the way down my neck into the small of
my back. Its epicentre seemed to be located just above my right ear.
Perhaps it was my imagination but this side of my head felt as
though it was swollen to twice its normal size.

When I tried to investigate with my hands, I couldn't. They were
tied together in front of me. My ankles were tied as well. As far as I
could tell, I was lying on the floor inside the cottage. I hadn't yet
attempted to open my eyes. This was something I'd postponed. For
the moment I was learning to live with the nausea and the pain.

While I lay there, I listened to the sounds around me. There
weren't very many of them. Most of those I could hear weren't in my
immediate vicinity. They appeared to come from a distance, from
outside the cottage. I could distinguish the wind in the trees and the
occasional crash of thunder. A door or window was creaking nearer
to hand. If Toni was anywhere around, he was keeping very quiet.
After a minute or two, I decided I was probably alone in the cottage.

Opening my eyes wasn't nearly as bad as I'd imagined. I already
knew my concussion couldn't be too serious, however much my head
hurt. I could remember everything that had happened, right up to
the moment Toni had hit me. This was a good sign. My eyes seemed
to function as well as my memory. Everything was hazy for a few
seconds. Then my eyes locked into focus.

It was fairly dark inside the cottage. Even so, there was enough
light for me to see that the interior was as dilapidated as the exterior.
Apart from a lot of dust and rubble, it wasn't exactly overfurnished.
There was a table with an unlit oil lamp on it a few feet away from
me. Otherwise it was simply a large, empty room. At least, I thought
it was empty until one of the shadows against the far wall moved. I'd
been wrong about Toni. He'd been standing there watching me.

"I was wondering when you'd wake up. I only gave you a little
tap."

Toni was crossing the room towards me. Outside there was a flash
of lightning. The thunder followed a few seconds later. It sounded as
though the storm was still building up over the sea. I doubted
whether it would be very long before it reached us.

"How do you feel?"

"Terrible."

"It could be a lot worse."

He proved his point by kicking me in the stomach. It wasn't a gentle kick. I brought my knees up to my chest and groaned. When the pain didn't subside, I groaned again.

There were too many tears in my eyes for me to see properly but I heard Toni move away from me again. He stopped and I heard the rasp of a match. Even through my tears, I could see the sudden flare of light. He used the match to light the oil lamp. When it was adjusted to his satisfaction, he came back towards me. As soon as he was within range, he kicked me again. This time he caught me on the shin. It hurt like hell and I managed a few more groans. My eyes were watering more than ever.

"I like hurting people," Toni announced. "It's a terrible thing to admit to but I always have. It makes me feel good."

There was no appropriate answer I could think of. Besides, I'd bitten my tongue. My mouth was filling with the salty taste of blood. I spat some of it onto the floor beside my head.

"I have some questions to ask you. You're going to answer them. If you don't, I shall hurt you very badly indeed before I kill you."

"And if I do answer them?" My voice was little more than a croak.

"In that case, I shall kill you painlessly."

Toni's smile was almost affectionate. This scared me more than anything else so far. He didn't see me as a human being. He saw me as a source of pleasure and entertainment.

"I offered more or less the same deal to your friend Latimer," he continued. "He chose to be difficult. Why don't you think about my proposition? We have plenty of time. Nobody will interrupt us."

He walked over to perch on the edge of the table next to the oil lamp. I lay on the floor and thought. Mostly I thought about killing Toni. It wasn't for Robert any more, or for Joaquim. It was for me. Toni scared me like nobody had ever frightened me before. If I did live, I had to kill him. Otherwise I'd always be looking back over my shoulder.

The questions were all written down on the back of an envelope. They were the kind of questions I'd have expected Adam to ask. What had I told the police about the shooting at da Silva's house? How much did Angela know about the diamonds? Who else had been told? What, if any, physical evidence did I have? They were entirely selfish. Adam was seeking to protect himself. None of the answers were absolutely vital to him but they'd all help. As Toni had missed me at da Silva's house, Adam had seized the opportunity to check his position.

I answered all of the questions truthfully. It was the only way to prevent Toni putting his threats into practice. In any case, nothing I said was likely to make a great deal of difference. When the questions were finished with, Toni would kill me. There was no doubt about this. Unless Toni left me alone for a few seconds, I failed to see how I could escape. This was why my replies were detailed as well as honest. The longer I could spin them out, the longer I put off the moment of truth.

Only a part of my mind was occupied with what I was saying. The rest was busy being annoyed with myself. Now that it was too late, I had the entire jigsaw pieced together. My beloved father-in-law had almost certainly been involved with da Silva from the very beginning. He'd probably helped to plan the diamond heist. Like da Silva, he'd been hit very hard by independence in Angola and Mozambique. He would have seen the diamonds as a heaven-sent opportunity to recoup some of his losses. The morality of what was being done wouldn't have bothered him at all. What was good for Adam Boulter must, by definition, be right.

I could even hazard a guess as to how the arrangement would have worked. Da Silva would have taken all the risks and been responsible for organization. Adam would have been lurking in the background as a consultant. He wouldn't have wanted to sully his hands with the sordid details. All he'd be interested in would be his cut of the proceeds.

Da Silva must have informed Adam about Robert's intervention. To Adam's way of thinking, this would have been sufficient reason to have him killed. He wouldn't have wanted Robert to discover that his father-in-law was a crook. More important, he wouldn't want

Angela or his wife to know. He couldn't afford to risk Robert making the connection between da Silva and himself. Although there was
very little proof to support my theory, I was positive that this was
what must have taken place. I couldn't think of any other reason
why Adam would have told Toni to kill Robert.

It was all such a bloody waste. Adam never had understood Robert. If Robert had discovered the truth, it would have tickled him
pink. He'd always considered Adam to be a sanctimonious prig.
Knowing about the skeleton in his cupboard would have been something for him to savour. But he would never have told anybody else,
least of all Angela. Robert would never do anything which might
hurt or upset her.

Of course, Robert's death hadn't been the end of it. Son-in-law
number two had arrived on the scene. At first, before I'd had an
opportunity to learn anything, Adam had tried to warn me off. Initially this had been done verbally. Then he'd had Toni put in some
practice with his silenced rifle. Neither approach had worked. For a
while Adam had been content to let matters lie. I hadn't appeared to
be making much progress. Besides, I'd sent Angela back to live at his
house. He'd been able to monitor developments through her. Toni
was close to hand if he should be needed. Adam must have been
feeling smug. He'd had everything tightly under control.

It was my fault Joaquim and da Silva were dead. There was nobody else I could blame. I'd actually told Adam I was in Nazaré; I'd
said I'd be staying for another night. This would have been sufficient
to shatter Adam's complacency. As far as he was concerned, Nazaré
could only mean da Silva. I'd become as much of a threat to him as
Robert had been.

Toni must have been sent on his way immediately. When he'd seen
me with da Silva, he'd known what he had to do. His employer
would only be safe with both of us dead. Adam's good name was far
more important to him than the diamonds. But Toni had messed it
up. He'd only managed to kill two out of three.

The failure must have been reported to Adam. As a result, Toni's
brief had been modified. I was still to be killed, of course. First,
though, I was to be encouraged to answer a few pertinent questions.
The notes on the envelope suggested that Adam had dictated them

over the phone. This was why I was doing most of the talking now while the storm rumbled closer and closer.

Surmise or not, I was confident that I must be very close to the truth. However, I wasn't particularly proud of my powers of deduction. They'd come up with the answers far too late to do me any good. I'd run out of things to say and Toni had almost run out of questions. He'd folded the envelope and put it away in his jacket pocket.

"Very good," Toni said. "Very good indeed. There's just one thing you omitted to mention. You forgot to say where you hid those diamonds you found."

This wasn't one of the questions he'd had on his list. It was one he'd thought of himself. I could detect a new note in Toni's voice. It sounded suspiciously like greed. I allowed myself a small flicker of hope.

"Who wants to know?" I enquired. "Is it you or Sr. Boulter?"

"That's immaterial. Just answer the question."

"I disagree with you." I was trying to choose my words carefully. The pain in my head didn't help at all. "I think it's vitally important. Presumably Sr. Boulter is paying you to kill me. I'm prepared to pay you to let me live. I have a lot more to offer than the diamonds."

"How much more?"

"Shall we say five thousand pounds sterling in cash?"

There was no mistaking Toni's interest. This was the first mention I'd made of the money in the shoe box. It was several seconds before he reluctantly shook his head.

"It wouldn't work, MacAllister. You know far too much for your own good. Sr. Boulter apart, I have to kill you to protect myself."

"All right." This wasn't a point I was prepared to argue. "I'll change my offer. Five thousand pounds for you to make one phone call for me. Does that tempt you? The diamonds and five thousand pounds for one lousy phone call."

Toni was tempted all right. Anybody would have been.

"Whom do I have to telephone? The police?"

"That would be very nice." Somehow I managed to produce a travesty of a smile. "Actually, I was thinking of Sr. Boulter."

"Sr. Boulter?" Toni was surprised. "What would you want me to say to him?"

"That there's no need to kill me. I don't want to die. I'll agree to any conditions he cares to make if he doesn't have me killed."

Sounding scared wasn't at all difficult. This was precisely how I felt.

"You'll be wasting your time."

"I don't see why. I'll give him all the assurances he wants. We must be able to work something out."

Toni shook his head.

"You're in cloud-cuckoo-land, MacAllister. He'll simply repeat what I've already told you. You know too much. Killing you is the only way he can be safe."

He was right, of course, but this wasn't the point. Somehow or other I had to persuade Toni to leave me alone in the cottage. It was the only chance I had.

"For Christ's sake," I said. "I'm his son-in-law. I was married to his daughter. Surely that must count for something."

"It didn't do your friend Latimer any good."

"But you have to try." The desperation in my voice came naturally. "I don't want to die. Anyway, I'm not offering to pay you by results. I'm paying you for making a phone call and asking."

Toni still hesitated for a moment. Then the obvious solution occurred to him. He held all the cards. He could have his cake and eat it too.

"O.K.," he agreed. "I'll make your phone call for you. Tell me where to find the diamonds and the money. Then I'll do it."

"No." I was very definite about this. "I can't trust you."

"So what do we do?"

"I'll tell you about the diamonds now. We can make arrangements about the money after you've spoken to Sr. Boulter."

Another obvious solution had occurred to Toni.

"Perhaps the phone call isn't necessary. I'm sure I can persuade you to tell me everything now."

"Maybe, but I wouldn't bank on it. I don't have a hell of a lot left to lose."

We'd reached an impasse of sorts. Toni obviously fancied the idea of forcing me to talk. Against this, it would be much easier for him to play along with me.

"We'll do it your way then," he decided. "Where are the diamonds?"

I told him. When I'd finished, he still had his reservations.

"How do I know you're telling the truth?"

"What have I got to gain by lying to you? The diamonds are no good to me."

"Perhaps I ought to hurt you a little, just to make sure."

"It won't make any difference."

He toyed with the idea for a while. It was probably the time factor which was the deciding influence.

"O.K. Let's leave it for the moment. We have a phone call to make."

When he reached down to pull me to my feet, I knew I'd lost. I'd hoped Toni would leave me behind while he phoned Adam. If he was taking me with him, I hadn't gained anything at all.

CHAPTER 15

I'd been vaguely aware of the rain for some time. However, it wasn't until we stepped outside that I realized just how heavy it was. With both of my ankles tied, I had to hop. The rain seemed to be coming down in solid sheets. Although it was only a metre or two to the Alfa, I was soaked through by the time I reached it. There was a flash of lightning as Toni yanked open the door. For an instant, the entire clearing was illuminated. Then it was dark again. The thunder which followed made the ground shake. By now the storm was almost directly overhead.

Toni wasn't enjoying the rain any more than I was. I could hear him swearing to himself under his breath. When he pushed me onto the floor in the back of the car, he wasn't gentle. I awkwardly tried to clamber up onto the seat but he used his foot to push me down again.

"You stay on the floor until I tell you to move." He had to shout to make himself heard.

"Why? I'm not going to try anything."

"Because I said so. Five thousand pounds or not, you upset me and you're dead."

This was a persuasive argument. The floor wasn't at all comfortable. While I'd been driving, I'd been unable to appreciate exactly how uneven the track was. Down on the floor, I was able to savour every bump. Within fifty metres my head was aching worse than ever. The incessant drumming of the rain on the roof did nothing to soothe it.

My head was the least of my worries. I was fast running out of time. Somehow or other I had to free myself. While we'd been at the cottage, I'd had plenty of opportunity to test the ropes around my wrists. There had been no give at all. I didn't fare much better in the back of the car. All I succeeded in doing was rubbing off a lot of skin. Even with the blood as a lubricant, the rope wasn't noticeably looser.

After a few minutes, I decided I was wasting time as well as skin. It made more sense to try for my ankles. Then, at least, I might be able to run.

As my hands had been tied in front of me, reaching my ankles was no great feat. The real problem was moving without Toni becoming aware of what I was doing. And untying the bloody knots. The rope around my wrists had cut off most of the circulation to my hands. It meant my fingers were as nimble as untrained bananas. For some time I picked away at the knots without making much progress. I still persevered. This wasn't a situation where I could afford to give up.

Some quarter of an hour later my perseverance was eventually rewarded. One of the knots was definitely beginning to give. Another couple of minutes and I had it undone. Unfortunately, Toni had left very little to chance. He'd used a double knot. I allowed myself a brief rest before I started again. By now the rope was very slippery. I wasn't sure whether this was sweat or blood. To make matters worse, there was virtually no feeling left in my fingers. It was difficult to get a proper grip. I was still grappling with the second knot when Toni stopped the car.

"All right. You can get up onto the seat now."

Toni sat half turned in his seat while I struggled up. And it was a struggle. My whole body ached, not simply my head.

We definitely weren't in Nazaré. The windows were too steamed up for me to see clearly but we appeared to be in a village. Perhaps it was Marinha Grande. Then again, perhaps it wasn't. Wherever we were, the Alfa was parked beside a public telephone. If the window had been open, I could have reached out and touched it. Always assuming that my hands had been free. Beyond it were the lights of a café. There would be people inside. For all the good they were to me, they might as well have been on the moon. It definitely wasn't the weather for pedestrians.

"You sit very still, MacAllister. I'll be watching you all the time."

"You know what to say?"

"Sure. Not that it's likely to do you any good."

On this cheerful note, Toni left. The ignition key went with him. He also left the door open so that the interior light stayed on.

For the first few seconds I stared at the glove compartment. The Savage automatic was still inside. At least, I thought it was. I mentally reviewed all the movements necessary to get the gun into my hand. There were far too many of them. They'd take far too long. But would I ever have another opportunity to try? A half chance was the very most Toni was likely to allow me. Could I afford to wait any longer?

I couldn't bring myself to commit suicide. This was what trying for the Savage would have amounted to. As he'd promised, Toni was watching from the telephone. He could shoot me before I was halfway to the glove compartment. If my hands had been free, I might still have risked it. As things were, I preferred to return my attention to the rope around my ankles.

The brief rest had worked wonders. It was only a matter of seconds before the second knot was loose as well. After this it was simply a question of unwinding the rope. It was time to check Toni again. He was talking on the phone. His head was still turned in my direction. While I flexed my toes and ankles, I stared at the glove compartment again. Perhaps it was an acceptable risk after all. With my legs free, I'd be that much faster. I'd also be considerably more manoeuvrable.

It was Toni who made up my mind for me. When he put down the telephone receiver, I relaxed in my seat again. In a way I was relieved. I still didn't think I'd have been fast enough.

"Well? What did he say?"

I barely allowed Toni time to close the door behind him. Not that I was really expecting good news. This was just as well. Toni was grinning as he gave me the thumbs-down.

"Your father-in-law wants you dead. End of message. If you remember, I did warn you what he'd say."

"Oh, shit."

This wasn't an expression of disappointment. I felt completely empty. I'd run out of time, just as I'd known I would. Now I wished I'd tried for the glove compartment after all. As I hadn't, I'd have to tackle Toni in the car. Dive over the back of the seat and somehow prevent him from using his own gun. I moved my feet slightly to give myself better leverage.

"What about this money you mentioned?" Toni enquired. "I've met my part of the bargain."

"The money is with the diamonds."

I was perfectly happy to keep Toni talking. My only hope was to take him completely by surprise.

"With the diamonds?"

"That's right. It's all in the shoe box together."

"You crafty bastard." There was grudging admiration in his voice. "You were stringing me along all the time. It was a good try."

"Not quite good enough." My legs were tensed, ready to drive me upwards and forwards. The adrenaline was already flowing. "What happens now?"

"I'm afraid you have to drop out of sight. Over a cliff to be exact."

"That doesn't sound much fun."

The words were meaningless. As I spoke, I came out of my seat. Every ounce of energy was channelled into this one explosive surge. My backside must have lifted a good six inches from the cushions before Toni's gun made violent contact with my head. Then everything suddenly went black.

For a while I flirted with consciousness. I stood on the threshold without actually stepping through. Everything was registering but nothing was making any impact. There was no real sense of urgency.

I could hear the purring of the Alfa's engine. It was almost drowned by the sound of the rain on the roof but I knew I was moving. Any possible doubts were dispelled by the jolting and bumping of the floor beneath me. I could smell the cigarette Toni was smoking. I could hear his tuneless whistling. All this was peripheral, without any great meaning. The central reality was the pain in my head. Everything hurt. Even my teeth were aching. Every pothole we hit banged my head against the floor. I could almost see the flashes of pain inside my cranium.

When I tried to move into a more comfortable position, nothing happened. Although my brain was sending out the appropriate signals, none of my limbs were listening. It vaguely occurred to me that I might be paralyzed. This didn't seem to be very important. Nor did the prospect of dying. Once I was dead, I wouldn't hurt any more. The thought was almost comforting.

I drifted again. After a time, the car stopped. Even with my eyes closed, I was aware of the interior light being switched on. The driving seat creaked. I assumed that Toni had turned to examine me. This was just fine by me. There was nothing I could do to stop him doing anything he wanted.

"MacAllister. Can you hear me?"

I didn't even attempt to answer. It would have been too much of an effort. Besides, now I had a secret. I could hear Toni and he didn't know it. I felt pleased with myself. Toni wasn't having things all his own way.

"MacAllister."

This time Toni spoke louder. He also prodded me. I was as responsive as a suet pudding. He leaned down and pinched the lobe of my ear. This probably hurt but I wasn't sure. The gesture didn't have any significance. The pain had stopped when the car had. I was happy the way I was. I was like a butterfly in its cocoon. Only I didn't want to break out. Sooner or later Toni would go away and leave me in peace.

He did as well. There was a click as one of the doors opened. I could hear Toni scrambling out. Then I was alone in the car. The rain sounded much heavier with the door open. It was strangely soothing. I lay on the floor and drifted. The pain still wasn't bothering me. Nothing did. *Que sera, sera.*

It was the clap of thunder which spoiled it. The noise was monstrous. It was as though the heavens were breaking apart. I started, banging my head against the door. The pain was monstrous as well. Waves of it lapped down from my head. Even my buttocks clenched. Suddenly, there was no cocoon any more. I screamed, a high-pitched whinny of anguish. I sounded like an animal.

"Get up, MacAllister." Even with the pain, the voice inside my head made itself heard. "If you don't, you're going to die."

I listened but I stayed where I was. Movement would mean more pain. I was trying to reconstruct my cocoon.

"Come on, you bastard." The voice wouldn't leave me alone. "Move."

Outside, a fork of lightning lit the sky. The thunder which followed was even louder than before. With that kind of backing, the voice couldn't be ignored. It would have been presumptuous to refuse it.

I started with my legs, moving them towards my head. My cheek was pressed hard against the carpet. My backside was sticking up in the air. This was where I stuck. I'd tried but it was no good. It was unreasonable to expect me to do more. I started drifting again.

"Move, you miserable bastard."

The voice still wasn't satisfied. It refused to leave me alone. So did the thunder. The next clap seemed to be inside the car with me.

I started up the back of the seat, whimpering with pain and terror. It was like the north face of the Eiger. Twice I slipped back. The third time I managed to hook my arms over the top of the seat. Then my chin was resting on it as well. I hung there for a second, staring out through the windscreen. There was nothing to see except rain. Even the powerful headlights couldn't make much of an impression. Besides, my eyes weren't working properly. They kept flickering in and out of focus. The dashboard was no more than a blur.

"Well done." The voice was trying praise now. "You can't give up. Toni will be back soon. You have to get out of the car."

Although there was no thunder this time, I'd enjoyed the praise. I wanted to earn more. Falling over the seat into the front was relatively easy. There was the minor problem of bringing my legs over after me but I managed it all right. I was beside the open door. It was simply a question of falling out and crawling.

Or was it? There was something I'd forgotten. There had to be a reason why I hadn't used one of the doors at the back. The pain made concentration difficult. My mind kept wandering and it was an effort to drag it back. Luckily, I had a voice to assist me.

"The glove compartment," it said. "You have to open the glove compartment."

This was an imperative. I didn't question why. I simply pushed the button and watched the flap fall open. The sight of the gun inside did nothing to excite me. It was heavy. It would be an encumbrance. All the same, I took it with me when I tumbled out of the car.

The rain was cool and refreshing. I could almost feel it washing the cobwebs away. Although the drops hurt my tender head, I didn't mind. I suddenly knew what I was doing. There was no longer any need to rely on mysterious voices or claps of thunder. I was a sentient being again. I'd remembered my ambition to live to be a hundred.

My immediate concern was where Toni might be. Unfortunately, my eyes still weren't working properly. The rain was as heavy as ever. I was trapped inside the small pool of light around the Alfa. Beyond it was a sound I couldn't immediately identify. Then I realized that it must be the sea. It was the noise of the Atlantic breakers driving in against the rocks. Toni had found his cliff. He must have gone to find a suitable spot to drop me over.

Now I had a definite sense of urgency. I might have lost track of time but one thing I knew. Toni was unlikely to be away much longer.

Standing up I could manage with the help of the car. Walking I couldn't. After I'd fallen down, I settled for crawling. My brain might be functioning again but the rest of me was lagging way behind. Progress was painfully slow. When I looked back, I'd only crawled a few yards. For a moment, I toyed with the idea of staying where I was. I could ambush Toni on his return to the Alfa. This was an attractive theory. At least, it would have been if I'd been able to hold the Savage steady. The way my hands were shaking, I'd be lucky to hit the car.

I started crawling again. Thirty seconds later I fell into the ditch. One instant I was scrambling forward as fast as I could over the sodden grass. The next, there was nothing beneath my elbows. Even before I struck bottom, I knew I was going to land on my head.

It was a hole, not a ditch. For a while, this wasn't a distinction I appreciated. I simply knelt in the water at the bottom and vomited. Even when there was nothing remaining in my stomach, I continued to retch. I felt completely and utterly wretched. For the moment, I couldn't have cared less about Toni. The water had cushioned my head when I'd fallen into the hole. It had also nearly drowned me. I'd swallowed several mouthfuls before I had my head above the surface. It was the vile taste which had made me sick. My stomach muscles were sore from the violent retching. My head ached, I was soaked to the skin and I felt feverish. Perhaps Toni would be doing me a favour if he put me out of my misery.

This was an attitude which ended with the retching. I wasn't entirely sure how I was going to do it but I knew what ought to be done. The hole was about four feet deep. It was almost as wide. I levered myself up and peered over the edge. The car seemed frighteningly close. I hadn't crawled more than fifteen metres before I'd discovered the hole. There was still no sign of Toni.

When I turned my head to look in the opposite direction, there was nothing at all to see. The rain and the darkness formed an impenetrable wall. It would have been a good moment for a flash of lightning to illuminate the scene. None came. Although the storm seemed to be dying down, the rain was as heavy as ever.

Toni was standing beside the car when I checked the Alfa again. Instinctively, I ducked down. I knew he couldn't possibly see me but this wasn't the point. The psychological balance was tilted irrevocably in his favour. He was the hunter and I was the hunted. He still scared the hell out of me. Back at the cottage, I'd fantasized about killing him. Now it came to it, all I wanted to do was escape. I'd fumbled the Savage out of my pocket but this was as meaningless as ducking down had been. Toni had dominated me for too long. I didn't have the confidence to tackle him unless I was forced to.

For several seconds, Toni remained by the Alfa, peering into the darkness. He'd know I hadn't had time to go very far. He was probably wondering how best to conduct the search. If so, it didn't take him long to decide. Toni climbed inside the car, closed the door and

started the engine. There was no particular urgency about his movements. Perhaps his overconfidence would work to my advantage. He
didn't know I was armed.

As the car began to turn, I crouched even lower. I could see the
twin beams of the headlights swinging across the entrance to the
hole. The car was moving slowly. It sounded as though it was coming directly towards me. I huddled at the bottom of the hole and
prayed I wouldn't be found. I knew I should use the gun but I still
couldn't trust my hands not to shake. The Alfa idled forwards, coming closer and closer. I thumbed off the safety catch of the Savage.
The car really was heading directly towards me. I tried to tell myself
to stand up and start shooting. I couldn't do it. It was much easier to
close my eyes and continue praying. My entire body was trembling. I
was convinced that Toni was playing a game with me. He'd known
where I was hiding all along.

Earth and small stones plopped into the water beside me. The
engine sounded as though it was right overhead. When I opened my
eyes again, I could see the bulk of the car looming above me. The
tyre was no more than a few inches from the edge of the hole. It
rolled past and a second tyre took its place. More earth tumbled
down on top of me. The second wheel was even closer.

Then the car was past me and I started breathing again. I poked
my head aboveground and watched the car drive away. I couldn't
watch for very long. After a few metres the car was swallowed up by
the rain. For a few seconds more, I could just distinguish the reflection of the headlights. After that there was nothing. The rain even
drowned the noise of the engine.

My euphoria was short-lived. If Toni was conducting a search, it
wouldn't be very long before he returned. I didn't think I was likely
to find a better hiding place than my hole. This seemed as good an
excuse as any for staying where I was.

Twenty minutes later, the car still hadn't returned. The luminous
hands of my watch said it was after two in the morning. I wondered
apprehensively what Toni was doing. I also wondered how long my
skin would remain waterproof. It was impossible to get any wetter.
Apart from the rain cascading down on my head, the water at the
bottom of the hole came up to mid-calf. The cold was beginning to

affect me. Even my bones felt chilled. Once or twice I'd had to fight back sneezes. On the credit side, my head had cleared a little. It still hurt but the pain had settled down to a persistent ache. I thought I could walk now. I decided to find out before I froze solid.

The direction I chose was at right angles to the one taken by the car. Because of the rain, I didn't have to worry about concealment. Unless I actually tripped over Toni, he wasn't likely to see me. My main concern was that the car might yet come back. If it did, the lights should give me a few seconds advance warning.

Within a few seconds I had a new concern. The sound of the sea was becoming louder. I wished I'd had a stick to test the ground in front of me. Falling into a hole had been good luck. Stepping over a cliff would be fatal. I'd no intention of doing Toni's work for him. It seemed safest to drop down onto my stomach to crawl. This would have been a lot easier if my wrists hadn't been tied.

Suddenly there was nothing solid beneath my hands. The noise of the waves was very loud now. I inched forward until my head was sticking out into space as well. There was no sensation of vertigo because there was nothing to see. The sound of the sea appeared to come from a long, long way below me. There was no escape there.

I eased myself back again, fighting down the panic. I estimated that I'd come approximately twenty-five metres from the hole. Although it was much too dark for me to have any point of reference, I couldn't have deviated too far from my intended course. I knew the sea had been in front of me while I'd been in the Alfa. Even in my confused state, this wasn't something I could have been mistaken about. Now I'd found the sea to one side as well. I thought I could understand why Toni hadn't returned with the Alfa. It would be nice to be wrong.

Navigation was equally difficult on the way back. As I missed the hole completely, I couldn't be sure I was going in the direction I wanted. However, I was positive that I hadn't travelled in a circle. Nor did I think I'd strayed too far to the right. Yet after a few minutes I could hear the pounding of the waves ahead of me again. On this occasion, I didn't go to the edge of the cliff to investigate. I didn't need to. I had the picture now. I was trapped on a promontory. Cliffs and sea surrounded me on three sides. The only way out was in the direction the Alfa had gone.

This was why Toni hadn't needed to come back. There was no point in him getting soaked while he searched for me in the darkness. It was far simpler for him to drive to the neck of the promontory. If he stayed there, he had me bottled up. He'd have known there was a fair chance I might manage to fall over a cliff on my own. If I didn't, I'd have to go straight to where he was waiting for me. Either way, Toni had me. He was probably prepared to remain where he was all night.

There were two courses open to me. One was to test my theory. I could head inland until I discovered whether or not Toni was waiting for me. Or I could try to locate my hole again. Whatever I did, confrontation seemed inevitable. I'd have to kill Toni to escape. It was this consideration which swayed me in favour of going to ground. I'd need every advantage I could grab. Let Toni come to my prepared position instead of the other way around. It should come as a big surprise to him.

Locating the hole again wasn't much easier than finding a needle in a haystack. I'd soon lost all sense of direction. Visibility was nil. The rain still poured down in torrents. If it hadn't been so important, I'd have given up. It was very tempting to simply lie on the ground and opt out. Only my hatred and fear kept me going. Crawling awkwardly, I must have crisscrossed the soggy turf dozens of times before I eventually struck lucky. On this occasion I even managed not to fall in. When I lowered myself into the hole, I discovered the water was slightly deeper than before. This didn't bother me at all. It was almost like returning home.

I couldn't afford to relax. With one problem out of the way, I had another to replace it. By now I'd lost all sensation in my hands. I had to take it on trust that they were still there. They'd been tightly tied for several hours. The constant soaking appeared to have made the rope shrink. Although there was no way to check in the darkness, I knew my hands would be swollen and puffy. Circulation was virtually cut off. If this continued for too long, gangrene might set in. This was merely a vague thought at the back of my mind. For the moment it had no real relevance. Gangrene only became significant if I lived.

Toni was somewhere out in the darkness. I didn't have to see him to be sure of this. He wouldn't leave until he was positive I was dead.

He couldn't afford to. As soon as it was light enough to see properly, he'd come looking for me again. Some time after dawn I'd almost certainly have to use the Savage. And I'd have to use it well. The only way to stop Toni was to kill him. It was a question of survival. To do this I'd need hands which functioned properly. Hands which could hold a gun steady. I'd need a finger which could pull a trigger when I wanted it to.

Somehow or other, I had to get rid of the rope around my wrists. And I had to do so soon. Even when the ropes were off, there would be a period when I couldn't use my hands at all. The returning circulation wouldn't be a pleasant experience. The pain was likely to make my headache seem like a fond memory.

My first idea didn't work. There was a gas lighter in my trouser pocket. Despite the rain, it should be able to burn through the rope. At least, this was the theory. Merely getting the lighter out of my pocket was an adventure. I couldn't tell whether my fingers were grasping it or not. All the instructions from my brain ran into a roadblock at my wrists. And this proved to be the easy part. When I had fumbled it out, I couldn't use the lighter. Igniting it was too intricate a manoeuvre for my hands to cope with. This was probably just as well. If the gas had lit, I might well have roasted my wrists. After I'd dropped the lighter for the third time, I didn't bother to retrieve it.

This left me with my teeth. They were healthy and strong. All of them were my own. Rats could gnaw through rope and so could I. Squatting in the water at the bottom of the hole, I started to chew. I chewed and I chewed. Blood from my gums must have mixed with blood from my wrists. After a while I lost all feeling in my mouth as well. This didn't stop me chewing. The process had become automatic. There was no other choice. The ropes had to come off. I'd keep going until they did.

It was almost mesmeric. The chomping of my jaws had taken on a life of their own. My gnawing was in rhythm with the rain falling on my head. I continued for a few seconds after I'd bitten through the strands of rope. I didn't realize I'd succeeded until I noticed that my wrists would move an inch or two further apart. There was no sense of elation. I had things to do and I was doing them to the best of my ability. I was too bone weary to concentrate on more than one thing at a time.

For a second or two I did indulge myself. I sat with my head back and my mouth open. The rainwater tasted pure and clean. Some I drank and the rest I used to rinse out my mouth. Then my teeth were back at work again, unwinding the rope from my wrists. It was just after half past three in the morning and my hands were free.

I was glad I couldn't see them. For the moment they were completely useless. They were simply appendages at the ends of my arms. I had to bring them right up in front of my face to be sure they were still there. Dawn should arrive at about five. Possibly it would be earlier. I had until then to work on them. I hoped this would be long enough.

It was the pain which told me I was winning. I'd been rubbing my wrists for several minutes before I felt the first twinge. There were more twinges which grew into acute pins and needles. The pins and needles became six-inch nails and red-hot rivets. I moaned to myself and kept rubbing. This soon became as automatic as the chewing had been. After a while I must have dozed.

It was the silence which roused me. It took me a minute or so to realize the rain had stopped. Although dawn was still some time away, it was also getting lighter. For the first time I could actually see the walls of the hole around me. I could also distinguish my hands. They were still badly swollen. The skin appeared to be discoloured and they ached. It was as though I had gout or arthritis. I flexed my fingers one by one. I couldn't make a proper fist but they all seemed to work. As long as I didn't ask them to play a piano or thread a needle, they'd do what I wanted.

They were like the rest of me. I felt sluggish and cramped. My head ached abominably. I felt bruised all over. My stomach muscles were still sore. The list went on and on but I was functioning. Provided I accepted the diminished efficiency, I was in full working order.

Dawn was closer than I'd thought. I realized this when I cautiously raised my head out of the hole. It was the half light which separated night from day. There was enough of it for me to examine my surroundings. As I'd already guessed, I was on a promontory.

My hole was in the centre of a narrow strip of land. The cliffs on either side were no more than twenty-five metres away. Ahead of me, the land sloped down for twice the distance before it dropped into the Atlantic. The sea itself was grey and turbulent.

Behind me, on the landward side, the promontory widened. However, its basic character remained unchanged. The short, springy grass extended as far back as I could see. Only an occasional rocky outcrop broke the surface. There were no trees or bushes. If there were any other holes, I couldn't see them. I'd been very fortunate the previous night.

Visibility still wasn't very good. The mainland was no more than an indistinct blur in the background. There were no signs of habitation that I could see. The same went for Toni and the Alfa. They'd be out there somewhere, though. I didn't attempt to generate any false optimism by pretending otherwise.

Nothing I could see tempted me to leave my hole. With no other cover, it still seemed the safest place to be. I squatted down again and took out the Savage. It was an ugly weapon. It felt heavy and cumbersome in my hands. I wondered what effect the previous night's soaking would have had on it. The rain certainly wouldn't have done the automatic any good—on the other hand, it shouldn't have done too much harm. Robert had maintained the weapon in good condition, and I'd stripped and cleaned it myself. The gun should be all right.

I slipped out the box magazine. All ten 7.65-mm. rounds were there in their staggered rows. While it was unloaded, I spent a minute or two testing the mechanism of the pistol. Everything appeared to work well enough. Although my hands were a bit unsteady, I thought I could manage. I'd be shooting at close range.

After I'd replaced the magazine, I popped my head above ground again. Now the sun was rising above the horizon, the light had improved dramatically. I could distinctly see the coastline. Toni had selected his spot well. There wasn't a single house in sight. Considering the cliffs, this was hardly surprising. Although they weren't on the scale of the cliff at Nazaré, they were high enough. They fell sheer, with no visible means of access to the narrow strip of beach below. There was no reason for anybody to live on top of them.

I still couldn't see Toni. The promontory had a slight hump on the landward side. To look over it, I had to rise higher out of the hole. As soon as I spotted the sun glinting off the Alfa, I dropped down again. It was parked approximately three hundred metres away at a point where the promontory narrowed again. I hadn't stayed up long enough to spot Toni but I knew he must be nearby. I didn't think he could have seen me.

Suddenly I felt trapped. The hole no longer seemed so secure. I checked again but there was no better hiding place. Nor were there any loose pieces of rock near to hand that I could use to construct a rampart. I'd have to make do with what I had. The trouble was, the hole was too big. In daylight, the entrance was bound to be visible from some distance away. It was wishful thinking to believe Toni would miss it. It was precisely the kind of hiding place he'd be searching for. I'd have to rely on surprise. Toni might spot the hole. He might guess I was huddled inside. What he couldn't possibly know was that I was armed. Or could he? What if he'd checked the glove compartment while I was a prisoner? What if . . . ?

It took a conscious effort to push my doubts to one side. There was plenty of mud at the bottom of the hole. I daubed liberal quantities of it over my face and ears, ignoring the stench of stale vomit. I plucked small clumps of grass from around the edges of the hole and sprinkled them over my hair. When I'd finished, I used my shirt to wipe the muck from my hands. It wouldn't do for them to be slippery.

Very, very cautiously, I raised my head from the hole. It was sudden movements which caught the eye. All the same, I felt awfully exposed, especially after I saw Toni. He'd left the Alfa and started down the promontory towards me. Although he looked casual enough, he was carefully checking all available cover as he came. He had his pistol in his hand.

I lowered myself as cautiously as I'd stood up. There was no time for any more indecision. I was committed now. It was simply a question of waiting a few more minutes until Toni was close enough. I'd have to rely on my hearing to warn me. There was a rocky outcrop about ten metres from the hole. Toni would have to check there. When he did, I'd take him.

Objective and subjective time ran their separate courses. The hands of my watch hardly seemed to move; the seconds ticked away like hours. In the background, the noise of the sea was a constant irritant. It made me doubt whether I'd hear the sounds of Toni's approach at all. The idea of popping up for another look grew from temptation to compulsion. I fought against it. I reminded myself that Toni wouldn't be rushing himself. He wouldn't be in range yet. I'd ruin everything if I showed my hand too soon.

Then I could hear Toni whistling. At first I'd assumed it must be the wind but the wind didn't whistle in tune. Besides, it was the same melody Toni had been whistling in the car. I was suddenly very calm. Relying on my ears alone, it was impossible to estimate distance or direction. He had to be very close, though. And he was definitely to landward of me. I cocked the Savage and gathered my legs beneath me. All my aches and pains had disappeared. There wasn't any place for them in the next few seconds.

The whistling stopped in mid-bar. Almost simultaneously, something plopped into the hole beside me. Panic struggled towards the surface. I didn't know what was happening. It wasn't until I saw the second stone bounce from the side of the hole that I realized.

"Is that where you've been hiding, MacAllister?" Toni's tone was almost conversational. Although he sounded very close, there was no shadow. "If so, you'd better come out. I'm most annoyed with you. You've put me to a great deal of inconvenience."

His voice was the marker I'd needed. I knew where Toni was now. As he'd pointed out, there was no sense in hiding any longer.

When I jumped up, the Savage was gripped firmly in both hands. Toni was standing exactly where I'd wanted him, over by the outcrop. He was no more than eight metres away. Despite what he'd said, my sudden appearance caught him off balance. He couldn't have been sure whether I was in the hole or not. More important, he definitely hadn't known about the Savage. Otherwise his own weapon wouldn't have been hanging at his side in his left hand. I had him and I knew it. I could savour the relief as my finger tightened on the trigger.

The third stone he'd lobbed at my hiding place nearly saved him. It was already on its way as I appeared from the ground. Peripheral vision picked it up as it came towards me. Reflex made me duck as I fired. Instead of taking him in the chest, the bullet struck him high on the shoulder. As the impact spun him around, I fired twice more.

One shot was low, hitting him in the thigh. The other missed completely.

Toni was on the ground by now, rolling desperately. He was looking for cover that wasn't there. I was firing more methodically now, spacing my shots. Three more bullets struck home and he still wouldn't die. His gun had fallen from his hand. He was attempting to drag himself across the turf towards it. A couple of feet short, he ran out of strength.

It didn't even occur to me to spare him. It didn't to Toni either. I could tell by the way he was staring at me, his lips drawn back over his teeth in a blood-flecked snarl. He didn't show mercy and he didn't expect it. I raised the Savage again, aiming between his eyes.

"This is for Robert and Joaquim," I told him.

Even as I spoke, I knew I was lying. Adam Boulter would be for them. Toni was all mine.

CHAPTER 16

By the time, almost thirty-six hours later, when I negotiated the drive leading to the Boulter mansion, the thunderstorm was no more than a memory. Since then the weather had settled down again. It had been a bright, sunny day with hardly any breeze. According to the pundits on the radio, it had been the warmest day of the year. I believed them. Even with the windows of the Alfa wound right down, it was almost stiflingly hot.

The heat did nothing to impair the smooth running of Adam's household. Heat wave, blizzard or monsoon, the staff were expected to maintain the same standards of efficiency. Otherwise, they didn't last very long. Batista, the majordomo, had the door of the house open before the Alfa had finished settling on its springs. He was at the bottom of the steps while I was still clambering out of the car.

"Good afternoon, Sr. MacAllister."

As Batista spoke, he closed the door of the car. Normal procedure would have been for him to make some enquiry about my health. The sticking plaster prominently displayed on my head made him decide it was more tactful to give this a miss.

"Good afternoon, Batista. Is the master at home?"

"I believe he's in the billiards room. Perhaps you'd like to wait for him out on the verandah? Sra. Angela is having her afternoon tea there."

"I'll join her later. I'd like a word in private with Sr. Boulter first."

I'd already started up the steps. Although he gave no impression of haste, Batista contrived to keep ahead of me. He was holding the door open for me by the time I reached the top.

"If you'd like to take a seat, I'll tell the master you're here."

"There's no need, thank you. I can find my own way through."

I wasn't playing by the rules and poor Batista was in a quandary. In Adam's house, guests didn't find their own way anywhere. They certainly didn't burst in on the master without being announced. Batista was clearly torn between the demands of protocol and his desire not to offend me. In the end, he compromised. He scurried along in front, making sure he reached the billiards room ahead of me. He tapped deferentially before he opened the door.

"Sr. MacAllister is here to see you, senhor."

Adam could see this for himself because I'd followed Batista inside. Grudging though it might have been, I felt a certain admiration for Adam's control. Being surprised went against his creed. Showing surprise would have been unforgivable. Adam simply looked up from the billiard table, nodded in my direction and then completed a tricky cannon before he stood away from the table to greet me properly. Although he was slightly paler than usual, there was no other visible reaction.

"Hello, Frank." His tone was cool and reserved. "I wasn't expecting you. Thank you, Batista. That will be all for now."

Neither of us attempted to speak until the door had closed behind Batista. Even then, I kept silent. I was leaving it to Adam. I was intrigued to see how he'd handle what must be a very awkward situation for him. Typically, he chose to meet me head on.

"I thought something must have gone wrong when Texeira didn't contact me again." I assumed that Texeira must be Toni. "Is he dead?"

"Very."

Adam nodded thoughtfully. By now I was no longer admiring his control. It simply served to remind me of what a heartless bastard he was.

"I can't pretend I'm sorry," he said. "He really was a most unpleasant man."

"I don't suppose you would have shed too many tears over me either."

"Unfortunately, that's perfectly true. I won't attempt to deny it. Your death would have solved a lot of problems for me. It was nothing personal, though. I can promise you that."

"That makes me feel much better about it all." I'd been nurturing my anger for two days now and I couldn't damp it down any longer. Adam was far too calm and collected. I couldn't detect the slightest trace of remorse or guilt. "I'm sorry you've been disappointed. Perhaps you'd like to finish off the job yourself. Or do you only operate through hired killers?"

I'd had Toni's Walther in my pocket. Now I threw it down onto the table. The Savage had gone into the sea together with Toni's body.

"Don't be so silly, Frank." Adam spoke as though I was a naughty child. He even took the time to check that the baize wasn't damaged when he removed the gun from the table, placing it on the mantelpiece. "There's no need for cheap melodrama. We have to discuss this sensibly. Why don't you sit down?"

I bit back an angry retort and went to sit in one of the armchairs beside the fireplace. Losing my temper wouldn't help at all. And, in a way, Adam was right. We did have things to discuss. I still wasn't sure what to do about Adam. Killing him was out of the question. Exposing him to Angela for what he was wasn't much of an alternative. The loss of Robert had been a terrible blow on its own. Discovering her father had been responsible for Robert's death might be something from which she'd never recover.

"Where have you been for the past couple of days, Frank?" Adam had put down his cue and seated himself in the armchair opposite. "I'd have thought you'd be in touch before now."

"I was in Caldas da Rainha. I needed time on my own to think."

"About me, I assume."

"About you," I agreed.

"And? Did you come to any decisions?"

"Not really. I decided I wasn't capable of killing you in cold blood. That was as far as I got."

"I can understand your dilemma." We might have been discussing the weather. "With both Texeira and da Silva dead, your hands are rather tied. There's no way you can connect me either with the diamonds or the deaths. You have no real proof to present to the police."

"Don't delude yourself. I have a lot of circumstantial evidence. It would take them very close to you."

"The delusion is all yours, Frank. This is Portugal, not England. You know how things work here as well as I do. It's wealth and position that count. The police wouldn't dare to move against me unless they had an absolutely cast-iron case. Even then they'd think twice."

This was undeniably true. All the same, Adam wasn't fooling me. His display of confidence was no more than a front. Underneath, he'd be scared stiff. His family honour and his own personal reputation were the most important things in his life. Having his name dragged through the mud was the worst thing which could possibly happen to him. Rumours could be as effective as weapons as hard facts. Both of us were aware of this.

If it hadn't been for Angela, I'd have had no compunction about it at all. I wanted Adam destroyed. I'd have taken the greatest pleasure in ripping down all the little castles he'd built in the air. Although Adam hadn't realized this yet, his daughter was his only safeguard. I couldn't destroy him without destroying part of her. Angela might not like him very much but Adam was still her father.

"It isn't only the police you have to worry about," I pointed out. There was no reason why Adam should know how I felt. "There's Angela to consider as well. She hired me to find out who killed Robert and why. She ought to be told."

"Angela wouldn't believe you."

"Oh yes, she would, and you know it."

For the first time, cracks were appearing in Adam's façade. Although his features were as impassive as ever, the fingers of one hand were drumming on his knee. It was a clue to his inner turmoil. I derived malicious satisfaction from twisting the knife a little more.

"How would you explain it to her, Adam? What possible reasons could you give her for murdering the man she loved?"

For once in his life, Adam didn't have a ready answer. Not a direct one, at least.

"You said that you hadn't reached any decision yet." Now the strain was beginning to show in his voice as well. "Does that mean you're still open to persuasion?"

"Possibly."

"Would money make any difference to you? If that's what you want, I can make you a very rich man."

I shook my head contemptuously.

"You never did understand me, Adam. Despite what you chose to think, your money never did mean anything to me. I wasn't a fortune hunter when I married your daughter. I haven't become one now."

"So what is your price? You only have to ask and it's yours."

Adam was virtually pleading with me now.

"I'm not sure there is one."

"There must be some thing you want."

I didn't answer immediately. No amount of malicious pleasure was sufficient. I wanted Adam punished. He had to pay for what he'd done. I still failed to see how I could manage this without punishing Angela as well.

"An explanation might help." It wouldn't, but it bought me a little more time. "Why on earth did you steal the diamonds in the first place? God knows, you certainly don't need the money."

"I didn't steal anything."

Adam was clearly upset by my accusation. It was a reaction which put his scale of values into perspective. He could admit to having people killed without a qualm. This was obviously something he could reconcile with his conscience. Call him a thief, though, and he was insulted. Gentlemen didn't steal.

"What exactly did you do, then? You're not going to tell me those diamonds were a gift."

"Of course I'm not. Da Silva took them. He arranged everything."

"But you were his partner."

"That wasn't until afterwards. Da Silva organized the theft on his own. It was his idea and he carried it out. I didn't discover what had happened until later."

"You're splitting hairs." I made no attempt to conceal my contempt. "You knew the diamonds were stolen. That makes you an accessory and a receiver."

"All right, but it wasn't as bad as you're trying to make it look. Some of the diamonds that da Silva stole were mine anyway. They were mined by one of my own companies. I was only retrieving something which belonged to me anyway."

It was a waste of time arguing with him. I knew that nothing I said would shake him. Adam had his own personal morality.

"How about Robert?" I asked. "I suppose you can justify killing him as well."

"It had to be done."

"Why?" My anger was boiling very close to the surface again. "That's what I'm asking you."

"You wouldn't understand."

The contempt was in Adam's voice now. I couldn't hope to comprehend his lofty ideals.

"You're probably right, but try me anyway."

"You know most of it already. Robert had reached da Silva. He knew all about the diamond smuggling. It was merely a matter of time before he established the connection with me."

"And this was sufficient reason to have him killed?"

"I thought so, yes. I considered it very carefully first but there was no alternative."

I shook my head in disbelief. Incredulity had temporarily replaced my anger. Although this was more or less what I'd suspected, suspicions were very different from Adam's bland admission. He'd been right. I didn't understand him at all. I didn't want to.

"What did you think Robert was likely to do if he did learn about your involvement? He wanted to be da Silva's partner, just like you. He was hardly likely to go to the police."

"That wasn't what concerned me."

"What did? That's what I'm trying to establish."

Adam shrugged. He clearly thought I was being obtuse.

"For one thing, he'd have told Angela."

"I very much doubt it, but what if he did? What harm would it do?"

"I knew you wouldn't understand." Adam made this sound like an accusation. "You couldn't. You've never appreciated what we Boulters stand for here in Portugal. We have a position and a reputation it's taken generations to establish. If you like, we've become part of the social fabric of the country. However much you might sneer, we have a position to uphold. People respect us. They look up to us and take us as a model. I couldn't simply stand by and permit the work of centuries to be destroyed."

"And Robert would have managed this just by telling Angela about you?"

"It wasn't only her. There would have been others as well. Robert only had to tell one or two people and the damage would have been done. I couldn't allow it to happen. I didn't like to have him killed but it was necessary."

Icy fingers were walking up my spine. If Adam wasn't actually insane, he was as close to it as anybody I'd ever met. He sincerely believed the gibberish he was spouting. He really did believe he'd acted honourably. The Boulter family name was his family grail. By invoking it, he could justify just about anything. It cut him off from reality. The simple truth was that Adam couldn't bear the prospect of being seen to have feet of clay. He couldn't be allowed to slip from the pedestal he occupied in his own mind. I'd have dearly loved to puncture the bubble but I doubted whether it could be done. There was far too much insulation to strip away.

"Why was Robert murdered in England? Was it to divert suspicion away from yourself?"

"That was the original idea. It hasn't worked out as well as I'd hoped."

Suddenly I wanted to put an end to it. However pathetic Adam might be, I didn't feel any sympathy for him. His misplaced sense of honour was a double-edged sword I could use against him.

"Well?" he enquired. "What do you intend to do? You know it all now."

He was trying to pretend he didn't care what my answer was. He'd failed to kill me and he was preparing himself for the role of misunderstood martyr.

"I'm going to allow you a chance to keep the Boulter family name untarnished."

"I don't follow you."

"It's quite simple, really. We play one frame of snooker. If you win, that's an end to it. I'll blame everything on da Silva. Your name won't be mentioned to Angela or the police."

"And if I lose?"

"Then it will be up to you. You'll have to decide exactly how much the Boulter good name is worth to you. I'll allow you twenty-four hours to make up your mind. If you decide you really are a man of honour, I'll still leave everything at da Silva's door. The Boulter name you hold so dear will be safe."

Adam knew precisely what I was talking about. He hadn't missed the sharp edge of sarcasm in my voice either. It was a challenge his pride wouldn't allow him to ignore.

"All right," he said. "Do we play now?"

"Why not? It's high time this was all ended one way or the other."

He seemed confident enough. He knew he was the better player. It might be very different when he started to think about the stakes.

Adam began to learn about pressure very early in the frame. He might have more skill but this was new to him. His problem was that he'd never had to compete before. Everything he'd ever needed had been handed to him on a silver platter. Besides, every true gentleman knew that winning or losing was irrelevant. The game was the thing. I knew otherwise and it didn't take Adam very long to appreciate the difference. In the game we were playing, winning was everything.

His normal play was based on a very simple principle. He tried to sink every ball, no matter how difficult the shot might be. This approach was fine when there was nothing at stake but it would have cost him a small fortune in the workingmen's clubs where I'd learned the game. In his present situation, it could prove even more expensive. Adam was forced to think about what might happen if he missed one of his speculative shots. He had to consider what he might be leaving on the table for me.

The fourth shot of the frame left Adam with an opportunity for a long red into one of the bottom pockets. It was risky but normally he wouldn't have thought twice about going for it. Eight times out of ten he would have put the red into the pocket. On this occasion, however, he hesitated. If the shot didn't come off, he was almost certain to leave something on for me. Adam decided to play safe and he made a hash of it. Safety shots were my speciality, not his. I potted two reds, a black and a green before he got back to the table. It was first blood to me.

I was playing well. A cold, fierce anger made concentration very easy. Although I'd offered Adam a sporting chance, I'd never had any intention of losing. I kept the game very tight, only going for those shots where the percentages were in my favour. If there was any doubt, I opted for safety, running the cue ball down into baulk. It might not have been very exciting to watch but it kept the pressure on Adam. I made sure I didn't leave him any easy shots.

Although Adam wasn't playing particularly badly, this style of game was totally alien to him. He was an instinctive player and thinking about his shots was a brand-new experience for him. No matter what he did, I kept my nose ahead. As he became increasingly anxious, he began to make more mistakes. His judgement became erratic. His cue action was no longer so fluent. He was losing and we both knew it. By the time we were down to the last two reds, I was seventeen points ahead.

And then I blew it. The penultimate red was right against the cushion. Although it was only a few inches from the pocket, it wouldn't be an easy shot. Normally I would have settled for safety but the other red was down at the baulk end of the table. It would be equally difficult to find a safe place to leave the cue ball. Besides, I knew I only needed the two reds, a black and another colour for the frame. Sink them and Adam would be left needing snookers.

I chalked my cue while I considered the situation carefully. The shot would have to be played very slowly, especially if I wanted to retain position on the black. I thought I could manage it but I thought wrong. I played the shot too slowly and, after wobbling a bit, the red stayed in the very jaws of the pocket. From behind me, I clearly heard Adam's sigh of relief.

I felt sick. This wasn't simply a reprieve. It was a golden opportunity for Adam to win the frame. With the possible exception of the blue, there weren't any really difficult balls. Everything depended on Adam's nerves and they appeared to be holding out pretty well. The two reds went into the pockets and he took the black with both of them. Although the strain was evident on his face, he was playing with great precision. Perhaps there was a competitor inside him after all. Now my advantage was down to a single point.

The yellow, green and brown balls were on their spots and Adam was in good position. All three of them went into the pockets cleanly. Adam was eight ahead with only eighteen points remaining on the table. It all hinged on the blue ball. If Adam potted that, the best I could manage was a draw. Even this was unlikely because the pink was invitingly close to a pocket.

It was Adam's turn to chalk his cue while he considered his position. If there hadn't been so much riding on the shot, it would have been relatively straightforward. It was a narrow angle and he'd have to cut it fine but this was no real problem.

Until this point we'd been playing in silence. We'd had nothing left to say to each other. I only spoke now in the hope that this would add to his tension. Sportsmanship had nothing to do with what we were about.

"Well, Adam," I said. "This looks like the big one."

Adam ignored me completely. Nobody needed to remind him of what was at stake. I'd never seen him sweat before but there were beads of perspiration on Adam's face as he settled himself for the shot. I was sweating as well. I was praying that Adam would miss but he didn't. The blue went right into the middle of the pocket and Adam stood up from the table. I could clearly see the flicker of triumph which crossed his face. It was premature. Adam had been concentrating exclusively on sinking the blue. He'd completely forgotten about the cue ball. Both of us watched as it trickled slowly but unerringly into the left-hand bottom pocket. Adam's face was grey with shock. It was almost as though he was ageing before my very eyes.

"Unlucky," I said. "That's twenty-five to you and four to me. Are you going to respot the blue or shall I?"

I had to do it myself because Adam seemed rooted to the spot. We both knew I wasn't going to make any more mistakes.

Angela didn't notice me immediately when I went out on to the verandah. She was looking out over the gardens, a teacup in one hand. Sitting there in her white dress, there was something childlike about her. She looked very small and vulnerable. I was suddenly afflicted by doubts: I was wondering whether I'd been correct in handling Adam the way I had. One thing was certain. What I'd done certainly wouldn't make life any easier for Angela. There would be more grief for her to face up to, and she'd have more pressures and responsibilities to cope with. Perhaps I'd been wrong. Perhaps I should have left well enough alone.

My doubts were only momentary. I knew I'd done the best I could. Although she hadn't phrased it like that, Angela had come to me for justice. This was more or less what I was giving her. Right at the beginning I'd told her that once the process was started it couldn't necessarily be controlled. I'd warned her that it might be painful.

"What it is to be rich and idle," I said from behind her. "It must be nice to be one of the privileged few."

"Frank." The sound of my voice had snapped her round in her seat. Some of the tea slopped onto her skirt but she ignored it. "Batista said you were here."

I could see the pleasure and relief in her face. She'd been worrying about me. The realization was sufficient to cause another brief stab of guilt.

"Your poor head." Now Angela had noticed the sticking plaster. "What happened to you? Are you all right?"

"It's nothing to be alarmed about. It looks far worse than it is." By this time I'd taken a chair opposite her. "The plaster is mainly for show. I enjoy playing the wounded hero."

"But what have you been doing? I haven't heard from you for days. There was a mysterious phone call to Daddy saying I didn't need a bodyguard any more. Then you simply vanished."

"I'm sorry. I should have contacted you before."

"Never mind that now. Tell me what's been happening."

"I've been tidying up a few loose ends. It's all over now."

"What's that supposed to mean? Have you found Robert's murderer?"

"Yes."

Angela was waiting for me to say more but I lit a cigarette instead. I wasn't simply being aggravating. The next few minutes would be crucial. Unless I wanted to be lying to her for the rest of my life, I had to head off the most awkward questions.

"I'm going to hit you in a moment, Frank MacAllister. You're doing it on purpose. Will you please tell me what you've been doing the last few days?"

"All right." I raised my head so I was looking Angela directly in the eye. I made my voice a flat monotone. "I tracked down the man who murdered Robert. He didn't like being tracked down, so he tried to murder me as well. It was a kill or be killed situation and I was the one who did the killing. I had to shoot him to protect myself. Then I threw his body over a cliff. It isn't something I particularly want to talk about."

"Oh my God."

One of Angela's hands had gone to her mouth. I'd known I could play on Angela's sympathy.

"He called himself Oliveira," I added as an apparent afterthought. "At least, he did some of the time. I doubt whether it was his real name."

Angela nodded and kept quiet. I was doing well. So far I hadn't had to tell any lies. I waited until Angela was just about to say something before I spoke again.

"I suppose you've heard about Joaquim."

"Yes. It was in all the newspapers. That's one of the reasons I've been so worried. You were actually there when it happened, weren't you?"

I managed a bitter laugh. The role was much easier to play than I'd imagined.

"I was the real target," I told her. "Joaquim only died because he had the bad luck to be sitting next to me. That's something else I'd rather not talk about. Maybe I will later but not now."

Angela was having a struggle to fight back her tears. I could be a real bastard when I put my mind to it.

"I'm so sorry, Frank." The words were almost a whisper. "If I'd had any idea what it would lead to, I'd never have asked you to come to Portugal."

"Don't be sorry, for God's sake. Apart from poor Joaquim, I don't regret anything that happened. It's simply that I didn't enjoy doing it."

For a minute or so we were silent. Angela was nervous. She didn't know what to say. Now she was the one who felt guilty.

"There's just one question." Angela sounded very hesitant. "I can understand you not wanting to talk about it but I have to know. Why was Robert killed? Did you manage to discover that?"

"It was those bloody diamonds." There were occasions when lying was the right thing to do. "Robert found out that Latimer SA was being used to smuggle them out of the country. Instead of going to the police straightaway, he tried to find out who was responsible on his own. He was too successful for his own good. The smugglers had him killed because he was getting too close. Da Silva, the man who was killed with Joaquim, was the smuggler-in-chief."

Angela nodded. Although my explanation had been cursory, it appeared to satisfy her. I'd given her a reason to hang on to. She had names even though she hadn't known the men they belonged to. Most important, I'd kept her image of Robert intact. She'd never know he'd wanted to be a diamond smuggler too.

"Did you tell all of this to Daddy?"

"Some of it. I also explained why I wouldn't be mentioning most of it to the police. There's nothing more for the authorities to do. If I told them the truth, I'd be in a very awkward position."

Angela nodded again. I was still making sense to her.

"What did Daddy have to say?"

"Not a lot. I think he was too surprised."

"I'll bet." Angela managed a laugh of sorts. "He never enjoys being proved wrong. Has he gone off somewhere to sulk?"

"That wasn't quite the way he phrased it." Now I was deliberately casual. "I think he's gone to the gun room. When he left me he was muttering something about cleaning his Purdy shotgun."

I guessed that Adam would be busy calculating how best to stage the accident. I was sure he'd arrange it with great efficiency. Suicide, like stealing and murder, was a pastime for the lower orders. Gentlemen only had accidents.

About the Author

RITCHIE PERRY is the author of ten previous novels about the British secret agent named Philis, including *Foul Up, Fool's Mate* and *Grand Slam. MacAllister* is his second novel for the Crime Club.